Where Our Paths Meet

D. Wells has written two previous novels, 6 Caledon Street and The Things We Regret. She lives in East Anglia with her husband, children and cat.

Where Our Paths Meet

Taverton Tales Series: Book One

By D. Wells

This novel is a work of fiction. Names and characters are the product of the author's imagination and any resemblance to actual persons, living or dead, is entirely coincidental.

Dedication

For my parents

Chapter One

2019

Evelyn Storford spun the pen between her fingertips, allowing it to whirl in circles on the counter. Struggling to stifle a yawn, she checked the clock; the third time in as many minutes.

She loved her job. She really did. After all, as an avid reader, who wouldn't love owning a small, quirky bookshop, set in an old Tudor building, in the middle of an historic Suffolk town? It was the stuff of dreams. Yet, far too many days ebbed along; the customers – flurries of them here and there, then vanishing for no apparent reason, left the shop empty and feeling unloved. An occasional quiet day was fine, but not when they were so frequent.

She hated that on those days she would tally up the books sold and how much meagre profit went towards the business expenses, her staff's salaries (all two of them) and then her own.

On the plus side quieter periods were golden moments to grab a book off one of the shelves, and ever so carefully, so as not to crease the spine, thumb through and absorb the flowing words. However, today she was restless.

None of the books she perused grabbed her attention and after several failed attempts she gave up, letting the idle pen in her hand drop with a thud against the oak surface. She entered the kitchenette, flicked the kettle on, deciding to up her caffeine content instead.

Smoothing her erratic dark curly hair behind her ears, she then reached for the sugar pot, adding a spoonful of sugar into the coffee, and embracing the mug with both hands. A small, polite cough stirred her from her thoughts.

Joe Sawyer swayed, his arms piled high with books, trying and failing to manoeuvre his slipping glasses by wrinkling his nose.

'May I?' Evelyn asked.

He nodded bashfully.

She put down her coffee mug and straightened the frame of his glasses. He tilted his head towards the books in his arms.

'Full set of Dickens.'

'Great. I might have something to read, after all,' she mused, lifting the first few books off the top of the pile.

Evelyn loved reading anything historical. She preferred non-fiction, but the fiction classics were a close second. There was something thrilling about reading about life in previous eras, the buzz of discovering some long-lost detail or event. It was even more thrilling to live in an area so rich with historical relevance.

'Can I leave these with you then?' Joe asked. The inflection in his voice was borderline desperate. He almost sagged as he placed the books on the desk. Straightening his slightly stocky frame, he ran a hand through his sandy brown hair, ruffling it up. Wearing a Jurassic Park t-shirt with an oatmeal-coloured open shirt over the top, it didn't match, but that was Joe, thought Evelyn. He was a style all of his own.

She contemplated her own attire. She wore one of her late mother's dresses; a simple blue dress which buttoned up at the front. Small white flowers danced across the fabric. Recently she and her father had begun the mammoth task of going through her mother's belongings. Starting with the wardrobe, Evelyn had been surprised by some of her mother's outfits; several of which would be considered vintage by today's standards. Her father, Ethan, nodded silently when she asked if she could keep them for herself. She wondered now if that had been a little insensitive.

'I'm going to grab a cup of tea,' Joe said, heading toward the back of the shop. 'Let me know if the delivery arrives with the crime thrillers. I've been waiting for days.'

The deliveries were sluggish of late. A change in suppliers had caused an inevitable trickle effect and now she was shielding phone calls from their few regular customers, irate and demanding to know where their orders had got to. Earlier one had phoned to cancel their order, claiming to be able to get it quicker online. Evelyn didn't doubt it.

'As soon as the stock is booked in,' she called to Joe, 'we must phone the customers. There have been enough delays this week.' He mumbled in agreement from behind the partition.

She thumbed through the large A3 diary in front of her. She still needed to organise their staff schedule for the coming month as well as book appointments with sales reps. A new seasonal window display needed to be designed too, now that the summer months were near. The endless weeks of pounding rain were ceasing and the pale blue sky endeavoured to make a valiant return.

It was early May. She noted the date with a slight pang. She breathed it away, refocusing her attention. One day at a time. Isn't that what she'd learned from Helen herself and from the crashing circumstances of her own personal life?

*

'I've put you and Lucie down for the next two Saturdays. Here,' she said, sticking the schedule under Joe's nose. 'Let me know if there's any problem.'

She moved into the small office at the back, which stood between the tiny cloakroom and the kitchenette area. She preferred to do her admin out front unless the shop was busy, which was rare, but it wasn't always convenient. She hated being shut away, behind a cheap desk, and in a darkened room, but at times it was necessary. It reminded her of the basement office in London, where she'd spent years archiving historical documents and records. There had been little sunlight in that room either. She grabbed a file of invoices out of the locked cabinet. Despite computers and databases, everything had a paper trail. She was a stickler for detail.

Returning to the warm and welcoming shop floor, she surveyed it with an intense pride. Regardless of the building's age, and the restrictions regarding what she could do to the place, she loved the Taverton Tales' curves and edges. Not one wall was the same. Different dimensions, different patterns of beams, different lights installed over different decades; it was an eclectic mix that she adored. Her previous modernistic existence faded to a vague memory here. Instead, she was reminded of growing up in the country, the endless summer days and dry sun-baked fields stretching out across a lilting distance. Memories of learning to drive down bumpy country roads, almost squealing in exhilarating fear at each blind corner, as her father glanced with a nervous expression over at the steering wheel.

And the fresh air, on occasion punctuated with manure from the farmer's fields, but more often abuzz with the pulsing haze of a summer's day. In winter the same landscapes seemed cosy, an enclosing blanket simultaneously stretched to the horizon, yet wrapped around her in each direction, making her feel secure.

Taking on the bookshop was both a literal and metaphorical coming home. She'd needed something, anything, to help her through the implosion of life in the city. The grief of her mother's death, the months of isolating fatigue as her marriage to Ishmael crumbled. She even reverted back to her maiden name. Although in hindsight it only highlighted what had been lost, rather than gained.

She willed herself against the memories, plonking the heavy file down on the shop desk. Joe, still busy in the task of stacking books from the previous delivery, gave a slight nod toward the schedule on the desk.

'All good,' he said, a slight pinking hue creeping across his cheeks.

Three months ago, she'd faced the reality of needing a third member of staff. Barely able to afford it, but unable to manage Taverton Tales between just the two of them, she took the plunge. Lucie was twenty-one, sweet and fresh in her youth, a pretty girl with long blonde hair and hazel eyes. She was a good worker, but kept herself to herself.

Evelyn noticed Joe's immediate reaction, but soon realised that Joe neither had the confidence to take his feelings further, nor did Lucie seem to notice him in any other capacity than as a colleague. Evelyn noted his slight embarrassment at any mention of Lucie's name.

The shop door opened and a group of pensioners arrived into the cosy space. They wore waterproof jackets, sensible after the recent wet weather, and Evelyn wondered if they were tourists. It was common for coaches to pass through the picturesque town, dropping off mostly retirees and pensioners. Tourists often made good customers and after the slow morning they'd had, any sales would be welcome.

After giving them an appropriate amount of time and space to peruse, Joe discreetly approached. 'May I help with anything? We have a vast array of classic fiction here, as well as a selection of popular modern titles. Here are the current bestsellers. Or perhaps a little local history is more your thing?'

Evelyn smiled, returning to her attention to the invoices.

*

Ethan Storford sat at the dull green kitchen table, scratching a persistent itch at the back of his neck with one hand and holding a loose page with the other. The kettle had just boiled in preparation for Evelyn's arrival. Their routine had become like clockwork over the months. Steady, comfortable.

He slid the paper back into the shoe box where it originated. He contemplated the farmhouse style kitchen, remembering the decades of memories that spilled out from its four corners. That first Christmas; the real tree chopped down from a local farmer's field, dropping its needles across the linoleum as they dragged it through the house. The day Helen had announced that she was pregnant with Evelyn; while he stood at the sink, a cup of tea in hand, about to leave for work. The happy noise and chaos of his two little girls, running around the house, making more mess than he and Helen ever had time to clear up. He remembered Evelyn, leaving home to go off to university, then Aimee heading off for yet another ill-judged adventure. His mind recollected visions of Helen, shuffling into the kitchen each morning in pain, but determined not to show it. His first day spent alone, in a house that ached with emptiness, the size too big for just one man.

Having Evelyn home again, despite her circumstances, had rescued him from loneliness. He knew it wasn't forever. It couldn't be. It shouldn't be. She was young, only thirty-one. She'd build her life back up and he would have to let her go. He must let her go and be content.

The front door clicked open and closed again with a muffled thud. Placing the shoe box lid back on, he pushed it away from him. Running a hand through his salt and pepper hair, he awaited his daughter's appearance.

'Tea?' he asked, as her head poked around the door frame.

'Oh, yes please.' She placed her purple leather handbag on one of the kitchen chairs and sat down, arms outstretched, hands clasped together in front of her.

'Good day at the bookshop?'

He poured the still boiling water into the mug, which bore a capital E on the side. Evelyn's favourite.

'Terrible morning,' she admitted, shifting in her chair. 'But Joe worked his magic on a group of tourists this afternoon and managed to sell about £200 worth of books between them. Then a flurry of people after that.'

'That boy is an asset.'

'He's not a boy, Dad. He's twenty-five.'

'I thought that was considered a boy these days,' Ethan laughed. 'I was married by twenty-five.'

'I wasn't far off,' muttered Evelyn, before falling silent. She wasn't willing to go there yet.

Sensing the shift in mood, Ethan handed her the tea and joined her at the table. He watched her awhile, marvelling at how much she took upon her own shoulders. How much was left unsaid. There was the struggling bookshop. And then there was the separation. She was so like Helen sometimes, it made him ache.

'Do you want to talk about it?'

She made eye contact with him for a brief second before dropping her gaze to the mug. 'Daddy, there is really nothing I want to say.'

The undertone of sadness clawed at him. But she had made it clear, the day she'd moved back home. This was her fight.

'What's this?' she asked, pointing at the shoe box.

'Something of Mum's,' he replied, hoisting it under his arm and standing up. He wasn't willing to share the contents yet. He also had his own fight to contend with.

'Is the clearing out going well? I'm sorry I've not been around to help much.' She sounded weary, as if the day was catching up with her.

'Slow, as expected. I can't just throw things away. I have to go through it all.'

He slid the shoe box to the top of a cupboard. 'I thought it would be quicker, but almost every item invokes some memory. I thought I'd be ready to say goodbye by now, but it's harder than I imagined. I should have done it earlier. I have put it off for too long.'

Several friends had suggested he clear out Helen's belongings after the first year. At the time it felt like stamping on her memory and he'd refused. But the longer he left it, the harder it was.

Three years ago. Three years this very week; which was why Ethan had announced to Evelyn, just days before, that the time had arrived. He saw that she was wearing one of Helen's dresses. He was pleased, although it brought with it a slight pang of wistfulness and regret.

It's only material, he reminded himself. He didn't even remember a specific occasion where Helen had worn that dress. Besides, Evelyn was so like her mother at times, that it made absolute sense for her to be wearing it. Aimee, on the other hand, he doubted would ever have given the clothing a second glance, and he was oddly grateful about that.

*

6

Evelyn drained the rest of her tea in quiet contemplation. Even after three years, her father was having trouble letting go. Would it be the same for her and her circumstances? It was a sobering thought and she willed her mind to dwell on happier things.

'There's soup in the fridge and the machine made a fresh loaf this morning.'

Ethan gestured toward the block shaped parcel on the counter top, wrapped in a clean tea towel. 'Oh, and Janice dropped off a cheesecake earlier.'

She grinned. Their next-door neighbour, a harassed looking divorcee of fifty, liked to pop in regularly with her various baking creations. With mousey grey-brown hair always scraped back into a ponytail, and a very slender frame giving a false impression of weakness, the woman had a relentless enthusiasm to bombard the attractive widower with her presence. Evelyn wondered if he even noticed Janice's obvious interest. He gave no outward sign that he did.

'That sounds perfect.' She didn't have energy to cook tonight. They shared the chore, although matching up their menus and shopping trips was more of an effort than the cooking itself. Some evenings they made up their own food, scraping together leftovers, or fixing egg on toast.

Adjusting to being back in the childhood home was an ever-evolving challenge. Ethan, sensitive to Evelyn's situation and the fact that she had had her own home for a number of years, kept the rules simple and few. They were both responsible for their own mess and they shared the cost of a cleaner, who scrubbed away the worst of the dirt once a week. They washed their own clothes and dishes, unless one offered to do the others. They shared responsibility for Randall, the aging and grumpy ginger cat. They bought their own food and when they remembered, wrote down their menu on their allocated days, on the board on the fridge.

Still, their situation felt like a bizarre limbo, ground-hog day concoction. Both realising its temporal nature, there wasn't ever a sense of feeling settled. Evelyn, on a monthly basis, reminded her father that she would move out as soon as the business supported her rent, while Ethan nodded in agreement, pretending that he didn't know that it would take far longer to get off the ground than she'd admit.

Evelyn had bought a floundering business. Despite it being a childhood dream, running the bookshop was a heavy learning curve and fifteen months later it was barely breaking even. Employing an extra staff member couldn't shift the truth. She would need to see substantial growth in the profits before the business was a success. Despite that, she wouldn't impose on her father another year. It had already been far longer than she'd planned.

Opening the fridge door, she viewed the tub of chicken soup on the middle shelf and she removed it, along with a block of cheese and another of butter. Pulling open the cupboards, she took out a pan, chopping board and knife. Ethan hunched over the post that had arrived that afternoon.

In his late fifties, he still carried himself well with a short slender frame, salt and pepper hair, and an unforced natural ability to look dapper. He always wore chinos (Evelyn suspected he owned several in every colour) and stylish shirts. On cooler days he would pair it with a body warmer, or even a waistcoat. His suit jackets were always smart as were his boots, despite the practical nature of wearing them in the countryside. She knew he hid an old pair of wellingtons caked in mud in the garage.

She felt a burst of pride as she watched him. He had always been the glue that kept their family together. Even now, after all the fragmentation, he was a presence of calm and solidity. If he hadn't taken her in, eighteen months ago, she didn't know what she would have done. He was her anchor and she was forever grateful.

Chapter Two

'Whatcha think Gordon?' Ethan grinned; his arms folded across his blue checked shirt. 'Ignored the sign again?'

'That's for sure. They always think they know best, Ethan,' Gordon shook his head, watching the chaos unfurl before them.

A lorry, far too unwieldy for the narrowing country lane was wedged between the hedgerows, after an ill-fated attempt to turn around. The driver shouted into his mobile phone, face bright red and sweating, spittle escaping the corners of his lips with uttered expletives.

'I've spent the best part of twenty minutes trying to help, but he's got himself right stuck now,' Gordon said, rubbing his white whiskery chin, which contrasted violently against his red weathered cheeks. He tilted his head toward Ethan. 'Of course, all he'll achieve is further damage to our lane. If I wasn't against the government taking our money, I'd be all for giving these loons a fine.'

Ethan chuckled, knowing better than to encourage Gordon in another anti-establishment rant. Fifteen years of being neighbours had taught him that.

'What on earth is going on?' Evelyn's voice drifted over his right shoulder, as she came into view. 'How the hell is he going to get out of that one?'

She reached the two men at the bottom of the drive, who stood watching in faint amusement. She expelled an exasperated laugh.

'Well, anyone who says that nothing happens in the countryside is fibbing.'

'You grew up here didn't ya? Pah, a few years in the city and you've forgotten it all,' Gordon mumbled with a hint of affection.

She pulled a playful expression then gestured towards the lorry. 'At least he's far away from the house.'

'If he'd gone any further in, he'd have risked hitting Janice's or mine,' Gordon grumbled. 'Right,' he announced, pulling his hands out of his pockets in decisive action. 'Best have another word. I can't stand here all day.'

'Me neither, I have to get to the bookshop.' Evelyn adjusted her bag across her shoulders. 'Will you be okay, Dad?'

'Yes, yes.'

She knew his mind was on other things. He'd taken two weeks off work to sort through Mum's stuff and it was obvious he wasn't relishing getting back to the task.

'Pop into the bookshop later. I just got in some fancy coffee. We can have a drink and a natter.'

He raised an eyebrow. 'Are things that quiet?'

Evelyn wished she hadn't said anything. The growing lull between customers was a worry. She expected it in midwinter. Few tourists visited the area then and the regulars just weren't regular enough. But now it was May, the weather was improving, the days lengthening and school holidays approaching; and yet, there was no improvement to the amount of people coming through the door.

'It's still picking up,' she replied in an evasive tone.

He studied her. After a pause, he gave her a slight nod, more in empathy than acquiescence.

'Off you go then.'

*

Evelyn flicked on the lights, watching in satisfaction as the bookshop came to life. The warm red carpet complimented the dark mahogany tables, which displayed books in neat piles, according to popularity and genre. Bookshelves clung to the walls, some short, some tall, according the ununiformed nature of the wall's dimensions. Little nooks and crannies concealed further shelves, which Evelyn absolutely loved. It was a feature that had sold the business to her. Being able to walk around a corner and discover another section delighted her. She'd lost count of how many customers commented on the almost magical nature of the shop's interior.

She unlocked the back rooms and fired up the computers and till, before counting the float and checking that the money tallied. It was small, systematic tasks like this that kept her on track. Whenever her mind had time to wander, it found things to dwell on that she either wanted to forget, or wasn't ready to analyse.

At some point she would need to face up to her circumstances. The business was far from just being a distraction, it was a childhood dream. Yet, it had somehow managed to fill the role of the former, which was not her intention.

She slammed shut the till drawer and placed her head in her hands, expressing a deep groan. She breathed out with precision. She hoped that today wouldn't be a bad one. It held all the tell-tale signs; the overwhelming tiredness, wandering thoughts, a heaviness building inside that she couldn't ignore. Evelyn thought of her dad and the re-emerged grief that he was fighting. He had lost the love of his life. The woman he was married to for nearly thirty-five years. Her own marriage hadn't made it to four.

Trying, but failing, to bring a little perspective, she made herself a cup of coffee instead. She may not have experienced the same level of grief as her father, but she *was* still grieving. Mum, Ishmael. They both left a painful void.

The front door opened and Joe waltzed in, swinging a plastic bag in his right hand. 'Have you seen the drama down your lane?' he laughed. 'They've had to call a tow truck, although I'm not quite sure how that'll fare against a lorry?'

'I feel very grateful to be walking distance from my job. Can you imagine the traffic delays this morning?'

'Nope, don't drive,' Joe said, absentmindedly. He placed the plastic bag on the desk and started rifling through. 'The co-op has a two for one on pasta,' he exclaimed, scooping out two containers of pre-prepared tomato and cheese pasta. 'Lunch is sorted,' he added in triumph. He headed for the kitchenette and the small bar fridge.

Joe Sawyer already worked in Taverton Tales when Evelyn bought it. The elderly couple running the place had had enough and just wanted to scrape as much profit as possible to see them through their twilight years.

Arriving at her father's door, with just two suitcases and her entire life savings in her bank account, the 'for sale' advert in the local paper seemed like a godsend. She needed focus. The business of her dreams would give her that. Grateful for small mercies; such as being a cash buyer (her lack of business experience was unlikely to secure her a bank loan), she made them an offer.

Keeping Joe on was a stroke of genius. Or rather he was. He knew books inside out. He knew the shop, knew the industry. He was exactly what she needed, while she pretended to know what she was doing. It was obvious that Joe had caught on to her lack of experience, but he was the kind of character to patiently get on with his own work and let her learn hers.

'There's still coffee in the pot,' she offered, as he passed.

Joe wrinkled his nose in disgust. 'Yuck, can't abide the stuff. Is there enough boiling water for tea?'

'There should be.'

She smiled into the still opened till drawer. Their mundane conversation was like a balm against the harsher realities of life.

'Oh, there's something else in that bag. You might be interested.'

'Unless it's a month's supply of chocolate, I doubt it,' she answered, coffee mug halfway to her lips.

'Better than that,' Joe said, poking his head around the door frame.

Intrigued, despite herself, she glanced inside. At the bottom lay a solitary banana, a Sudoku book and a newspaper. That was it.

'Um, Joe, you are going to have to explain this one.'

He returned to the shop floor, mug of tea in hand and nodded toward the bag.

'The local newspaper, check out page eight.' He sat down behind the desk with a heavy grunt and stretched his legs out. 'Go on, have a read.'

Evelyn removed the newspaper from the bag and opened it up. A brief pause later, she raised her head and grinned.

'The festival?'

'It's a perfect opportunity, if you ask me.'

She read the article again, her mind already ticking over ideas. The town's summer festival, held every August, was a brilliant way to attract tourists and a brilliant boost for local shops and businesses. And this year the festival was growing, to include local arts, culture and writers. The organisers were advertising, requesting business owners to book their slots and tables. They were also advertising for a team to help organise the extra events.

This might be their chance to get Taverton Tales on the map. It might even be enough to help them turn a corner. They already represented the bookshop at various local events, but not to the crowds the festival would attract.

'You could buy your own month's supply of chocolate after that,' Joe joked, butting into her thoughts.

She laughed loudly.

Chapter Three

2009

He had been Steve's friend. That's how she knew him. Studious, clever, kept his nose in a book or hung out in Steve's room, playing bad guitar and sipping soda. She had never paid much attention to him before. After all, her housemate's friends were not her friends.

She'd known Kate, her other housemate, since halls and had shared a place ever since. Evelyn still wasn't sure where Steve came from. Kate knew him and he was 'a decent sort', and back then, naïve and youthful, that was good enough reason to move into a house share together.

But Steve's friend - she wasn't expecting to like him.

It started when she noticed him perusing the paperbacks on the bookshelf in the lounge. They all belonged to her; Kate wasn't a reader and Steve was possessive over his books, choosing to keep them in his bedroom. He'd pulled out several, thumbing through the pages, reading each blurb with interest. What impressed her was how he placed them back in their exact spots, pushing them flush against the others so they all lined up as before. It either demonstrated consideration or slight OCD tendencies. She didn't mind which, she was still impressed.

Then there was the trip to the pub, situated at the end of a street known for student housing. Evenings there got rowdy, but Arnold the publican took it in good humour. After all, he made a small fortune from them all.

Evelyn and Kate had hauled themselves off the sofa, a rare night where they were both in the house and hadn't made any other plans.

There was little to spark their interest on the television, so they'd glanced across at one another and shrugged.

'Drink at the pub?' Kate enquired, lifting an eyebrow.

'Hmm,' Evelyn managed, not in the mood, but desperate to escape the four walls now associated with endless hours of writing her dissertation. 'I don't know if I can be bothered.'

'One drink, come on. It's Friday night. We used to go clubbing on a Friday night. Now it's all bad telly and cheap cider. And studying, too much studying,' Kate whined.

'Well I do want to pass my degree,' Evelyn offered in defence. It was an excuse though. How could one drink hurt, other than to her purse, of course?

'Fine, I'll come.'

'Great!' Kate jumped up from the sofa. 'Give me half an hour.'

'What do you need half an hour for?'

'I need to change and freshen up,' she said, shrugging. Evelyn knew that meant the full works; make up, shaved legs, trying on a dozen different outfits.

'We know everyone down the pub. They'll all be in their crappy clothes too. Your Prince Charming is unlikely to make a sudden appearance.'

'I don't need a man. I just want to look nice, that's all.'

Forty-five minutes later, they were ready to leave. Evelyn had deigned to make a small effort, changing her top and brushing her hair. If Kate was going all out, in smart new jeans, a sparkly black top, and washed and styled hair, Evelyn would feel underdressed if she did nothing at all.

They reached the pub, already fit to burst with patrons, and squeezed inside. The tables and chairs were all occupied and along the bar smaller groups of people congregated, laughing and shouting. The deep oak beams above them made the space cramped. With the crowds beneath, it was claustrophobic. Pushing their way through, Kate and Evelyn reached the bar and placed their order.

Evelyn spotted Steve at the pool table, accompanied by a couple of friends. The one who had shown interest in her books was there too, standing against the wall, pool cue resting upright in his arms, laughing at someone's joke.

There was something natural about him. Every day she was surrounded by people who were either trying to fit in with the crowd, or being belligerent in opposition to fitting in. He was neither. He

14

seemed comfortable with himself. Of course, she didn't know him, to be sure of that. He just exuded an air of natural confidence.

'Oh, it's Steve,' Kate said with excitement, and dragged Evelyn over, drinks and all. It wasn't so much Steve she was excited to see, but Evelyn rather suspected the group of men hanging around the pool tables with him.

There was a slightly awkward pause at their arrival which made her wince. Kate, ignoring the atmosphere, zeroed in on one guy and Evelyn was left with an annoyed Steve.

'Hi,' she waved, self-consciously.

'I'm going to the loo,' Steve said, indignant. He stalked off. She wondered what had bothered him more; his housemates ruining his evening out, or Kate already getting on famously with the guy on his right.

Evelyn's gaze fell on Steve's friend. He was looking at her too and gave her a nonchalant nod. She nodded back.

'Do you play pool?' he asked, holding out a spare cue. His hands were sinewy and strong, which belied his short frame. His black hair was cut short against his olive complexion. His brown eyes were dark and intense.

'I was always told not to play pool with strangers,' she said, shrugging.

He laughed. He had a nice laugh.

'I'm Ishmael,' he said, holding out his other hand to shake hers. 'See, we're not strangers anymore.'

'I've never met an Ishmael before,' she said in contemplation, returning his handshake. 'I'm Evelyn.'

'I've genuinely never met an Evelyn before, either.'

'I was named after my gran.'

'I wasn't,' he replied. Now they were both grinning. 'So, pool?'

'Sure,' she said, definitively.

Chapter Four

2019

Lucie Chase entered the bookshop, trying in vain to wipe away the exhaustion of a broken night's sleep. Shaking off her red waterproof, she carried it through the shop floor to the rooms at the back. Joe was counting the float and gave her a self-conscious greeting.

'You all right?' he asked clumsily.

'I didn't sleep well,' she murmured, her eyes downcast. She didn't want to elaborate and hoped he'd change the subject.

'Oh, why was that?'

Her heart sank. She took a moment to put her jacket away and compile her thoughts.

'Just one of those things, I guess. Do you want a cup of tea?'

'I've just poured one. The water should still be hot.'

She grabbed a mottled grey mug with faded writing on the side and chucked in a tea bag. Reaching into her black trouser pocket, she withdrew a hairband and tied her long straight hair back, away from her eyes. She yawned.

Gathering her last vestiges of energy, she stared unfocused into the mug as the tea bag brewed. She needed to get a grip. Life wasn't going to become easier anytime soon and she couldn't fault her mother's help. 'It's a season,' her mother told her almost daily. It seemed a long one, and one that appeared to be beating her.

Smoothing down her purple blouse, old fashioned but all that was in her budget, she added a dash of milk and a large spoonful of sugar to

17

her drink and joined Joe on the shop floor. Suppressing a yawn, she sipped her tea.

'We got a new batch of Jenny Colgans in,' Joe nodded toward one of centre tables. 'I kept one aside. Perhaps you'd read it and review it for the bookshop blog? I know you like her books.'

Joe was a nice guy, she thought. 'Thanks, I'd love to. I just... it might be a while before I can finish it. I don't have a lot of time.'

'Perhaps, if you're not sleeping, you can read it then. I've bought it, so you can keep it and take it home.'

'Hmm.'

Joe took the hint, changing the subject.

'We've had loads of deliveries. They seemed to arrive in one go, so they're already out on the shelves. If you can just serve the customers when they arrive - Evelyn's left me with some phone calls to make, so I'll get on with that.'

'Sure,' Lucie replied, distracted. 'Did you say you've bought me the book?' She lifted her head, surprised.

'Well, yes.' His cheeks blushed slightly, his eyes fixed on the order book. 'But,' he added. 'You only work here once or twice a week, so I thought you wouldn't have much time, as you said, to read it while you were here. So, this way you can take it home and it won't put added pressure on you to try and get through it on those few shifts, and you can update the blog at your leisure.'

This was a long explanation for Joe, and Lucie rather imagined he had pulled it out of thin air, but she was grateful anyway. Not wanting to examine the real reason he had bought her the book, she thanked him instead.

'No problem,' He walked to the front door and flipped the sign. 'Right, here we go. Let's hope Saturday is a good one.'

*

'What have you found?' Evelyn asked, crouching down to her father's level. He was inside the large white cupboard under the stairs, rifling through various boxes. His exclamation had drawn her from the kitchen.

'I didn't know she'd kept these,' Ethan said, shaking his head. He was bent over and Evelyn couldn't see what he was referencing.

'Kept what?'

He glanced up at her and she was alarmed to see a slight glaze in his eyes. She felt guilty for trying to rush him. He wriggled his way past the decades of stored debris and out to where she was standing.

'I need a coffee,' he said, handing her the items that had caused his outburst.

A bundle of fabric petals, scrunched together and creased over, lay in her palm. She remembered that her mother had had a fondness for fabric flowers, before they lost popularity and were replaced with real and difficult-to-keep-alive orchids. However, she didn't remember these particular ones. They were short stemmed, singular and all individual colours; pink, russet red, deep purple and cobalt blue.

She stepped into the kitchen. Ethan's back was turned, his shoulders hunched as he watched the kettle.

'Dad, are you okay?' She placed the flowers on the kitchen table and stood a couple of metres behind him, unsure whether to approach.

'I'm just surprised she kept them. They were the first gifts I gave her. I didn't think… things were different then,' he added vaguely.

'Mum was always sentimental. She kept all mine and Aimee's Mother's Day cards.'

'That's different. Most mothers do that. When I gave her those, we weren't dating. It was a difficult time. It was the last thing I expected to find, to be honest.'

'Well, that's good then?'

'Yes,' his mind elsewhere. 'I suppose it is.'

She noticed the brief flash in his eyes. Almost a haunted glimmer, as if the flowers had stirred an unwanted memory. It scared her a little, but already the moment had passed. He poured his coffee, offered her one, to which she shook her head.

'I'll be out in the garden for a while,' he said and then he was gone.

Chapter Five

I hope summer never ends. Each day the sun shines brightly, the buzz across the fields filter through the streets, bringing with it a never-ending helpless hope for the future - for our future.

I know I've met the one for me. It has made me poetic. I am writing lots of poetry. All I want to do is spend time with him and write of how he makes me feel.

I cannot believe that even two months ago I knew nothing of his existence. It is inconceivable that someone, who is already so important, was unknown to me just weeks ago! Yet all has changed since he arrived.

Caroline Andrews was the first to spot him. I thought I'd lost all chance then. The boys always choose her over me. But no, Laurence's gaze slipped from hers to mine in a single breathtaking second. He got out of his car and started talking to us... no, started talking to me. He only had eyes for me.

And he has a car! His own one too. His family must be rich, but it's a little rude to ask. None of the boys here can even drive yet, and there's no way any family in town can afford a second car for their teenage offspring.

I am too nervous to ask, to be honest. Our conversations are so exciting, so full of promise that trivialities such as his family's wealth pale into pointless speculation. I don't care less whether he is rich or not. I want him, not his money!

I told him yesterday about my poetry. I almost expected him to laugh, as my parents do whenever I raise the subject. But Laurence pointed up at the clouds above us, as we lay in the meadow, and said, 'These clouds take their own form. They don't follow anyone else's rules.'

What a perfect response. It makes me love him even more. And yes, I do love him. I cannot believe my good luck, that I have found the perfect one so soon. Caroline Andrews will be seething in jealousy!

Chapter Six

Saturday afternoon was too quiet. While the respite of the family home, in the midst of the Suffolk countryside, was a needed salve, Evelyn on occasion missed the non-stop thrill of life in London. There was never a lack of things to do, never a lull in noise or chatter.

Here, the foxes made a racket in the evening. Their high pitched mating squeals were followed later by the piercing, desperate shrieks of a rabbit caught within their jaws. The birds chattered in the twilight as they prepared to roost for the night and deep haunting hoots of owls echoed through the trees. There were endless unidentifiable sounds that carried across the fields, from the woodlands beyond. Yet, in the deep dead of night there was an almost finite blanket of dense quiet.

She loved it, yet hated the comparisons it provoked: memories of nights out with friends, of entertaining back at their flat. She and Ishmael pouring glasses of wine on top of spotless modern countertops, laughing and joking as they served up bowls of homemade versions of whichever food was fashionable. They had an unspoken understanding. They were in sync with one another, moving around their kitchen with ease. Yet when the guests went home, it was another story.

Saturday afternoon in the small market town of Taverton was vastly different. No preparing for a big night out; unless you were planning on being a bar fly at the pub, or a member of Mavis Vettigrew's book club (although Evelyn was incredibly grateful for their unwavering support, buying copies of each month's book from the shop), or preparing the flowers at the local church, ready for the Sunday morning service.

No that was unfair. There were coffee shops, popular during the day, and residents often socialised in one another's houses at night, not to mention the various social clubs on during the week too, or a night out to one of the nearby larger towns. But it wasn't what she'd grown used to in London. After fifteen months, she was still making that adjustment, despite her relief to be home.

Now, in the silence of the house, Ethan having retired to his workshop, and the last of the afternoon sun plunging most of the living space into shadow, she felt lonely. She missed her friends. They seldom visited. She missed Ishmael, despite everything, despite what they had decided.

It had been long enough, surely, to get over a failed marriage, especially one that had only lasted four years in the first place. Everyone expected her to be over it by now. Text messages from friends and comments on her social media posts all leant towards one conclusion:

You seem so happy!
So good to see you doing so well!
Any men on the horizon yet?!

They might be shocked to realise that a cute bookshop didn't bring in a proper income and that the stunning scenery hadn't filled the cracks of a broken heart. That no man had even turned her head, not while the separation was still open-ended with no official paperwork in sight.

Beneath it all was the squirming grief of losing her mum. Something she had never really dealt with, even after she'd moved home. She had realised that the location made no significant difference to her healing, not when the healing had to be worked from the inside out.

A sudden chill blanketed the house and Evelyn dialled the thermostat up, hearing the boiler fire up inside the kitchen cupboard. She made her way upstairs. The house boasted four spacious bedrooms and Evelyn had naturally moved back into hers. Before she'd left home the bedroom's décor was a peculiar hybrid of primary school days and teenage angst. Posters of Paramore and the Foo Fighters had hidden the peeling Disney wallpaper. Red, blue and black paint had been splashed across the book shelves and chest of drawers in an ill-judged attempt to repaint, leaving peeling and chalky surfaces instead. Her parents were apoplectic at the time, as she hadn't asked permission and had also ruined the furniture.

Now the room was sunny and bright, shades of ivory and sand complimenting the walls and the wrecked shelves and drawers replaced with a handsome oak stained wardrobe and a matching bookshelf. Evelyn added her own stamp on the bedroom; framing a few favourite locally drawn sketches and artwork, and layering the numerous books she liked to collect across the book shelves. It was peaceful. There was no tension here. All that had been left behind in London.

The view outside the window was the most impressive part of the room and lent itself to the serene atmosphere inside. The back garden wrapped around the corner and towards a partially hidden orchard, where apple and pear trees grew. Running the length of the garden was a tumbledown wooden fence. Beyond that chicken wire highlighted the boundary of the farmer's fields. The view was partly obscured by trees, growing in a thin diagonal band off to the left, meeting with a broader area of woodland in the near distance. The rest of the view opened up to the fields behind; wheat fields, still green and awaiting the emergence of their ears mid-June, and the still neat meadows beyond that. In two months the ears would stand golden and tall, awaiting the harvester, while the meadow would display a cascade of wild and untamed beauty; burnt oranges, vibrant pinks, deep purples, yellow feather like grasses. It was her favourite time of year and her favourite view ever.

Evelyn withdrew a book from the shelf and flicked through it for a few minutes, before putting it down on the bed, distracted. She had decided against her usual weekend jaunt into the countryside, rediscovering and appreciating the scenery around her, scenery she'd never seemed to notice while growing up. She'd spent a lot of her free time visiting local landmarks, castles, or remains, anything that stirred the sense of the history of the area. But today she'd stayed at home to help Ethan clear through her late mother's things. She regretted it. She was in the way. Ethan needed space to work through it in his own time. He was also being mysterious and the thought of it picked away at her. Had her parents had secrets? In one way, it seemed a ridiculous question. Of course they had. All humans do. But, were those secrets the kind that drew a couple together, in a blanket of security, or were they the sort that cause endless pain and trouble, even decades later?

She couldn't quite believe they'd faced similar problems as she and Ishmael had. It was inconceivable. Mum and Dad always seemed together, in more than one sense; solid, a unit. Sure, there were arguments. She remembered one occasion in particular, where she and Aimee had hidden at the top of the stairs, shushing each other and listening in on the rumble of loud voices from behind the kitchen door. In her eight year old wisdom, she had told a four year old Aimee that Mummy and Daddy weren't fighting each other, but rather shouting at the naughty dragon who lived at the bottom of the garden, and who was now trying to steal the cat's dinner. Aimee had had recurrent nightmares for two years after that.

Was there something else that left an undercurrent between her parents that only now was emerging? Could this be why Dad hadn't yet moved on from her mum? Was it down to unresolved issues, rather than an overwhelming grief?

She considered this for a few moments, hearing but not registering the echoing sound of a woodpecker in a nearby tree and the faint twitter of birds nesting in the higher branches. She pulled her thoughts together and approached the door.

*

The garden was cast into shadow in the late afternoon shade. There was a cool crispness in the air. The leaves above Evelyn's head rustled delicately and the grass beneath her feet was cold already, the chill permeating her thin pumps. She wrapped her arms around her, pulling the dusky pink Arran cardigan tighter across her chest. Walking round the back of the house, she reached the workshop.

The faint glare of a light inside hinted at its occupancy. She peered around the open double doors. The workshop, built fifteen years ago, was Ethan's attempt to escape the erratic moods of his two pubescent daughters. What originated as a glorified shed had evolved into a productive work space. Here he had built raised flower bed boxes, remote control cars, elaborate bird feeders, kitchen stools, mirror frames and dado rails, to replace the ancient ones falling off the walls in the house. He also kept a dart board and related paraphernalia there, just for fun.

It was a place for introspection too. It was somewhere to sit and contemplate, to reflect on, or to draw up new plans. Evelyn didn't remember the last time she had disturbed him here. It was always a no-go area, but back then she had been a teenager, living under a set of strict parental rules that no longer applied.

She breathed in the scent of metallic tools and sawdust. Beyond the glare of the bare light bulb, she saw Ethan sitting in a single chair. It had once belonged to an old sofa suite her parents owned years before. A faded red colour, wearing thin on the armrests, it still looked comfortable. It brought back memories. She was glad he had kept it and requisitioned it for his workshop.

'Dad?' she ventured, moving into the room.

26

He offered a tired smile. 'I thought you might have gone out.'

'I had hoped to stay here and help you sort through stuff.'

Rubbing a hand across his brow, he sighed. 'I'm not sure I'm up to that.'

She moved closer. He appeared older in the half-light, his frame bent over within the confines of the chair.

'I'm here, you know? You can talk to me. I can help... if you like. If you need,' she added, after a brief pause.

'Evelyn, I wouldn't know where to begin. Besides, my burdens are not yours. I don't want that. Helen wouldn't have wanted that either.'

'You're scaring me talking like that.'

He gave a short laugh. 'Don't be scared. As you know, sometimes being a grown up can hurt. It will all be fine.'

He stood up and headed over to the counter top on the far wall. Above it were shelves full of tools, boxes of nuts and bolts, nondescript bottles and jars; their contents unclear. On the counter stood a travel kettle and a couple of cake tins, the kind you find on sale at Christmas time, with snow scenes and West Highland Terriers on the front. He opened one and offered it to her. Inside were packets of sweets; mints, lollipops, mini chocolate bars. She raised an eyebrow.

He laughed. 'Some of these have been in here for months. I crave something sweet when I'm working. But, seeing as you are a guest', he said, thinking. 'I don't believe you've ever set foot in here before.'

'No,' Evelyn said slowly, a blush reaching her cheeks as she remembered sneaking in with Aimee on a couple of occasions in years past.

He flashed a knowing grin. Embarrassed, Evelyn plucked out a lollipop and waved it. 'Thank you.'

He gestured to a wooden rocking chair next to his and she sat down.

'You should be out having fun. Why don't you go into London and visit some friends?'

Evelyn felt a twinge of sorrow at the thought. 'Most of my friends are Ishmael's,' she replied, studying the lolly which remained unwrapped in her hand.

'What, they can't be yours now?'

'It's difficult. He's there, I'm miles away. Of course they see him more. Some of them were his friends to begin with anyway.'

'You're becoming isolated.'

'In that marriage, I think I always was.'

They sat in companionable silence, the faint ticking of a wooden clock, which Ethan had in the distant past made from scratch, the only sound permeating the encroaching shadows.

Chapter Seven

2009

'You all right?' she said with an attempt of nonchalance, leaning against the kitchen sink and stirring a spoon through her tea. Her heart pounded at his sudden appearance.

'Yeah,' Ishmael replied, a playful expression dancing through his eyes.

He knew, she thought. It was no surprise, not after the other evening. Back in the pub, Friday night, after two rounds of pool (Steve having skulked off back to the house) and at least two more drinks, they'd laughed, joked (they had a similar sense of humour) and shared horror stories and fond recollections of the still vibrant memories of living in halls.

He'd insisted that he walk her home. Despite her idealistic feminism at the time, she grew bashful by how much she enjoyed the potential romance of it all. That was rather spoilt with the awkward goodbye, where his attempted kiss on her cheek instead caught the side of her nose.

Now on Sunday morning, having spent the entire Saturday regretting not giving him her phone number and wondering how she might broach the subject with Steve, and whether he would feel charitable enough to pass on Ishmael's number to her, here he was; in her house.

Steve entered the kitchen, giving her a glare that translated as 'he's my friend,' and 'watch it, I'm onto you.'

'Tea?' he asked Ishmael, his voice gruff.

'Yeah, thanks.' Ishmael replied, never once breaking eye contact with Evelyn.

A blush spread over her cheeks. She was the first to glance away.

'We have lots of work to do,' Steve piped up, for her benefit she was sure. Evelyn wondered if it was the hijacking of his night out that bothered him more, or the attempted acquisition of his friend's attention.

'I'll be in the lounge,' she announced, attempting a calm, poised manner. Inside, her body felt very different, her nerves at edge, and an uncharacteristic clumsiness invading her limbs. The cup was heavy in her hand, every sense on heightened alert.

Sitting on the sofa, she opened a dog-eared magazine, trying to ignore the muffled masculine voices through the wall. Her mind, not taking in a single word from the glossy stylised pages, instead panicked amongst the thoughts of what would happen next. Would Ishmael draw attention to the other evening? Would he want to go out on a proper date, or was it just banter that kept him by her side that evening? What did she want to happen? It was obvious from her mental and physical reaction to his sudden appearance that she was attracted to him.

She'd only had one serious boyfriend before. A musician called Frankie; talented but clueless to living life in the real world. She took two years to tire of coming second to his music and his irrepressible dreams for his band, to tire of his lack of desire to get a day job to tide him over. He had slouched around halls and later her first house share, hanging out in her room, eating her snacks, laughing at her taste in music, and still she had daydreamed of becoming the loving lifelong companion of a rock star.

It was nothing more than a teenage fantasy for both of them and Evelyn grew up. The day she ended it was scored into her memory; his dingy flat with the heavy grey curtains that were always drawn, his bed hair (which he never seemed to know how to brush) sticking out in all directions, the utter disbelief on his face as she explained, that despite it all, they just wouldn't work. It was sad. She was sad. So much so, that other than a handful of unsuccessful dates since, she focused instead on her studies, ignoring men altogether.

She was twenty-one. She had years to worry about relationships and she was in no rush. Her degree and subsequent career needed to come first. But Friday night she'd met Ishmael as his own man, rather than just as a silent companion to her awkward housemate. Now he was an acquaintance, someone who had nuances and unique characteristics that made her stomach lurch in an uncomfortable but exciting way.

The kitchen door flung open into the lounge and Steve and Ishmael walked through. Passing Evelyn on the slouchy blue sofa, Steve ignored her, while Ishmael regarded her, locking eye contact. Evelyn's body froze into inaction. She couldn't believe she was reacting this way to a man.

Kate clattered through the front door at the other end of the room, cutting off Steve and Ishmael from their escape upstairs. She had just arrived back from the shop, her plastic bag overflowing with junk food. Evelyn saw several tubes of Pringles and the shape of a box of chocolates inside. How Kate managed to retain such a slender figure, let alone how she afforded to eat rubbish all the time, remained a mystery.

Kate shook her long dark honey locks over her one shoulder, while Steve stopped and stared. Evelyn felt embarrassed for him; his crush was obvious. Coughing, he ran a hand through his short dark hair and then absently across the front of his black and white checked shirt. Either oblivious or unconcerned by his reaction to her, Kate ignored him and walked past, just as he managed to utter a 'you all right?' reminiscent of Evelyn's own attempt, to Kate's retreating figure.

Ishmael grinned at Evelyn, who grinned back. Steve composed himself. 'Right, come on then,' he said to Ishmael, his voice cracked.

'I'll just pop to the toilet. I'll be up in a minute.'

Steve stared at them both and exhaled. 'Whatever.' He stomped up the stairs a little harder than necessary.

'I do need the toilet,' Ishmael admitted, his smile endearing. 'But first... well, it's entirely up to you what you do with this. It's a bit old fashioned, I admit... but I just wanted you to have it.' He paused, digging into his back pocket. He withdrew a scrap of paper.

Placing it in her hands, he nodded with shyness and retreated from the room. She opened her palm and uncurled the strip of white paper with her other hand. Scrawled in blue ink across the surface was a series of digits. He had given her his phone number.

*

As the dissertation deadline loomed, Evelyn found it harder to steal time away to be with Ishmael. In the first few weeks, a coffee date here and there had had to be enough. Friday evenings at the pub were a given. But now it was changing. Dates transformed into entire days together. Weekends couldn't pass by without seeing each other. He was always at the house.

Steve begrudgingly accepted their blossoming relationship and his eye rolling became less frequent. Evelyn wasn't sure that Kate had even noticed their relationship.

As the weeks passed, they bonded over their studies; some evenings up until the early hours, heads in their books, taking turns to make each other massive mugs of tea. He was approaching the end of his Engineering degree and her own degree for English Literature, seemed trivial in comparison. But his fervour for his studies encouraged her to work harder. She put extra research and hours in her dissertation, deepening the words, creating a stronger framework. She liked the influence he had on her life. Already they showed signs of being a great team.

'We need some fresh air,' he announced unexpectedly, stretching his arms behind his head, the table in front of them covered in books, their laptops sitting a little too close to the edge for comfort.

'But I have just ten days until the deadline,' she wailed, feeling a sudden prickle of panic at the thought. 'I still have so much to do.'

'You're stressing yourself out. I can see it oozing out of you.'

'Well, that's pleasant,' she muttered, her attention still on the book splayed out on her lap.

'Quite,' he said. 'That's my point. We need a break and some fresh air. Ice creams in the park? Maybe a quick bite to eat?'

One thing that irritated her and it was a tiny thing she reasoned, was his flippancy about money. She'd had to work through her degree and still barely scraped by. Sometimes Mum and Dad would transfer a little extra into her account as a gift, something she was always grateful for but never reliant on. Ishmael's parents had paid for his degree, all four years of it, upfront. They often sent him extra, which he didn't need as he wasn't workshy and was quite happy to earn his own, so it would get spent on unnecessary extras. It was their family, their rules, so she tried not to judge. It just niggled at her sometimes.

'I can't afford that right now,' she said, holding up her hand as she realised he was about to offer to pay. 'You are not paying for me,' she added emphatically.

He seemed put out, but composed himself. 'Okay, just a walk then. Come on. We've been stuck in all weekend.'

She acquiesced and they headed out toward the common behind her house. The promise of a hot summer ahead was in the air. The gentle breeze held the heady scent of nearby flowers, the astringent odour of city pollution and the growing heat from the sun permeating through it. They held hands, walking down to where a pond was already gathering algae and weeds surrounded its perimeter. They passed numerous families, dog walkers and other students; most of whom had hogged the limited shade under the nearby oak trees.

Ishmael stopped, wrapping his arms around her and pulling her towards him. She loved it when he did this. It showed a vulnerable side to him, a side that needed her. He wasn't often expressive and Evelyn respected that, but where she'd gush lyrical about him, he never seemed to be able to do the same for her. But behind closed doors, when it was just the two of them, she never doubted the strength of his feelings. And when those dark eyes would delve into hers; they would swim with an expression of there being no one else more desirable on the planet. To be comfortable to show his affection in public reassured her. They had only been together a few months. It was too soon for declarations of love, she reminded herself.

'We both finish our degrees soon,' he whispered into her hair. As his arms tightened around her, she felt the first stab of alarm at the realisation. What would happen then? She would go home to Suffolk, he would return to the Midlands… not a million miles away from each other, but still a distance that a relationship in its infancy might not survive.

'Yes,' she said with a croak, her mind darting as she considered their limited options. Already, she knew that if their relationship ended she would be devastated. They may not have said 'I love you' yet, but she was already there.

'We have some decisions to make Evie,' he spoke into her thick dark hair.

She didn't like him calling her that, but now was not the time to mention it.

'Let's get our dissertations out of the way then we can sort the rest out.'

It was more of a statement than a suggestion. Rather feeling the decision was being made for her, but grateful that he at least hadn't ended the relationship, she nodded. She'd be devastated if she lost him.

They made their way back to the house, back to the books, and the yawning void of what would come next.

*

33

Evelyn's part time job, at a café on the river front, stretched into the summer holidays. Her rental contract finished in early September, so she'd made the decision to stay where she was until then.

Ishmael decided to do the same, so despite the unspoken question mark between them, they spent their spare summer days relaxing in the park, hanging out all evening, falling in love with each other. By mid-August she didn't want to imagine a future without him. Plucking up the courage, she told him she loved him, feeling an immense joy – and relief – when he told her the same.

For years, that summer would remain her favourite. Young love, amid dreaming underneath the hot summer sky, the days blending together in a perfect haze.

One late evening, the odd star punctuating the perpetual smog of the city, as they sat outside on rickety patio chairs, a bottle of beer in her hand and a can of coke in his, Ishmael cleared his throat.

'I have a job interview in London,' he said, his gaze steady on hers. 'In fact, I have two. They're pretty good positions, considering I'm just finishing Uni.'

'Wow,' Evelyn managed, swallowing down a mouthful of beer with difficulty. She guessed London would be a little easier to get to from Suffolk. She suppressed her irritation that he hadn't mentioned applying for the jobs in the first place, or that he'd made plans without consulting her. They'd been a couple for five months, she kept reminding herself. She wasn't his keeper, even if they did do everything together.

'Yes,' he said, taking her exclamation as an opportunity to launch into a speech, detailing the benefits of being in the capital and what jobs might open up there in the future.

She sat and listened, her own dreams and plans floating somewhere up towards the lone star above them. It was then that she had a first glimpse that her career might always be a secondary consideration if she and Ishmael were to have a future together.

There was a sudden lull in his monologue and she tried to refocus her thoughts. He was staring at her, his eyes expectant.

'Well?' he said, pressingly. 'It makes perfect sense, doesn't it? We want to be together, right?'

Her mind sharpened, relaying his spiel as she frantically tried to recall what he'd said. Eyes widening, her memory hit on the last minute or so of their one-sided conversation. He had been talking about moving to London, regardless of whether he got one of the jobs or not.

'You should move there with me,' he'd enthused. 'I'm sure there'll be plenty of jobs there for you too.'

An afterthought.

She loved him so much. He was the kindest, sweetest man. A troubling thought that he sometimes liked to control their narrative impressed on her, but she rebuffed it. No one had held her like he did, running strands of her hair through his fingers, as she rested her head on his shoulder. She loved the way he treated her as if she was the only creature in the world able to enrapture him. She lost herself in his deep eyes. They made a great team already, the endless weeks of studying proved that. It made sense for them to continue in that vein; moving to London together, forging their careers together.

Evelyn nodded and Ishmael grinned back, relief spreading across his features. She loved that grin of his. It lit up his entire face.

'Yes, I want to be with you,' she said, her voice unsteady. 'I...,' she choked over the words and a sliver of anxiety grew in the pit of her stomach. 'It's so soon. We've not even met each other's families. I'm not sure my parents would like the idea of their daughter running off to London with some guy they've never met.'

'Then I meet them,' he shrugged, as if it wasn't a big deal at all. 'It'll take weeks until I have secured a job, after all. We've time to get them used to the idea.'

'And meet your family too?' Evelyn ventured.

'Of course,' he said, yet she noticed that he averted his eyes from her as he replied.

'Then... okay,' she confirmed. 'Let's do this.'

Chapter Eight

2019

Evelyn stared at the mobile in her hand and a particular name in her contacts list. It seemed to throb into her conscience. Ethan's words echoed through her thoughts, 'you're becoming isolated.'

She couldn't deny the truth. She *was* becoming isolated. What had birthed as an escape back home and a chance to heal, had developed into an incubus of seclusion. With the day to day running of the shop, Evelyn hadn't noticed it happening. But as much as she enjoyed spending her day with her colleagues Joe and Lucie, at the end of their working hours they went home to their own family and friends. They didn't hang out together outside of the shop.

Instead, Evelyn would return to the comfort of the family home and often to Ethan. But even he, she reminded herself, had a social life and half the week wasn't even around. She'd somehow managed to become a hermit.

Finger hovering over the green button, she paused. It seemed a bit presumptuous, after months of no contact, to just call; to expect to pick up from where they'd left off, as if she hadn't dropped off the face of the globe. She read the name of her best friend one last time, swallowed down the disappointment, exited the screen, and dropped the phone back into her pocket.

It needed to be done. She knew that. Just not today; she didn't have the strength today.

Leaving the office, she entered the shop floor. Joe was serving a customer, their reusable bag stacked full with paperbacks. If anyone could persuade people to part with their money and buy multiple books at a time, it was Joe.

Despite being a natural introvert, he was approachable and always friendly with customers. In a few short questions he'd ascertain what the potential customer was searching for, suggest various titles and several alternatives to tempt them to try something different, all the while making them feel like the most important person in the room. She'd never seen a customer finish a conversation with Joe without a grin on their face, and more than not, at least one book.

As the customer departed Joe caught her eye. 'What do you think?' he asked, whipping out his mobile phone from beneath the counter top and showing her a picture of the flyer he'd designed.

As a general rule phones were banned from the shop floor, but Evelyn figured that as she'd asked him to do the errand, and they were all grown-ups who knew how to be professional at work, she didn't have to enforce the rule too often. The flyer was Evelyn's idea, off the back of strategising about the upcoming festival. She'd always planned to run events at Taverton Tales and had already hosted several launches for local authors, but regular events took more planning and advertising and she hadn't got there yet.

Trying to find ways to monopolise on the festival, and to try to increase local interest in the bookshop, she'd decided to launch a storytelling hour. Every Friday morning they would create a dedicated space for parents and their pre-schoolers and Joe, upon a little encouragement, would put his impressive storytelling skills to good use, followed with book related colouring in and the chance to buy whichever children's books had special promotions running.

Evelyn knew it wasn't a revolutionary idea, but there was nothing similar locally. The town was popular with young families. Applying for the relevant police checks and an examination into their insurance policy confirmed that they'd be able to go ahead and make plans. Evelyn hoped to host the first morning in the beginning half of June, should their police clearances arrive in time.

The flyer included Joe's own sketches of various children's book characters, dotted around the page and framing the font. She grinned. She loved it.

'This is fantastic, Joe. If you can send me the file, I'll get them printed. It's about time we were doing things like this. This is just the start, believe me.'

'Let me know if you need anything else designed. I quite enjoy it,' he said, taking the phone and moving back behind the counter. 'You know I went to Art College?'

'No, I didn't. But it doesn't surprise me.'

His expression narrowed. 'Was that a compliment, or mockery? I can never tell with you.'

She laughed. 'I would never mock you, Joe. Art College... it all suddenly makes sense.'

He mimed throwing a nearby book at her and she grinned. The sound of someone clearing their throat startled them, and they turned to see a wide-eyed customer a couple of feet from the desk.

'I just wanted to buy this one, please,' an elderly lady stepped forward, placing the novel on the counter top with delicate movements. Her eyes were a little wary underneath her dark green beanie. Joe coughed to clear his throat and took the book from the surface.

'Of course,' he said, back to his usual soft tones. 'And, would you like a bag for that?'

Evelyn busied herself with a pile of books, ready to be shelved, and hid her smile behind them.

*

Wedging the shoe box back above the cupboard, Ethan grimaced. Helen was gone. Nothing changed that and hunting for clues in her journal pages wouldn't change anything about the life they'd carved out together.

Miniscule doubts that gathered like dust over the years now left a downy film of unanswered questions. While Helen was alive, being an attentive mother and wife, he'd been able to push those concerns to one side. Now his memory of her was fading, it seemed to only emphasise the shaky foundation they'd based their relationship on. But did it matter? They had been happily married after all. Whatever the original reasons behind their marriage, they had created a wonderful life as husband and wife.

Revisiting the cupboard under the stairs, where half an hour before he'd abandoned the sorting, he pulled out a box into the light in the hallway. Already opened, he removed an armful of items, placing them on the carpeted floor beneath him. There were several old fashioned photo albums and reference books that Helen had bought, with plans to start yet another new hobby but soon abandoned; painting, cake decorating, a book on tracing the family tree.

Ethan shook his head with fondness. This was Helen through and through. She'd always had a curiosity for the unknown and a desire to try something new. But she'd often start a new hobby then lost interest. It had been a mild irritant during their years together, now it was a characteristic he found endearing and he missed it. She'd passed on the same characteristic to Aimee, he realised, and he laughed.

Placing the books in a pile, ready to take to one of the local charity shops, he opened the top photo album. Inside, stuck down with yellowing glue, were watermarked and aged photographs of Helen as a child. There were numerous snapshots of her and her two brothers, Michael and Philip; her mother and father much younger and youthful, despite the tell-tale signs of parental exhaustion behind their eyes. Helen's father had died ten years ago and her mother was now in a care home. Ethan, whose own parents had already passed, still visited his mother-in-law every month.

He scanned through the pages, taking in the visual details of Helen as a child; pink and yellow checked flannel dungarees, a simple but pretty white dress with knee high socks, auburn hair in bunches, cute upturned nose, an infectious grin.

The last page stopped him short. Here she was, late-teens, not long before they became a couple. The features on her face were maturing, the angles youthful yet recognisable as the woman he would soon fall in love with.

A punch of guilt winded him then. These days grief was more of an incessant ache, but this time it was sharp and painful. Already kneeling down on the carpeted floor he replaced the photo album on the pile and wept.

*

'You realise of course, old Harriet Brown was a right trollop in her day,' Betty Longhorn stated matter of fact, whilst Joe ducked under the counter amid spasms of hysterics. Next to her feet, his eyes bulged with the effort to control himself.

'Is that right, Mrs Longhorn?' Evelyn enquired, her mouth twitching. 'I'm not sure though, that she'd appreciate you saying things like that about her in public. Some might consider it unkind.'

'Pah,' Betty scoffed. 'She was quite happy to flounce about with that reputation when we were younger. She almost held it up as a badge of honour. Of course,' she leaned in conspiratorially, her finger pointed.

'Her daddy was rich round these parts, so no one would have dared name call, like they did poor Penny Brooker.'

'Besides,' Betty said, shrugging off the entire conversation. 'Harriet is losing her marbles these days. She wouldn't remember anything after a few minutes, even if she did take offense.'

Evelyn couldn't, for the life of her, remember how the conversation had steered so far off course. They'd been talking about the weather a couple of minutes ago. Betty Longhorn liked to visit the bookshop once a week, often to share some juicy titbit about someone in the town, and would then inspect the Maeve Binchys and stalk out again. On the occasion she did buy or order a book, she would return to give a full and frank review of it to the bookshop's amused staff members.

In her mid-eighties, Betty was a firecracker of a personality, a personality that belied her fragile shell. Whiskery and slight, stooped at the shoulders, deep grey hair in a bun, and almost always clad in tweed, she was rather a formidable matriarch.

With an opinion of everybody, Evelyn had no doubt that she herself had been the subject of at least one of Betty's public conversations. A failed marriage at thirty, running home from the big city, to her widower father, with her tail between her legs; the source of plenty of gossip, she imagined.

'Is that boy okay down there?' Betty's voice cut into her thoughts.

'Yes.' His reply was muffled. 'Thank you, Mrs Longhorn. I'm just... rearranging the bags.'

So, Mrs Longhorn,' Evelyn piped up, trying to distract her. Betty was peering around the side of the desk, suspiciously doubting Joe's version of events. 'Are you going to try the novel?'

She held out the copy of Pride and Prejudice that Betty had brought over, several minutes before the conversation skewed, asking if was worth reading 'at my age.'

'I can't believe you haven't read it,' she laughed, kindly. 'It's a classic and an absolute must read.'

Betty looked unimpressed. 'I was busy raising five children,' she answered, her tone gruff, in justification for having never picked up a Jane Austen novel in her nine decades.

'It is wonderful.' Evelyn held it out as an encouragement. 'You won't regret it.'

'You'd be surprised what I've regretted,' Betty muttered, but nevertheless removed a note from her purse.

Evelyn ran up the purchase and handed over the change. Joe made an awkward and reluctant return to her side and they waved Mrs Longhorn off, neither daring to catch the other's eye.

Evelyn was still giggling under her breath hours later, shop closed for the day and now heading up the main street towards home.

*

Warm and comforting smells greeted her as she pushed her way through the front porch, into the hallway beyond. The kitchen door was ajar opposite, the light blaring out from the crack, and the melodious hum of the radio escaping with it.

The door widened and Randall squeezed through the gap with his white and ginger striped body. He sniffed at her with an air of indifference and stalked across the hallway toward the lounge.

'Thanks for the welcome Randall,' she said, dropping her bag on the mahogany sideboard and hanging her coat up on the hook above.

The rest of the house was plunging into darkness, twilight having descended outside, painting its layers darker as the minutes ticked by. Shadows filled the corners of the olive-green wallpapered hallway and Evelyn pushed her way into the kitchen, the light enveloping her in its all-encompassing warmth.

Ethan was stirring the contents of the cast iron pot upon the stove. The table was set, a glass of red wine already poured out. He acknowledged her presence, but kept his eyes on the food.

'Sit down and relax. The glass of red is for you.'

'Hi Dad,' she replied, giving him a side hug. He shifted the tea towel across his shoulders, moving it out of her way. His spare arm embraced her.

'Better day?'

'Yes,' she said beaming. Moving over to the table she picked up the glass and took a long, satisfying, mouthful. 'The stall is booked for the festival. Joe is keen to help the organisers behind the scenes as well, so that's great. We're also planning to launch the storytelling hour and I have lots of other events I want to add to the schedule too. And, I spent a good hour posting across our social media accounts, after shutting shop. I need to post more regularly.'

'I'm realising this is going take a longer time than I imagined. We need to build the place up from scratch again. At the moment it's just another 'small town' bookshop. I want it to become the place that tourists have heard about and come to visit because it's a focal point.

And of course, I want the business to meet the locals' needs as they are the ones who will bring in the regular sales.'

Ethan turned round, folding his arms against his chest. 'Sounds like you're coming up with a plan. It'll be nice to see the place transformed.'

'It'll take time though, Dad. We're breaking even, but we can't launch too quickly or spend much money. That limits my options.'

'You have a vision. It might take longer, but you're focused on what you want to achieve. That puts you ahead in my book.'

'I will move out… soon.' She swallowed down a large gulp of wine. 'I don't want to outstay my welcome.'

'You're my daughter. You're welcome here.'

'I know,' she said, inspecting the wine glass with both hands, shoulders slumped. 'I can't be a burden though. I won't be. I will stand on my own two feet. You have already done more than enough.'

He stayed silent, watching her a while. When she did regain eye contact, he gave her a tender, encouraging smile. Sometimes words weren't enough.

*

'That was amazing.' Evelyn lay the fork and knife down across the empty plate. A full glass of red wine and warming plate of chilli-con-carne had done the trick. She was ready for a good night's sleep.

'It's your turn to cook tomorrow, unless you have other plans of course, in which case I'd settle for egg on toast.'

The insinuation was unmistakable. How would she break it him that she had no plans, yet again? That she'd even chickened out of phoning her best friend? The first friend she'd made in London and who she used to see every week without fail.

'No plans,' she whispered. Picking up the wine glass, now empty, she stared into it. A small rim of red coated the bottom, hiding the join between the glass and the stem. She swirled it around.

'I didn't want to leave the house for months after your mother died,' Ethan admitted, clearing his throat. 'I had to of course. I had a job for a start. I learned that the world doesn't stop spinning for everyone else. It's a painful realisation, but a necessary one.'

He stood from the table, scooping up both his and Evelyn's empty plates and taking them to the sink.

'I had to put myself out there, Evelyn. It wasn't easy at all, but life improved a little the more I did it.'

43

Evelyn nodded, the threat of tears stuck in her throat. She hadn't cried for months and she suppressed the urge.

'It wasn't deliberate.'

'I know, but it has happened and you need to rectify it. If they're true friends, they'll forgive you. I know the shop has kept you busy, but before you plunge into the next busy phase, I think you'd benefit from mending a few bridges.'

He left it at that, as she gave a tight, unsteady smile and nodded again. She stood, approaching the sink to do the washing up. Opening the hot water tap, she placed the plug into place and added the washing up liquid. Watching the water swirl into the bowl, her gaze shimmered with unspent tears.

She hadn't just lost Ishmael. She'd lost her friends, left her job and turned her back on her entire life. It may not have been a life of her choosing, but it had become her comfort zone, her source of reference. The relief she imagined she'd feel, gaining control of her own circumstances again, hadn't materialised. Instead, she felt bereft. She felt alone.

She had an amazing business, with great potential, and she was back in the childhood town she adored. But her heart had been totally, and wholly, shattered. She didn't know how to repair that. She didn't know, even after a year and a half, where to begin.

Evelyn hid an escaped gasp of sorrow beneath the noise of the running tap. She hoped Ethan hadn't heard. Composing herself, she busied her hands with the dirty dishes, all the while not noticing her father standing, watching.

Chapter Nine

I showed him my poems and sketches today. I have not shown another soul before. I felt as anxious as if he had kissed me for the first time and as breathless as I had then. I so wanted him to like what I had written. They are abstract, but I hoped he noticed that they were all about him.

He laughed as he read them which worried me, my heart plummeting in disappointment. He can sometimes make me feel so naïve, so innocent. It annoys me no end, but I guess a country girl of seventeen, who'd never been kissed before, will leave that impression on a nineteen year old man. For that is what Laurence is, a man. The other boys in town pale into comparison.

But he raised his eyebrows in enthusiasm and that warmed me. He liked them! I saw the merriment in his eyes.

'My little field mouse, a brilliant poet and artist!' he said, his expression teasing. 'Or maybe, I should call you a kestrel from now on; your words are fiercer than you look.'

I hit his arm playfully, snatching back my notebook and we both laughed. Then he kissed me hard on the lips. And I forgot to reply.

Chapter Ten

2009

Ishmael accepted an offer for the second job, phoning Evelyn to tell her the news and how he was due to start in a fortnight. Her heart constricting with the pace that everything was moving, amid the anxiety of her own job search, she fought to sound pleased.

'Ishmael, that's great news.'

She almost heard him grinning down the phone, his excitement was so tangible.

'I know!' he laughed.

She swallowed with difficulty. He was so thrilled. She tried to forget her parents' words from the night before. They'd only met Ishmael twice and were worried that she was willing to follow him, to the depths of the capital, with no secure job of her own.

'He's a lovely man,' Helen said, placing her hand over Evelyn's. 'We do like him. It just seems a bit quick to be setting up together.' She glanced at Ethan for support, who nodded in agreement.

Evelyn suppressed a flash of anger, trying to reason where her parents were coming from. 'But we're not. Setting up together, I mean. He's searching for work there, and it makes sense for me to as well. After all, what better place is there to find work than London, right? There won't be as much on offer for me here.'

Helen and Ethan couldn't deny that.

'We'll have to find a house share at first,' she admitted. 'There's no way we'll be able to afford a place of our own. And as you said, it's very soon. We might not be living together anyway. We've already agreed that if we can't find work in the same part of London, we'll each find our own house share, just to start. We can make other plans later on.'

They'd added this caveat for two reasons. Firstly, to convince both sets of parents that heading off into the sunset, after only five months of dating, was not a disaster waiting to happen. And, secondly, as reality hit at just how big London was and how spread out their job search would be.

Meeting Ishmael's parents had taken all her nerve. Ishmael seemed to fluctuate between silent respect and deference to flickers of annoyance at any mention of them. There were unspoken issues there. It had surprised her then, upon that first visit, just how much she adored his mother; softly spoken, petite, but with a real sense of strength of character. Ania was a head shorter than her son, who was quite short himself, with a smart black bob and neat-as-a-pin clothing. She exuded the impression of a woman in control and secure within her role in the family. She didn't have to raise her voice to convey this. Ania was polite and a perfect hostess and Evelyn felt relief to see a sparkle and friendliness in her eyes as they engaged in conversation with each other.

Ishmael's father was the strong, silent type and it was here that Evelyn suspected the root of Ishmael's reticence lay. Wealthy and successful, evident by the large and beautifully decorated house, the brand new BMW in the driveway, and the expensive cut of his tailored suit, Benesh possessed the stance of someone secure in his own self-made empire. He had stronger features than Ishmael, an angular definition in his jaw that Ishmael's brother shared. Ishmael took after his mother.

There was an unspoken air of tension between the two men, and Ania, aware of it but never bringing attention to it, smoothed out the atmosphere, bringing out regular plates of food and diverting the conversation when necessary.

Benesh didn't pay particular attention to Evelyn and she noticed the flash of challenge behind Ishmael's eyes. If he thought his father might comment, he was left disappointed. Benesh kept their interaction civil.

Once, she caught a three-way glance between them all, during a discussion about jobs and how Ishmael expected to afford London. They offered money, which he refused.

She'd always assumed that Ismael was comfortable to receive money from his parents, helping him sail through university without the burden of debt. Now, a betraying thought considered whether his flippant spending of their money was on purpose.

The evening threatened to dip into darker territory when Ishmael's parents addressed the elephant in the room. Ania, ignoring her son's wearing impatience next to her, asked:

'You have been together just a few months. Moving is a very stressful experience, especially to a city so large and demanding. Have you thought this through?'

Ishmael cleared his throat in anger. 'We've been together five months, nearly six,' he stated, as if that made all the difference. He didn't answer her question.

Evelyn almost buckled at the truth of Ania's words. This was huge. She loved him, so very much, but this was bigger than anything else she'd faced in her twenty-one years. Yet, she knew her future was intrinsically linked to his. She felt it. Why put off what they knew to be true? They belonged together.

'We love each other,' she'd stated. 'This is part of our adventure.'

She'd imagined she'd feel emboldened as those words tumbled out. They had sounded so strong, so self-assured in her head. As they emerged though, she had a striking glimpse of their immaturity and naiveté. She kept still and poised, maintaining eye contact with Ania. She dared not blink.

Ania studied her, her expression giving nothing away. She then turned to her son and nodded.

'So be it.'

*

As with life, nothing went quite to plan. Jobless and with no money in her bank account, it was Ishmael who headed to London first. Due to start his new job, he found a grimy but reasonable house share, and off he went.

Poring over job adverts, numerous cups of coffee littering the kitchen table, Evelyn was nevertheless unperturbed. Back home with her parents, she took the train into London for interviews, trying not to get disheartened each time she received a 'no.'

If anything, her resolve grew. She missed Ishmael so much it hurt. His features were as familiar to her as any member of her family. She knew his dreams, his insecurities, and quirks. Moving to London to be with him became an almost obsessive focus. Indeed, it did wonders at removing any filaments of doubt. She hated living without him. If that wasn't confirmation that they were meant to be together, she didn't know what was.

Three months later, with two large suitcases to manoeuvre through the dense London crowds, she arrived. Securing a job as an administrative assistant, on a basic wage, wasn't quite the dream she'd imagined. Ignoring the betraying thought that she would have got a job like that back in Suffolk, at far cheaper the living expense, she instead focused on the thought that it was a stepping stone to getting to London, and being with Ishmael.

They had endured three months of seeing each other at weekends, and the odd snatched lunch break whenever she travelled in for an interview. They'd spent her twenty-second birthday miles apart from one another. Now she couldn't wait to see him after work every day.

She arrived at the flat where she'd be sharing with two other women. Niamh worked in finance and Gemma was a nurse. They'd both seemed friendly when she and Ishmael had viewed her room a couple of weekends before. It beat the alternatives; one flat was disgusting, mould creeping up the walls and with what looked like a cluster of mushrooms growing through lounge carpet. Another house share was weird – some of the housemates glared at her while others ignored her presence. The last one they didn't even view, arriving at the address to a house with metal carcasses of various broken-down appliances dumped in the front yard, and a front door step that was covered in what appeared to be vomit. Ishmael took her hand and led her away, not even saying a word and without having knocked on the door.

Viewing the last flat had been a relief to both of them. While the décor was a little tired, it was a warm and light space, and a quick inspection of the bookshelf alerted Evelyn to the similar reading tastes of her potential new housemates. Securing a rolling month contract, she'd settle into the job, and in a few months when Ishmael's rental contract ended, they'd be in a position to find somewhere together.

That first evening, unpacking her things and laughing at Ishmael's anecdotes about life in London, she felt daunted yet excited for what lay ahead.

Chapter Eleven

2019

Joe prised open the sci-fi novel with care so as not to crease the spine. He read a few paragraphs then placed it down on the counter, distracted.

Lucie was on her lunch break. She never stayed in the shop during that hour, which of course, he reasoned, was her prerogative. Sometimes he liked to wander too, even though every inch of the street, every shop front, every alleyway, was as familiar to him as the lines on the palm of his hand. He had grown up in Taverton, and other than his years at art college, had no inclination to ever leave.

Lucie had lived in the town for a couple of years; he knew that as she'd told him. Perhaps she was still getting to know the place and exploring the town on her time off. Or perhaps she headed back home to have her lunch. Back to her family, her friends, maybe even a boyfriend. He realised he thought about Lucie a little too much.

His mind forced itself to Evelyn. Six years younger than Evelyn, he didn't remember her much from their childhood in Taverton, meeting properly for the first time when she bought the shop. But he remembered her mother well as she'd been one of his teachers at High School.

He admired Evelyn's determination to take on a failing business, and through sheer grit and stubbornness, try to turn it around. He didn't know a lot about her, even less about Lucie. Evelyn mentioned once that she had split with her husband, but hadn't elaborated. She kept the rest of her life private too. It felt strange knowing so little about his co-workers. Edward and Margaret Denyer, the previous owners, were always sniping at each other. He'd known *all* their business.

In all honesty he preferred his work place to be drama free, as fond as he had been of Mr and Mrs Denyer. It was refreshing not to keep his head down and mouth shut quite so much. He didn't make a habit of getting involved with other people's domestic or emotional outbursts. He just wanted to get on with his job and read his books.

Running a finger down the cover, he contemplated giving the book another chance. The shop was quiet, with the flurry of lunchtime customers dissipating and the bookshop empty for the last twenty minutes. His stomach rumbled with hunger and his eyes flickered to the clock on the wall. Lucie would be back soon.

He grabbed the book, determined to finish the first chapter before his own search for food. Two pages later, now engrossed, he ignored the jangle of the bell and didn't register Lucie's presence until she was standing next to him at the desk.

He jumped in his chair, heart pounding.

'Are you all right?' Her eyes were wide and alert. 'I didn't mean to scare you.'

'Hmm, no… no you're good,' he said, composing himself. 'I mean, I'm good.' He cleared his throat. 'Did you have a nice lunch break?'

'Yes. It was fine, thanks.'

She averted her eyes as if trying to avoid revealing something. Perhaps she had a secret boyfriend, he thought in dismay. That would be it. He'd been stupid enough to let on his attraction, so she was keeping her relationship a secret for his benefit. He was embarrassed. He'd never been great with women, but now they were actually feeling sorry for him. He winced.

'Are you happy to hold the fort?' Joe said, shaking off his mortification. 'I need to head out for a bit.'

'Sure.'

Lucie hung her bag and jacket up in the back room and logged into the computer and till. Within seconds he was out the door, his cheeks glowing red and his gaze fixed on the pavement below his feet.

*

He marched up the hill toward the Norman church at the top. Shops lined either side of the street, with the odd antiques place and tearooms dotted in between. In the summer months, tourists would pour into town and the streets would buzz with chatter and the heavy footfall of visitors. However, this time of year, it was down to the local residents to keep the commercial centre going. Some shops didn't try, reducing their opening hours or even shutting during the quieter months.

Joe reached the top of the hill and skirted the graveyard surrounding the church. Imposing yew trees framed the plot, casting a shadow across the path and his feet. Fresh mown grass left a peaty, vaguely citrus, scent to the air. To his left the entrance of an alley led to a small common area. There he hoisted the shop-bought sandwich box out of his jacket pocket, taking a seat on a nearby bench. He ate the BLT sandwich with enthusiasm, musing on his love life, or lack thereof.

He'd had one girlfriend in college. A bolshie, headstrong girl called Lana, who took control of their entire relationship and bossed him into submission. He did everything she asked and unsurprisingly, a year later, was miserable. Yet, he hadn't had the guts to end it. She did in the end, swapping the subservient Joe for a stereotypical 'bad boy' who treated her like dirt. She seemed happy enough though. He had moved on from that relationship, with a confused shake of the head and a minuscule remnant of confidence.

There had been plenty of terrible dates; one girl barked like a seal when she laughed, another mentioned her ex a record thirty-four times during dinner. Joe had counted.

Then he'd met Holly. Red hair, pretty freckles, and a face that would light up the darkest room, he fell instantly in love. She laughed at all his jokes, never seemed ashamed or embarrassed to be seen out with him, and perhaps most importantly had a love for books as deep as his.

Dating for two years, they'd slipped into a comfortable synchronicity. Friday nights were always date night, either indoors with a takeaway and DVD, or out for dinner the first Friday after payday. On Saturday and Sunday, they would mostly do their own thing, but meet for a drink or for Sunday lunch at one of the parents' homes. During the week, they'd hang out after work, either at her place or his. Those evenings usually consisted of reading or discussing books, him strumming his guitar, or her talking about the local gossip.

It wasn't fireworks and candlelight, but a steady comforting routine he'd grown accustomed to. The day she pulled the rug out beneath them was unexpected and it blindsided him.

'Fancy a cuppa?' he'd asked, as she arrived at his flat, cheeks red from the cold night air. They clashed against her red hair, but he liked it.

'Sure, Joe,' her answer seemed distracted, but he ignored the warning sign.

Stepping into the tiny kitchenette in the corner of his glorified studio flat, he filled the kettle and absentmindedly waited for it to boil. Despite its tiny dimensions, he loved the place. It was his. It was all he could afford on a bookshop salary, and desperate not to live with his mother forever, he hadn't needed much persuasion to take the place.

Holly stepped in behind him. She hovered. He leaned over to kiss her and felt her body tense.

'Joe, we need to have a chat,' she sniffed, pushing a section of hair behind her ears.

'Let's just make the tea first,' he'd replied, with a growing prickle of awareness. He still grimaced at the memory of those words. He knew what was coming, but typical, polite to-the-end Joe, ignored it to produce the perfect cuppa.

It was a coping mechanism and it served him well for the next half an hour, as Holly poured out all her concerns, and un-negotiable reasons why their relationship wasn't working. He sat, stunned, as her words spilled forth.

'Is this all we want from life?' she'd gesticulated. 'To sit on each other's couches and watch life go by?'

He liked sitting on the couch with her.

'I know I can't do this year in, year out,' she'd continued, eyes glazing with tears. 'It's not that I don't care for you…'

No mention of love, he noted.

'But I need more purpose, more passion, more fire,' she declared.

She'd clearly been rehearsing this speech.

'We don't even talk about the future,' she raised her hands in demonstration. 'We have no direction!'

He replied to this. It seemed to shake him from his reverie.

'I do want to marry you,' he said, in earnest. 'I just wasn't sure whether you were ready. You've never mentioned it.'

She balked. 'I… I don't want to marry you, Joe.'

And so, there it was. And there, the relationship ended. He hadn't dated since. Not because he was still in love with Holly, or even still hurt by her words, but because love seemed far too complicated to put in the effort.

Then along came Lucie. He'd groaned when, within a couple of shifts, he recognised the tell-tale signs of his attraction to her. Of course, you can't go through life without being attracted to people, he knew that. But the proximity of their job roles, the frequency at which they worked together didn't give him any breathing space to get over his crush. Even one shift together each week was too frequent, he found, and so Joe's attraction kept ticking over, tightening its grip, instead of fluttering loosely away as he'd hoped.

It didn't help that Lucie was both sweet and pretty. Even though she kept herself to herself much of the time, she had a genuine interest in other people and what they had to say.

Joe was faced with the realisation that potential love at twenty-five years old was just as ugly and confusing as it had been at twenty-one, which was the last time he'd been in this situation. He bit into the rest of his sandwich angrily. When was it ever going to get easier? And when would he fall for someone who liked him in return, instead of either another unrequited situation, or a disinterested girlfriend, who'd dump him within a couple of years, bored and unsatisfied?

Feeling that one sandwich had not been nearly enough, he got up, forced his hands dejectedly into his pockets and slouched his way down the hill, back to the bookshop. He'd spend the rest of his lunch break hidden behind the words of a novel. The literary world was far less complicated.

Chapter Twelve

'I'm unable to take your call right now, please leave a message after the tone. You know, if you can be bothered, otherwise I suppose you could try again later.'

The recorded voicemail message made Evelyn laugh. She could almost hear the shrug in her best friend's voice. The beep signalled the start of the recording.

'Hi,' she paused. 'Hi Caren, it's me. Evelyn. I know I haven't been in touch for a while. I'm hoping you don't hate me for that.' She took a breath. 'If you still like me, call back. Otherwise I will try again later, and you're welcome to shout at me if you want. Bye.'

She pressed the button to disconnect the call and bit her lip. Now she just had to wait.

Caren was her oldest friend from London and by far her closest. Born to South African parents and raised in the UK since her teens, Caren (whose name was pronounced 'Car-en' instead of the British pronouncement of 'Ka-ren') had a no-nonsense exterior, but a soft-in-the-centre fondness for those she loved. Six years older than Evelyn, she'd been among the first to take her under her wing, as Evelyn tried to navigate life in London.

She remembered back to when they first met. Just a few weeks into the new job and the cracks were already showing. From the horrid commute each morning, to the office where she was treated as everyone's lackey and resolutely ignored in a surreal paradox. Having felt grown up moving to London, she ended up catapulted back into an adult version of the school playground.

In comparison Ishmael's job was going swimmingly well. He had his appraisal, accompanied with heaped praise and faint promises of a charmed future with the company. He'd made a few friends, one of whom, Adrian, was in a relationship with a woman called Caren and Evelyn had agreed to a double date. She felt isolated and lonely, so despite a reticence at the thought of meeting Ishmael's colleague and their partner, she wasn't about to give up an opportunity to socialise either.

Caren had been a welcome surprise. Confident, outspoken, but with a maternal edge, Evelyn was drawn to the other woman's strength. It exuded from her, whereas Evelyn's own had been dripping away amid the stress of trying to settle into city life.

As those early months passed, Caren was the one she leaned on when she needed a stern word to get back on track, or an avenue to vent her frustrations – often over a drink or two. As the years passed she made more friends, especially when she moved on from the job she hated, to working at the archive office. But Caren, these days knee-deep in nappies and play dough with two small children, as well as juggling a day job for a multinational company, remained the closest and most genuine of all Evelyn's friendships.

A minute passed before the familiar ringtone interrupted her contemplative silence. Evelyn grabbed up the phone and hit the answer button with a stabbing motion.

'Hello?'

'You're lucky I checked my phone. It's quicker to get me on my work mobile. I have a lunch meeting with my boss Denholm, so I can't talk for long. Perhaps if you hadn't vanished into thin air, you'd know I always have a business lunch on Monday,' was the peppered response.

Evelyn grinned. From anyone else it would have come across as an admonishment. With Caren it was a statement of fact. If she was angry, she wouldn't have called back.

'I've been a terrible friend.'

'Yes you have,' Caren stated. 'I guessed you needed time to lick your wounds.'

'Perhaps, but the bookshop has kept me busy too.'

'Oh, yes. The bookshop,' the pause afterwards was loaded. 'Is it a distraction or a new direction Evelyn?'

Struck by her friend's ability to hone in on the real matter and the uncanny ability to just stay shy of the line of causing offence, Evelyn was stunned into silence. She decided not to answer that question.

'I want to come and visit,' she said instead. 'I know you may be upset with me – perhaps you won't want to see me at all. But if there's a chance, I'd like to meet and apologise. And build bridges too.'

'Evelyn,' Caren said with emphasis. Evelyn imagined her waving her arms in frustration. 'What do you need to apologise for? You moved away. Life gets busy. It happens to us all.'

'Yes, but, I should have made more effort to stay in touch. If I'm honest, I've isolated myself. I've been lonely and that's my own fault. But that's not why I'm calling.' She took a deep breath. 'I am calling because I've been an idiot.'

'Denholm wants me to increase my hours, even though I have two pre-schoolers. The childcare fees will be insane. He also wants me to take work home every evening and work through my summer holiday. I am now on my way to persuade him otherwise. *He* is the idiot, Evelyn. Not you. Okay?'

Evelyn laughed. 'Okay, Caren. Okay.'

*

'I made apple pie,' Janice muttered in a monotone, the pie outstretched in her hands.

'Morning, Janice,' Ethan said in polite greeting, the front door open in his hand.

'Yes,' she said, distracted. She wore her purple rain mac, even though the sky was blue and clear, with a nondescript grey t-shirt and olive-green trousers underneath.

'Cup of tea?' he offered. She nodded and stepped through the door. He took the still warm pie and walked to the kitchen. She followed behind.

'Can I take your coat?'

'Oh no, that's quite all right.' She sat on the kitchen chair with a bump.

'I'll put the kettle on then,' Ethan said, attempting to break the awkward atmosphere that fell between them. 'You're very kind. For bringing food over so often, I mean. I hope you don't feel you have to in any way.'

'I bake a lot when I'm not working. What's this?' she asked, pointing to a small box on the kitchen table in front of her.

Ethan stared at the box. 'I'm clearing out Helen's things.'

Janice appeared startled. 'Well, I… that must be… indeed.'

Even after three years, the unexpected mention of his late wife still provoked an awkward reaction in people.

'I took two weeks off work to sort through it all, but it wasn't long enough,' he admitted. 'I'm still sifting through random boxes.'

And the contents of the shoe box, he thought. The journal entries were taking a long time to read through, process and try to put into a sense of order. In addition, boxes of knitting needles, folders of planning materials from her teaching years, the girls' various scribbles, should have seemed trivial in comparison, yet they hadn't. Everything seemed to require consideration, all of which took time.

'So, you're back at work, but still at home today?' she asked, eyes darting around the kitchen. 'I knew you were at home. I saw your car in the drive.'

A little uncomfortable, Ethan busied himself making their tea. 'I'm working from home today.'

He passed her mug across the table and sat opposite. Her gaze was fixed on his and he smiled in politeness, taking a sip from his own mug. He had known Janice for two years. She'd moved into her two-bed bungalow, situated halfway down the quiet lane, upon the completion of her divorce. She'd lived for many years in a neighbouring village and found a new start in Taverton more appealing than living near her ex-husband.

She spent an inordinate amount of time baking and dropping off the results. He'd initially considered this as nothing more than wanting to be a good neighbour. Now, as the months progressed, he suspected an underlining motive.

'How's life treating you Janice?'

She withdrew her watery gaze from him and sniffed, nose pointed in the air. Her fingers stroked the rim of the mug, but she made no attempt to pick it up and drink from it.

'Well, as you know, being on your own is no picnic at times. These big empty houses with just me and you rattling around inside, it can play on one's mind.'

'Sure...' he answered, not sure he wanted to know where she was going with the conversation. 'You have a daughter, right?'

'She went off to university and never came back.' She sniffed again.

'Well, maybe you could visit her. A change is as good as a holiday, as they say.'

'Oh, she won't be interested in that.'

Ethan rather felt the direction of the conversation was being shut down. 'Right, well... baking is a good hobby to have. Have you thought of selling some of your cakes to one of the local tearooms?'

'Yes... yes,' she replied, still gazing off to the distance.

After a short silence, Ethan heard the front door click and inwardly sighed in relief. Evelyn was home.

'Hi Dad,' he heard her call from the hallway.

Ethan noticed Janice stiffen even further, if that was possible, then her shoulders slumped. He felt sorry for her. It couldn't be easy living all alone, divorced, her adult daughter no longer interested. He wasn't convinced he was the solution though.

Evelyn entered the kitchen, raising her eyebrows as she noticed Janice's presence.

'Afternoon Janice,' she said, giving Ethan a side eye. Moving over to the just boiled kettle, Evelyn tested the side to make sure it was still hot enough and poured herself a cup of tea.

'Good day off?'

'Yes,' Evelyn said, mulling over the phone conversation with Caren. 'I did some shopping. The rest... I'll tell you about it later.'

Janice squirmed in her chair. 'I should be leaving,' she said.

'Don't let me chase you away,' Evelyn said, winking at her father. 'I'll be in the lounge, if I'm needed.'

Ethan stood. 'How about we all go into the lounge?' He gave his daughter a look as she tried to hide her smirk behind her mug of tea. 'Then we can all have a nice chat.'

Her face fell and it was his turn to hide a grin.

*

'She likes you, you know,' Evelyn said later, feet up and resting on the arm rest as the wood burning stove warmed the room. The night air was uncharacteristically cold for May and she hadn't needed much of an excuse to start a fire.

Ethan peered at her over the rim of his reading glasses, a dog-eared paperback in his hands. 'I presume you are referring to Janice?'

Evelyn rested her head against the back of the chair, staring into the fire, and pushed a thick strand of dark hair out of her eyes.

'Yup,' she said, sounding tired.

'I've realised. I'm still trying to decide if I need to address it, or just let it pass.'

'It may be beyond the point of just ignoring the problem.'

'She is popping over with more frequency,' Ethan admitted. Over thirty years of marriage and he hadn't had to worry about unrequited attraction and crushes. Life was simpler that way. He'd been on a couple of dates since Helen's death and each one had felt forced and unnatural. He'd expected to be married until old age, not to have to consider a future relationship at some point. Not that there was any chance of that with Janice. He wasn't attracted to her.

Ethan and Evelyn sat in contemplative silence, the sky darkening outside the windows, the curtains yet to be drawn. A casserole was cooking in the oven, the smells permeating the house in a pleasing and comforting way. Summer would be arriving soon, but on a chilly late spring day, it made a welcome change to stay warm and cosy indoors.

'I phoned Caren,' Evelyn spoke into the stillness. She kept her gaze on the hypnotic and calming flames.

'And, how did that go?'

'I'm heading into London next Sunday. We're meeting for lunch.'

Ethan nodded. 'I'm pleased to hear that. You need friends, Evelyn. Loss is lonely enough without hiding yourself away.'

He got up from the chair and made his way over to the door, which led to the hallway beyond.

'Would you like a glass of red?'

'Please, Daddy,' she said in a whisper, never taking her eyes off the crackling flames.

Chapter Thirteen

I don't want to grow up. I thought that I did, but life seems full of responsibilities and decisions all too complicated. All I want to do is to spend my days with him. But no! Come September and I must leave here, and I'll be miles away from his embrace.

I cried tonight. I promised myself I wouldn't, not in front of him. But I did. How mortifying. He just glared at me and said, 'if you don't want to leave, don't go. It's your life. I know what I need to do to be free of them all.' He shrugged, as if it was the simplest of decisions to make and I was making an almighty fuss over nothing.

Does he not understand that the choice was made a long time ago? My parents have saved for this, have supported me in every way, yet he says it as if those things are disposable or worthless. Before tonight I had not imagined a single word from his lips to be wrong. But now, oh how my heart aches!

I want to lie in golden fields with him forever. I want our summer of romance to stretch into the years ahead and not be cut short by my education. I cannot imagine another ever holding me as he does, cannot imagine anyone, or anything else, being as important as he is to me. Yet, even I, in all my romance, know that I must get a job one day. Going to college is the best option. At least it was until I met him. Now I am so conflicted.

Laurence met me tonight under the large oak by Dawson Street. It was late, the darkness already punctuating the midsummer sky. He smoked a cigarette while I leaned against the tree, staring up at the emerging stars. I worry our future is beginning to trickle away, but he stood there unconcerned, while I couldn't stop the tears welling up.

Why can't he at least pretend, for me? Now I am not sure he will fight for us at all. Will he even know how?

He cupped my face in his hands and kissed me. I got lost in those kisses. For a while I forgot my fears, but as I write this now, that heavy burden returns again. For weeks I have known no other's company but his. My parents still have no idea this is how I spend my summer days. They assume I am with Caroline, Andrea, Ethan or one of the others. But, I have not seen them at all.

It is all about him. It is all for him. From the moment he saw me, from out the window of his car, to the first evening we stole away from our friends; his finger brushing across the hem of my short sleeve t-shirt, running down my arm to my own fingers, the shiver through my spine, I was lost in his eyes. I still am.

There is no one else. There never would be. Not for me. But what does he feel? I fear if he does not fight for us, he will walk away forever. Oh, how my heart aches!

Chapter Fourteen

The sun rose with its heady warmth permeating the sodden ground, still wet from an overnight drizzle. The horizon was hazy, its steady line having lost its sharp focus amid the promising heat. A golden beam cast across the endless fields, like a sheet, chasing away the shadows of the night. It was going to be a beautiful day.

Like the unfurling of a flower's petals to the sun, the streets awoke. The first cars entered town, their occupants heading off to early shifts. The surrounding farms started work at dawn; Taverton's residents still tucked up in their beds as the farmers stepped out into the silently charged air. A rumbling lorry thundered down the main street, manoeuvring into the narrow road behind the convenience store, fresh deliveries ready for unloading. The family run bakery pumped out warm scents of crisp mouth-watering bread and sweet, indulgent pastries.

An hour later the first shops opened. The sun, now higher in the sky, beat down its radiating warmth, already too scorching to wear the light jackets and jumpers thrown on in haste to get out of the door in time.

Joe strolled down the street, keys swinging from his palm. He was opening up the shop this morning. He'd spent the previous evening sitting in on the planning meeting for the summer festival and he was keen to fill Evelyn in on all the details. He quickened his pace.

The familiar maroon shop front loomed. Swinging the bag from off his shoulders, he crouched down at the keyhole, placing the key in the lock, giving it a shimmy as it got stuck in the process. The door open, the alarm peeped in warning and Joe tapped the four-digit code into the box on the wall. Silence met his ears.

Savouring the smell of books, admiring the uniqueness of the quirky shelving as he did every shift, he breathed in the comforting realisation of being at home. That feeling was strengthened with the flick of the kettle, the surreptitious sniff to test the freshness of the milk, and his favourite mug with a faded Charlie Brown on the surface.

Twenty minutes later, the mug empty and drying on the rack, Evelyn bustled in. Traipsing past she threw her belongings into the back office, where she'd be spending the morning. The growing piles of paperwork that littered her desk were one of the downsides of running a small business.

'The DBS checks haven't arrived yet,' Joe mentioned to her retreating back, referring to the police checks they'd applied for. 'The website is saying up to eight weeks.'

Evelyn appeared in the door frame, exasperation marring her features. 'Really? Oh, well that's just perfect!' She threw her arms up in frustration.

'Didn't think you'd like that,' he mumbled. 'We'll have to wait until July for the first storytelling hour.'

'No, that's a terrible time. The schools will be out for the summer before the end of the month. It'll be better to launch in September. But that's so far away...' she paused, mulling the issue over. 'But... actually that's great! We can promote the event at the festival. Get some interest built up.'

Joe nodded sagely.

'You already knew that, didn't you? I sometimes believe you'd be better at running this place.'

Joe shuddered. 'No thanks. I don't like admin.'

'I'm with you there.'

She glanced back towards her cluttered office with a grimace.

'We need to chat about the planning meeting last night. It won't take long, but I've got some ideas.'

'What on earth would I do without you?' she asked in all sincerity.

*

Even with all the windows and doors open they couldn't relieve the bookshop from the stifling heat. Wishing she had the money to install air conditioning, Evelyn instead took the opportunity in her lunch break to go home and change her clothes.

The house stood silent. Ethan was in the office and Randall the cat was nowhere obvious. The kitchen was as they'd left it first thing that morning; empty coffee mugs in the sink, the dirty pan soaking in a layer of water, remnants of scrambled egg floating on the surface, the blinds still shut against the blaring sun outside. Evelyn took a glass from the cupboard and poured herself a drink of fresh orange juice from the carton in the fridge.

With an energy boost from the sugar, she bounded upstairs, replacing her black trousers and blue short-sleeve blouse with a charcoal and white patterned summer dress. Kicking off her socks, she rummaged through the wardrobe to find a pair of sensible sandals and then grabbed a hairband to put up her thick hair. The sudden lick of air around her neck was a welcome improvement.

Peering into the mirror, ignoring the clammy wisps of hair around her temples, she studied her reflection. She hadn't been sleeping well since her phone conversation with Caren. It wasn't her friend that she worried about, but the actual visit to London. Last time she'd been in the city, she was literally fleeing. The flat sold fast. After three months of upending, soul-destroying uncertainty, she had money in the bank, a couple of suitcases to hand, and a spontaneous ticket purchase in her back pocket. Evelyn ran home and had not looked back.

Her eyes were heavy and tired, the tell-tale shadowing underneath her cornflower blue pupils. Frown lines etched across her brow. She didn't remember when they'd first appeared, but she hazarded a guess at eighteen months ago.

She wasn't a quitter. It wasn't in her nature. What occurred the day Evelyn jumped on a train, without questioning her decision, was the result of their entire world and relationship crashing into oblivion. The alternative would have been a pokey house share, or to remain on the temporary bed on Caren's sofa, where she'd already spent several uncertain months of her life. Perhaps it should have been the answer rather than running away. But London was never her home, or her idea. It was where Ishmael was comfortable, not her.

The lane back into town offered little relief from the heat, despite the thick foliage either side just shy of meeting in an arch above. Randall stalked along the bottom of the hedgerow a few metres ahead. Hearing her approach, he threw an expression of immense disgust. That cat had always hated her. It was refreshing. She knew where she stood with the old, bad tempered feline. Waving to him as he slinked away, unimpressed, Evelyn laughed.

At the end of the sheltered lane, a further wave of heat assaulted her body. It was heavy and dense, the static haze floating in the air. The high street wound its way down the hill towards the bookshop. The street was teeming with people enjoying the unexpected heatwave.

With a swing of the shop door she left the scalding rays of sunshine behind. Inside the air was sticky, but a small swirl of fresh air emerged from the back door. There were a few potential customers browsing the books and she nodded politely as she took her place behind the desk. Joe hovered, wiping his sweaty brow with the back of his hand.

'It's your turn.'

'Oh, thank God,' he exhaled.

He dashed out of the shop, throwing Evelyn a look of utter dismay over his shoulder as the thick wall of heat walloped into him.

Allowing the potential customers to peruse the books in peace, some of whom she suspected of only being there to hide from the temperature outside, Evelyn read the contents of her thick notepad. Written across the top three pages were notes from Joe's meeting with the festival planners.

Some of his suggestions, while great, were too expensive to attempt right now. Other ideas, such as the posters and banners and drafting in local authors were effective and more affordable. She had had similar ideas herself, but it was great to know they were on the same page. She often questioned her depth of knowledge and ability. Running a business wasn't easy and her lack of experience was alarmingly evident at times. Knowing that she and Joe, who had years of industry experience under his belt, were coming up with comparable ideas, was reassuring.

They'd agreed on book readings and Q&As with local authors; a literary related 'treasure hunt' through the shop at a designated time during the festival; designing and printing a loyalty card for the bookshop to be launched on the day; setting up a monthly e-newsletter for people to sign up to. She'd need to print off leaflets to hand out at the stall.

The festival was over two months away, but she suspected time would pass rapidly. As well as providing a sense of excitement and the possibility of boosting the lagging morale of the bookshop, the festival also promised to be a good distraction from her personal life. She grimaced. The last fifteen months of running a business could be accused of the same.

*

'Fancy an ice cream?' Joe ventured.

Evelyn had just returned from the back room, abandoning her attempt to chase up orders amid the stifling air inside the room.

'They would melt before you'd get them back.'

He pondered this for a moment, as she approached the open front door, desperate to hunt down any hint of fresh air. Far from sated, she groaned in discomfort.

'This weather is ridiculous for May.'

'Ice cream,' Joe repeated. 'It will help.'

She raised an eyebrow in his direction. 'Thought of a solution?'

'My best offer,' he said, pacing before realising it was too hot to do so, and sitting down on the chair instead. 'Is that we take it in turns, while the shop is quiet, to run to the co-op and eat our ice cream. Or we can measure how far we make it back before it melts. Or ask Jessie if we can eat it inside, next to the air-con,' he suggested, referring to the manager of the shop.

'I like the second option better. The first seems suspiciously like a competition. It's too hot to be competitive.' Evelyn wiped her brow with the back of her hand to make her point.

Joe's expression indicated that no weather was too extreme to negate the need for a competition.

'Okay,' she acquiesced. 'I'll get my purse. You can go first, seeing as it was your idea.'

'Nah,' he waved. 'Ladies go first.'

Amusement twitched the corner of her lips. She knew some would be offended, wrongly perceiving his words of sexist undertones. But you couldn't get upset with Joe. He was as genuine as they came. She wondered, not for the first time, how he was still single.

'Right, I'm going to do it.'

She willed herself to brave the intensity outside. Taking a few pounds out of her purse, she held the coins in an already sweaty palm and faced the door. The heat was like a vacuum, sucking the air from the atmosphere. She gasped, crossing the street, quickening her pace in the desire to reach shelter. Her skin prickled under the intense rays of the sun.

The cold blast of the air con in the co-op was a simultaneous relief and a violent assault on the senses. In a ridiculous contradiction she shivered. The ice cream freezer was almost empty. There wasn't a lot of choice; a few orange flavoured ice lollies and several chocolate enrobed ice creams which seemed far too sickly and rich to eat in a hurry. She rummaged to the bottom, extracting a lemonade flavoured lolly. Having paid, she headed outside, keen to get back so Joe wouldn't miss out. As much as she preferred the cooler temperatures in store, Jessie wasn't working anyway.

She placed the packaging in the red plastic bin outside the door and crossed the road, the refreshing lolly cooling her dry and parched throat. Drips of sticky, melting liquid already slid down her fingers. She resisted breaking into a run risking sensitive teeth instead as she bit down to take a proper bite.

Eyes adjusting to the crowds, amid the glare of white hot sunlight, she halted, the lemonade ice pop forgotten in an instant. In the distance someone watched her and the emotional punch to her stomach was almost physical in intensity. Heading down a side alley, the familiar figure moved out of her eye line.

Her hand was sticky with synthetic flavouring but she ignored the sensation. She no longer craved the ice lolly. It lay heavy in her hand, an unwanted distraction.

'What are you doing here?' she whispered in the direction of the now retreating figure.

Wearing his familiar salmon pink shirt, his dark hair with a smattering of attractive salt and pepper curls around the temples, and his light brown skin that she hadn't embraced in over a year and half, brought back a thousand colliding memories. What was Ishmael doing here? She wanted to chase him and find out, but her feet felt cloggy and burdened, pinned to the ground instead.

A few minutes later, Evelyn pushed open the shop door, her lolly little more than a stump, her hand drenched with yellow stained drips. Joe laughed.

'Ha! I have a winning chance after all!' His well-natured smirk disappeared at the expression on her face.

'What happened?' he asked nervously.

She raised her eyes to his, a sob collecting in her throat. Peering down at her ice lolly, as if noticing its sorry state for the first time, she glanced back up at him.

'Your turn,' she managed, pitifully.

Chapter Fifteen

2013

Ishmael dug his spoon into the soggy cereal, stirring it before scooping up the next mouthful. Evelyn twiddled her engagement ring around with her thumb. It felt strange on her finger. At one carat the diamond was a little too large to not be cumbersome, although she wouldn't quibble about that. She loved the simple design; the princess cut standing proud against the plain platinum band. But it was taking a while to get used to.

Four weeks ago on their first holiday abroad in the sun-baked streets of Southern France, amid the darkening of the sky, a thunderstorm across the hills in the distance beyond, Ishmael proposed.

The dramatic backdrop heightened the romance and swept up in it all, Evelyn squealed a 'yes', tears playing at her eyes and her heart pounding in excitement. They'd been together for four years. She knew everything about Ishmael, as he did her, and couldn't imagine building a life with anyone else. Through an unsettling start in London, a terrible first job, spades of loneliness and uncertainty, she'd leant on him and as a result he wasn't just a boyfriend, or lover, but her best friend.

Forever the pragmatic, she hadn't yet launched into wedding plans, instead allowing the comforting glow of being promised to another seep through her, anchoring her in the promise of what the future might bring.

'It is real.'

He was watching her over the cereal bowl, his head low, reading glasses resting across the bridge of his nose. His hand rested on top of the pile of paperwork he'd have to wade through.

Nodding at the engagement ring he was referring to, she laughed. 'I know.'

'Still getting used to it?' he asked, taking the glasses off and swinging them in his left hand, a smile playing on his lips.

'I've scratched myself twice,' she said, grinning. 'And, I'm genuinely concerned I'm going to take a gouge out of something.'

He snorted in amusement. 'Honestly Evelyn. You're the only woman I know who'd have preferred a smaller diamond.'

'I hope that's a compliment.'

'Well, I do want to marry you, not them.' He stood, dropping his now empty bowl into the sink and sighed. 'I've got paperwork and meetings coming out of my ears at the moment.' He rubbed his nose with his finger, his expression distracted.

'You need to work late?'

'This project is going to be a massive one.' He nodded to the pile of files that lay on the table. 'It will showcase what I'm capable of. There might be some late nights for a while.'

'Right,' she replied, taking a breath. 'So, I'll be planning this wedding on my own then?'

'Evelyn.' The impatience in his tone was unmistakeable. 'I'll help where I can, but you know how important this is to my career. Besides don't most grooms just pitch up on the day anyway?'

'I was hoping to plan this with you,' she said, pushing the point home. 'I'm not going to be some Bridezilla who plans and controls everything down to the minute detail. I want something simple and elegant, but I also want your input. It's your day too.'

'The marriage is more important,' he answered, grabbing up the top couple of inches of files from the table. 'I need to get going. The first meeting is at nine.'

He sighed again, deeper this time, and placed his hand on her shoulder. 'I'm sorry Evelyn, of course I care. I do want to help. I just… work is a killer right now.'

He leant down to kiss her on the head then hurried from the kitchen, leaving the issue hanging between them.

*

Evelyn placed the phone back into the cradle, breathing slowly to control her erratic emotions. Leaning against the wall, she closed her eyes, the stinging beneath her lids almost too painful to bear.

The flat had sunk into darkness. Yellow streetlights outside the windows cast a small but inefficient light into the interior. The curtains had yet to be drawn. The phone call to her parents had lasted over an hour. It hadn't been dark then. Now it was, and she stood alone, not at all reassured by her own words that concluded the call; that she would be fine.

A sob rose and she struggled, and failed, to swallow it down. Returning to the tiny living space, she kicked aside the open wedding magazines which littered the old-fashioned carpet. Her mind danced over thoughts of her wedding dress. Helen and Aimee had accompanied her to the boutique, just weeks ago, and they'd spent an hour casting delight over every dress Evelyn tried on, their voices rising to a crescendo of excited shrieks as she emerged from the changing room with a huge wide grin, confirming she'd found the one.

Thinking back now, Helen had seemed tired and her skin pale. But Evelyn was so distracted with her own excitement. Now she kicked herself. The signs were there.

Mum insisted over the phone that she would do everything to fight the cancer that was invading her body. Evelyn stood in stunned silence, the phone against her ear, as Helen adopted the motherly role of reassuring the child, whereas Evelyn felt she should have been reassuring her mother instead.

'I'm not going anywhere in a hurry,' Helen said. The determination in her voice was clear. 'And there's no chance I'm missing this wedding.'

'But it's still a year away… what if?'

'What do you mean 'what if?' She replied crossly. 'We are not going to talk like that. I will be at your wedding, whether I still have this bastard cancer or not!'

The anger, and fear, behind her mother's words was deafening.

'Okay, Mummy,' she whispered.

Another hour passed before Ishmael arrived home. He appeared distracted, his briefcase in one hand and a pile of folders under his arm. A quick nod at the door to the living room was the solitary acknowledgement she received. Her tearstained cheeks unnoticed, as did the unusual event of sitting alone in the dark. She suppressed the dull ache of disappointment that her fiancé was too busy and too focused on his world, to notice that something was wrong in hers. He crashed around the kitchen making a snack, oblivious.

He didn't join her in the living room afterwards, instead calling out that he had work to do, and making his way to the little desk in the corner of their bedroom, shutting the door behind him. She made her way to bed, being careful not to disturb him, spent from emotion and too exhausted to explain why.

It was the following evening before she shared the news. He enveloped her in his arms as she cried it out. All the while she tried to ignore the niggling sensation that despite being in the process of combining their lives to one another, there seemed to be a strange, lingering distance growing between them. Not understanding the reason why, Evelyn held onto him, burying her face into his shoulder. There was too much else to worry about, too much else to focus on. This was a problem for another day.

Chapter Sixteen

2019

'Time in the country suits you,' Caren exclaimed as Evelyn stepped off the train and they embraced on the bustling platform.

Wearing blue skinny jeans, an off-white embroidered blouse and a thin black jacket over her shoulders, Evelyn's dark curly hair bounced against the top of her shoulders, full and glossy. Her complexion glowed.

'You seem disgustingly healthy.' Caren screwed up her nose in mock distaste. 'All down to fresh air and country pursuits, I suppose?'

'I doubt it,' Evelyn said with a grin. 'I spend most of my life in an under-lit bookshop.'

'You're happy then?'

'I've been lonely at times. I missed you. But, I've also been happier than I have been in years. That's not easy to admit to.'

They both let the silence hang at that statement, then Caren grabbed Evelyn's left hand, dragging her towards the nearest wine bar.

'We have a lot to catch up on,' Caren said. 'I haven't seen you in five months, and that was because it was Christmas. But Evelyn,' Caren stopped and faced her then, almost bashing into a group of young women behind them.

'I don't want us to be the kind of friends that only hang out when it's a special occasion. We used to go out together all the time. I know,' she raised her hand, as Evelyn opened her mouth to reply. 'You live miles away now. I have two children and never seem to have time to pee, let alone visit you. But we both need to do better, otherwise,' she paused. 'Otherwise, I can see this slipping away from us, until there's no option for a U-turn.'

'Agreed, I've been a terrible friend.'

'You needed to get away. It's understandable. Now, let's get a drink.'

They stepped across the street into a bar. Brass finishings and deep red walls gave the venue a sumptuous atmosphere, its small dimensions cluttered with the buzz of chatter and crowds of people. Caren ordered a large white wine and Evelyn a gin and tonic. With no available tables, they sat alongside the bar. Caren smoothed her jet black bob behind her ears, her perfect posture highlighting the sculptured blue dress that hugged her curves. She wasn't known for casual dress, not in public at least, unless she was headed to the gym. Her pristine exterior emphasised her organised nature and Evelyn felt a pang at how much she'd missed her best friend. Caren ran a finger around the rim of her wine glass as they chatted, catching up on the months since they'd last seen each other.

Evelyn danced around the subject of living back home with her dad. She doubted Caren would have been able to relate. And in all honesty, she still wasn't sure what the solution to that issue might be. Both Evelyn and Ethan seemed to be approaching a crossroads in their lives. At some point, a decision would have to be made. Instead she focused on talking about the bookshop, keen to impress the importance it played in her life.

Caren listened, nodding at all the right moments, smiling at the anecdotes, sipping her drink in between shows of solidarity. But as Evelyn tailed off to a natural silence, Caren placed her hand over hers.

'I have something to tell you.'

Evelyn tensed.

'I wasn't planning on saying anything. I didn't want to make a 'thing' of it. But now you're here, I just…' she paused.

Evelyn's eyes darted around the bar and a prickle of anxiety crept across her neck. She wasn't sure she wanted to know what might be coming.

'A few weeks ago it was Guy's fortieth,' Caren said, referring to a mutual friend from Adrian and Ishmael's workplace. 'Well, Adrian was insistent we go, although a warm bath and early night was far more appealing than a drunken party, after four hours sleep with a teething toddler the night before. Ishmael was there,' she paused again.

'Guy and Ishmael have been friends for years,' Evelyn said, managing to swallow down her apprehension.

'He wasn't there alone, Evelyn. He had a friend, a female friend, with him.'

'You mean a date?' She asked. Her vision blurred, which alarmed her, and she recognised the faint prickle of tears gathering.

'Yes. That's how he introduced her.'

'Right,' Evelyn said, keeping her head low, studying her drink. She lifted the glass and took a long sip. 'Well, it has been a year and a half.'

Silence fell between the two friends.

'He didn't want to be with me anymore, so he's done rather well to wait so long, really.' An unconvincing laugh burst forth, as she tried to process the fog of emotions pouring through her thoughts.

Ishmael had held off a decision about a divorce after discovering they would need to be separated for two years before they could apply. Although she'd agreed to the separation, and subsequent sale of their flat, the lack of divorce papers led to an almost comfortable ceasefire, which she realised now may have also fanned the briefest flicker of hope they'd turn their situation around. Running back to Suffolk and starting afresh was a clear indication that she wasn't going to rely on a change of heart from either party. But there was always that miniscule, lingering possibility.

Now her thoughts raced through the options of why he might have visited Taverton. After that hot May afternoon, she'd convinced herself that she was mistaken. It seemed an impossibility that Ishmael would have travelled up to Suffolk on a week day, almost a two hours commute from London, only to skulk in the street and walk away before talking with her. That wasn't the Ishmael she knew. It must have been someone else. But now Evelyn wondered.

There was a new woman on the scene. Was she his girlfriend? Were they serious? Had that confirmed his decision about a divorce? Is that why he was in Taverton? And if so, why didn't he talk with her? Her head pounded with unanswered questions.

'I'm sorry,' Caren interjected. 'I don't know where you are 'at' right now. Maybe you're over him, and you've been on dozens of dates already. I just thought you should know.'

Evelyn took a giant gulp of the gin and tonic. 'I accepted my marriage was over a long time ago. I wish that meant it didn't hurt anymore, but my emotions haven't caught up with my brain yet.'

'You'd better have another drink then,' Caren surmised.

*

The metallic clattering of train tracks was rhythmic and calming. The hour late, the twilight sky threw romantic illusions across the countryside, beyond the smeared windows of the carriage. Far off lights pinpointed distant dwellings. The darkened meadows stretched out past where the fading light reached.

Evelyn attempted to stay awake. The swaying of the carriage combined with the drinks she'd enjoyed lulled her to close her eyes. She was spent. The emotional investment of catching up with Caren after so long and the revelation of Ishmael's private life had taken its toll. Her head leaning against the train window, the vibration quietened her to a level of tiredness that demanded no more thought or analysis. All afternoon she'd tried to process the information Caren provided. She'd tried to rationalise her reaction, failing to understand why now, after eighteen months, she cared so much. If they'd wanted to get back together, surely that conversation would have come up already? Or was it just the shock of the news that provoked the confusion?

Using all her energy to focus, amid a torrent of thoughts, Evelyn hadn't even asked Caren the one question she'd prepared. Did Caren know why Ishmael had come to Taverton? She was annoyed with herself for not asking, but given Caren's revelation she was also relieved. There was enough injury already, without adding to it. If Ishmael wanted a divorce, she would deal with it when it happened. The speculation would pick away at her otherwise.

Evelyn pinched her nose between her thumb and forefinger and drew a deep breath. She'd returned to Suffolk and taken over the bookshop to try and simplify her life and move it in a new direction. Now the past was rearing its head. Of course, they couldn't stay separated forever. Divorce was the permanent solution, not a separation. But there had been that tiny fleck of hope, not obsessed on, but floating delicately like an ember into a smoky night sky. Ignored, for want of a better solution, it had been kept at bay. But now it danced its way into her vision and she couldn't shake the thought: did she still want Ishmael? And what, if anything would she do about it?

Chapter Seventeen

⤙

I leave for college in two weeks. My heart cannot bear it. He still laughs off my concerns, distracting me with his kisses instead. Why does he not take it seriously? I am beginning to fear that maybe Caroline is right. Am I just a summer romance? I knew, from the first time we met, that he was the one. Does he not feel it too?

He took me out in his car yesterday. We drove to the coast. I listened to the insects buzzing in the air through the open car window and watched the endless fields stretch to the horizon. He drives fast, which scares me a little, but it's exhilarating too. I guess those feelings sum up our relationship. There is nothing safe about him.

When we arrived it was all laughing, kissing, long lingering looks of intent. But he still talks nothing of the future. He still evades my concerns. My love for him deepens each day and I cannot imagine a life that doesn't include him. I worry that his love doesn't run as deep, but then I remember that he is one for living in the moment. Free from constraint. That doesn't mean that he doesn't care for me as much as I do him. He just processes our relationship in a different way. I long to have that carefree approach to life, to not mull on things so deeply, to live for the thrill of the now, but alas that is not me.

And now I worry further, that I am to head off, that even our future isn't secure. Perhaps I shouldn't go to college at all? If that is how I can keep him, then I am willing to take the risk. If it keeps him with me, then it is all worth it.

Chapter Eighteen

Lucie sat on the carpet, the only sound coming from the price gun as she stamped bookmarks, pens and other small gift items with self-adhesive labels. With a headache brewing she found the task comforting and therapeutic.

Evelyn had phoned the evening before, asking if she was available for an extra shift. Usually, at such short notice, she would have turned it down. But Lucie needed an escape from the same four walls. Evelyn and Joe were busy finalising plans for the festival. Notebooks, pens and folders spread across the office desk, their low hum of conversation a white noise against the silence of the bookshop.

The shop was empty again and Lucie was grateful. Tired and sore, she already regretted saying yes to the extra shift. She wanted to sleep. She needed a holiday; somewhere warm and sunny, somewhere on her own, all by herself. But that was unlikely on a part time salary, let alone for any other reason. Blinking back tears, Lucie pressed down hard on the trigger of the price gun, jamming it in an instant.

She stifled a curse. Opening the cartridge she attempted to prize the spool out. Her slender fingers grappled to secure a grip and a blur of tears obscured her vision. She was not having a good day. She fought the urge to sob. The bell rang above the door and she noticed a shadow emerge beside her.

'Sorry to startle you.' Ethan waved at the young woman sitting cross legged on the floor, surrounded by stock, her eyes wide. 'I need to talk to Evelyn.'

'Oh, she's in a meeting right now.' Lucie stood with effort, grabbing a notebook and pen from the till counter. 'Can I take a message?'

'No, I'll just wait. I am Evelyn's father,' he clarified, as her eyes widened further at his polite refusal to leave the shop.

'Ah. It's nice to meet you,' she said, in relief. 'I don't know how much longer she'll be.'

'That's fine, I can browse. I haven't read a good book in ages. Perhaps I'll find something,' he said, already wandering over to the nearest shelf. 'Don't let me disturb you,' he added, waving towards the pile of stock waiting their labels.

Lucie hovered for a few seconds, before crouching back down to her task.

*

Ethan examined the shelves for several minutes, picking up a book here and there and reading the blurb. As much as he'd love to purchase a book, he hadn't thought to bring any money with him. He had needed to get out of the house. He wanted to see Evelyn too. Her behaviour had been strange the last few days and between both their jobs there had been little chance to get to the bottom of why.

Determined not to distract the young woman sitting on the floor, who from the red-rimmed eyes seemed to be having a tough day herself, he moved around the shop, picking up random books and wishing that he had remembered his wallet.

'Dad?'

Evelyn crossed the shop floor to join him. 'I thought you were at work today. Is everything all right?'

'Everything's fine,' he replied, running a hand through his dark hair. It was a coping mechanism and Evelyn's raised eyebrow indicated that she recognised it. 'I thought I'd work from home again.'

'Why? Is there a problem at the office?'

'No, not at all,' he gave a short laugh. 'If you can't take advantage of working from home occasionally when you run the company... Well, that would be rather disappointing, wouldn't it?'

She wrinkled her nose at his explanation.

'Would you mind if I took my lunch break first?' she called across to Joe, now stood back behind the till.

'Go ahead.'

'Thanks. Dad,' she addressed Ethan. 'Give me five minutes.'

*

'So,' she said with emphasis, forcing her hands into her jacket pockets as they walked down the street. The weather had cooled again with rain showers ushering in the first week of June. She shivered. 'You've not visited the shop in months.'

She left the comment hanging, hoping he'd fill in the gaps. Silence met her ears. 'Home for a sandwich?' she suggested.

'Soon,' he replied. She peered down at her shoes as they walked.

'What happened in London?'

Living back home had its disadvantages, such as her father picking up on her recent mood change. He wasn't the type to meddle in her personal life, but she had to admit she hadn't attempted to hide her emotions since the trip to London. Tear stained and dishevelled, she'd made excuses, headed for bed and avoided questions. She'd evaded staying too long in any one room, except for her bedroom, to prolong the inevitable.

'Is it Ishmael?'

His question caught at her throat. She had difficulty swallowing. What was happening to her? She thought she'd dealt with her failed marriage. Why was this suddenly proving an issue? She stopped walking and waited for a mother and her two small children to pass.

'Visiting Caren brought up some bad memories,' she offered, shrugging, hoping the small morsel of information was good enough to explain her distant behaviour.

'Like Ishmael?' Ethan probed.

'Yes, Dad, like my estranged husband. Is that so hard to comprehend?'

'Of course it isn't. You were married. You were in love. Breaking up is painful.'

She kept her head down, eyes focusing on the crack between two paving stones beneath her feet. She wondered how much she could bear sharing.

'You lost Mum. We all did. What I'm going through is nothing in comparison.'

'That's utter rubbish and you know it,' Ethan said, his voice raised in frustration. 'Since you've come back, talking about your ex has remained off limits. I've respected that. But the last few months... you're struggling Evelyn. You've isolated yourself from your friends, you've sunk your energy and money into the business, but there's no balance in your life otherwise. And now you return from London, so evidentially in pain that it makes my heart ache. I'm your father. I want to be able to help, even if it's just to listen.'

'What about you?' she exclaimed, diverting attention as his words pierced her. 'You're working from home again. You can't face dealing with Mum's things, but at the same time you can't keep away.'

'You don't have the faintest idea what you're talking about.'

'And you do?'

Not waiting for a reply, Evelyn strode on up the hill, Ethan left dragging behind.

'I'm trying to understand, Evelyn,' he called after her. 'But I'm only given fragments of information. There's not a lot I can go on.'

'Well, perhaps it's not natural for a thirty-one year old woman to confide everything to her father,' she retorted, not slowing her pace.

'Doesn't that just prove my point? You've isolated yourself so much that you don't even have anyone to share with.'

'We are not so different,' she stopped, spinning around in fury. 'What have you shared with me? You hang around that house like it is some memorial or shrine, yet you don't want to talk about it. You've been secretive since you started going through Mum's stuff, like you discovered something horrific.'

She ceased ranting and stared at him. 'Did you find something horrific?'

He held her gaze. A flash of uncertainty flickered across the furrows of his brow. Alarm coursed through her.

'Dad?' Her voice wavered in fear.

'No, nothing horrific Evelyn, just... complicated.'

'Well, that makes me feel better,' she exclaimed, storming ahead again. Clearly, they were going to get nowhere. They were both as stubborn as the other. Ethan had always compared her to her mother; saying they were so alike. He didn't seem to realise how many personality traits he also shared with his eldest daughter.

Ethan's mobile phone rang behind her. She marched on, using the time to take deep breaths and calm down. A couple of minutes later and the soft, but increasing volume of footfall echoed behind her. Ethan caught up.

'I just had a call.'

'I heard the ring tone.'

He placed a hand on her arm to slow her down. She searched his expression.

'It was your sister,' he explained. 'Aimee is coming home.'

*

Joe risked a glance in Lucie's direction. She was still sitting cross-legged on the floor, piles of bookmarks, postcards and notebooks splayed before her. The price gun emitted a constant and satisfying series of clicks, as she priced each item.

Only the smaller items were priced like this. Books, apart from those with special offer stickers, were barcoded into the computer system. Joe didn't mind doing the task, but as it ate into his book perusal time he was pleased that Lucie had relished the opportunity. She told him she enjoyed the quietness of it. It was a strange comment to make, and he wondered what was so chaotic in her life that a mundane task like pricing was considered a welcome relief.

'Have you got any plans this weekend?' Joe asked, choking a little on the words. He berated himself for being awkward.

Lucie startled, as if her thoughts had been far away from the bookshop. 'I am working here on Saturday with Evelyn. But I've no other plans.'

'I thought twenty-one year olds spent their nights on the town,' Joe said, trying to crack a joke, but wincing at how pathetic his words sounded. Being an introvert suited him most of the time. At least until he had to attempt a decent conversation.

Lucie raised her eyebrows. 'Aren't you only a few years older than me?'

'I'll be twenty-six soon,' he replied, before turning away in embarrassment. This was not going well.

She laughed, not unkindly, as his cheeks flushed.

'Hey,' he shrugged. 'I have no social life.'

He resorted to self-deprecation, his default mode when the conversation got away from him. It happened with frequency.

'Well,' Lucie admitted, shifting her gaze between him to the pile of stock and back again, 'neither have I.'

'Why not?' he asked, surprised by her answer.

She paused, narrowing her eyes, considering him for a moment.

'There isn't much to do in a small town.'

Joe kept her in his vision for a few minutes, mulling over her words. Lucie was hiding something. That much was obvious. Whether he ought to investigate further, or let it lie as per his usual nature, he couldn't quite decide.

*

Evelyn placed the hot mug of tea in front of Ethan and took a seat. She sipped her own drink in silence. After their awkward exchange in the street, followed by the unexpected call from her sister, they had entered an unspoken impasse.

She hated falling out with her dad. They were so close, especially since she'd moved back home. They'd backed themselves into a corner though and the atmosphere between them was uncomfortable.

It was the first time he'd asked about Ishmael. It was astonishing really. Evelyn imagined what her mother's reaction might have been. Helen wouldn't have held back for a year and a half. She would have questioned her daughter, until she had mapped out the full landscape of Evelyn's marital decline. Ethan was so different, and Evelyn appreciated it, although it gave her a sharp pang to realise how much she missed having her mother to confide in.

Knowing that Aimee was not a suitable alternative and that she was about to return gave no comfort. Aimee was abrupt and lacked the sensitivity of their mother. Rather than listen, she often forced her solutions and analysis on everybody else's problems, while ignoring her own shortcomings.

No, it was fair to conclude that Evelyn was not looking forward to a visit from her younger sister. And now she didn't have Ethan on side, although she reasoned that he didn't hold grudges and their spat would be forgotten by dinner time. Regardless, he wouldn't raise it again, at least not for a while, but it would sit between them and fester.

'Aimee arrives next Thursday,' Ethan said, breaking the reflective silence. 'She didn't say how long she'll be with us.' He shook his head with both affection and resignation. Aimee had always done things her own way.

Evelyn didn't answer.

'Are you still mad at me?'

She took another sip of tea. 'No. But I can't communicate what I don't understand.'

He held the mug of tea in both hands and replied with a soft snort. 'Oh, I know that feeling well.'

'And here's you thinking I'm a carbon copy of Mum,' she teased.

He grinned at that. 'You have her steadiness and stubbornness, but more than a drop of my reticence.'

'What about Aimee?'

He snorted louder this time. 'Oh, she got all the adventure and none of the sensibility.'

They both laughed and fell into silence again, drinking their tea. The ticking hands of the clock ushered toward the end of her lunch break. Her stomach rumbled, the tea a poor substitute for food.

Ethan noticed and raised an eyebrow. 'Got time for a quick sandwich?'

'Sure.'

A few minutes later he handed her a plate with two slices of wonky cut farmhouse bread, locally reared ham and a smear of mayonnaise and mustard inside.

'Peace offering?' he asked, as she took the plate from him.

'My favourite sandwich filling?' she said, with amusement. 'Consider the argument forgotten.'

Chapter Nineteen

The sun rose over the fields beyond the house, highlighting the thin sheen of dew that draped the ends of the wild grass. It was early, the birds still emerging from their roost, the dawn chorus yet to reach a crescendo.

A fox slunk homewards, belly full from a night of hunting. A gentle warm breeze swirled around the tree tops, the tantalising promise of hotter temperatures ahead. Squirrels darted between trees, playful and searching for food. A pair of grey pointed ears poked up from behind a fallen trunk, twitching, trying to establish whether the coast was clear. With a moment of considered pause, out from behind the trunk hopped a small rabbit. Seconds later a second joined the first and a game of chase commenced.

Wrapped in his wax jacket, Ethan watched from the backdoor. He brought a mug of steaming coffee to his lips and surveyed the garden. After thirty-four years of living in the same house, viewing the same horizon and countryside, he never got tired of admiring its epical nature.

He finished off the dregs of coffee. He'd need the caffeine boost if he was to face the office today. Evelyn was right in her summarisation; he was finding it difficult to tear himself away from the house and Helen's belongings.

Discovering the loose pages of her journal had been a shock. The questions they raised reminded him of a puzzle which needed to be to solved, but he didn't even know where all the pieces were stashed, let alone how to put them together into something cohesive.

Add to that Aimee's impending arrival and sleep eluded him. Of course, he loved his younger daughter as much as he loved Evelyn. Aimee hadn't been home for almost two years. Her flighty nature left her easily bored and she had spent most of her adult life bouncing from one questionable decision to another. In all fairness, she avoided getting into too much bother. There was just one occasion, where Ethan had rescued her from a small, but substantial enough debt that stood out amongst the others. Most of her bad decisions revolved around jobs and relationships, all the while appearing oblivious to their repercussions.

But it was her sharp tongue that had the potential to cause the most damage. And given that both he and Evelyn were hurting, and trying to heal, this worried him far more than any new situation Aimee may have wandered into. It was selfish, he knew. He didn't want to be told by his twenty-seven year old daughter that he needed get over his late wife, nor hint that she knew plenty of young, single, pretty women who liked a distinguished older man. Aimee's lack of filter caused problems. It caused a lot of unnecessary hurt.

He imagined Aimee's reaction to Evelyn and Ishmael's situation. She'd already thrown caustic comments his way during the rare phone calls home. He hadn't passed on her opinions to Evelyn. He hoped he could stop his daughters sparring. They'd got on well as children, despite the four year age gap. It was when they reached adulthood that they'd drifted apart, their opposing personalities causing major clashes between them.

Aimee had considered Evelyn too young to get married, regardless of the years she'd already spent with Ishmael. Ethan doubted that age had been the real problem in the relationship. Evelyn thought Aimee irresponsible, especially after her summer post-exams, where she'd ran off to Greece with friends; contacting a frantic Helen and Ethan once she'd got there. What Evelyn didn't know, and what scared Ethan more, were the similarities between Aimee's actions and that of another teenage girl he'd known when he was younger. Desperate to please, desperate to prove herself, she'd also made some spontaneous and dangerous decisions.

*

Caren had been messaging all morning. Two small children, a dog who'd spent the weekend digging holes in her landscaped garden, and a sports-mad husband were getting on Caren's wick. She was desperate to make plans to meet up again.

Evelyn could complain about the direction her own life had taken, but at least outside of business hours she was her own agent. Apart from living with her father, the grumpiest cat in the world, and having little social life, of course. Despite that though, the previous month's takings at the shop were increasing, and this month had started with promise. With the festival ahead, she began to believe the shop would turn a corner in time and maybe the rest of her life would follow suit.

Across the room from Evelyn, Joe lovingly restocked the J.R.R. Tolkien books. The sky outside was bright and warm, shooting illuminating rays in through the windows and lifting the atmosphere. The last week now a memory, she felt happier and confident again. If Ishmael was dating, that was his prerogative and she wouldn't lose sleep over it. Instead, she'd focus on what was going well and what she was able to control, or at least steer.

'What do you know about Lucie?' Joe asked, startling her out of her reverie. She hadn't even noticed him sidle up to her.

'Why?'

'Oh, I just wondered,' he said, the tips of his ears pinking. 'She's quite new to Taverton, isn't she?'

'I think she's been here a year or two, but I don't know for sure.'

He hovered behind her shoulder.

'Yes, Joe?' she asked, flicking through the box of orders waiting to be collected. 'Is there something else?'

'Hmm… well… I guess… She is very cagey about her private life. She doesn't share much. Like going on her break now; she never shares where she goes and she never stays in the shop for her lunch sometimes, like we do.'

'She's not obliged to tell us, Joe. She's here to work, and if she prefers to do that without spilling her secrets, then that makes life easier for me. As her boss,' she added, for clarification. 'Do you want to know more about her?'

Joe's crush was obvious.

He stared over at the sci-fi section for a moment, lost in thought.

'I don't think it's that simple.'

'Oh, I don't know,' Evelyn said, shrugging. She moved into the backroom, collecting the hard copies of the online orders, checking everything tallied with the computer records. 'If she wants to share, she will. Or perhaps she just needs to feel comfortable first. She's not been working here that long, after all.'

'You do realise,' she added, her voice softening. 'That workplace relationships can be complicated and a potential minefield?'

Joe's eyes widened.

'Well, this is embarrassing.' He stuffed his hands into his pockets. His entire face bloomed red.

'There's no way Lucie is interested in me. She's... nice, just as a friend,' he stuttered. He paused then shot Evelyn a furtive glance. 'Did you buy any of that?'

Taking pity on him, she gave him an encouraging smile. 'Of course,' she answered, returning her attention to the orders.

*

'I bet you can't wait to put your feet up this evening?' Joe asked, as he and Lucie left the shop. Evelyn had stayed behind to send some emails. 'You seem tired today.'

Lucie tipped her head towards him, narrowing her eyes as she did. 'Are you saying I look terrible?' her voice pitching.

'No!' Joe exclaimed with alarm. 'I said tired, not terrible!'

'Isn't that the same thing?'

'I didn't think it was. Is it the same thing? You don't look terrible, just like you're not sleeping well again.'

'I'm not.'

They trudged up the high street. 'Can't your doctor prescribe anything?'

'It's not... I... My house is just here.' She indicated the narrow, cobbled lane that swept off to the left, across from the main road. Ivy hung in swathes against the ancient brick walls that lined the lane. Attractive whitewashed cottages stood further down, away from the visibility of the high street, masked by large billowing willow trees.

'Right,' he replied, rubbing his chin with his fist. The day's stubble extinguished the itch spreading across his knuckles. 'I'll see you next weekend then.'

She hesitated. 'Yes.'

Giving a quick wave, Lucie crossed the street. Her faux leather shoulder bag bashed against her hip as she walked, and her long blonde hair swayed within the constraints of her ponytail. Watching, Joe shook himself.

'Not a chance,' he muttered under his breath. 'Not a chance mate.'

*

'Betty Longhorn is on the festival committee.' Joe's face had turned a grey-yellow shade of shock.

Evelyn suppressed an urge to grin. He looked terrified.

'She joined last night. She just arrived at the meeting, announcing that she'll be helping make all the decisions,' he added.

'Can she do that?'

'Her late husband was quite influential back in the day. So much so, that she thinks she can still waltz in unelected and command everyone.'

'She's not that bad,' Evelyn said, with her arms folded. 'She's just a grumpy old lady.'

'She told me to stop breathing so loudly.'

Evelyn bit her lip to prevent laughing out loud. She grabbed a pile of delivered books and headed to their respective shelves. A moment's silence followed as she slid them into place, matching up their spines. She had a brief recollection of Ishmael doing the same, back before she even knew his name. She forced her thoughts to the present. How many times in this job had she performed the exact same action, placing books on their shelves? Hundreds, she guessed. It was ridiculous to allow such a mundane task to remind her of her husband.

'So,' she asked, attempting to distract herself. 'How are you going to handle Mrs Longhorn?'

'I hear the Mediterranean is warming up,' he said, in defeat. 'Maybe I can hide out there.'

'That might work, if you weren't so bone achingly British.'

'Hey, I've travelled,' Joe stated in indignation. 'There was that trip to Benidorm with my brother.' He shuddered. 'And then a couple of French exchanges at school…' he trailed off at that, clearly at the end of his short list of overseas adventures.

'You'll be fine Joe. You've grown up here. You know this town better than I do. You know how to handle her residents,' she concluded with a grin.

He shook his head, solemn. 'Try getting hauled out of her garden by your ear.'

'When was that?! And what were you doing in her garden?'

'I was twelve. It was a dare.'

Evelyn burst out laughing. 'Well, all part of growing up then.'

His cheeks bright red, he looked away bashfully. Evelyn returned to the desk, swiping up an old hardback with yellowing pages.

'I picked this up at the antique shop,' Evelyn said, waving it around, which was no easy feat given the depth and weight of the tome. 'It's an encyclopaedia of Suffolk. Listen to this...' she said, opening it to where a distressed leather bookmark nestled inside.

'Elizabeth Garrett, born in Aldeburgh in 1836, took advantage of the Society of Apothecaries rules to admit any person for examination, in order to secure a medical education which was unavailable to women at the time. She gained a licence to practise, before their rules were amended in response to her actions. She opened the first hospital in Europe staffed by women, in Marylebone. She received an MD degree from Paris and was admitted to membership with the British Medical Association. Her other achievements include becoming a lecturer at the London School for Medical Women and president of the East Anglian branch of the Medical Association. She was elected the mayor of Aldeburgh and was the first woman in England elected as chief magistrate. Wow. Her younger sister Millicent was one of the pioneer suffragettes and devoted her life's work to championing the cause.'

'Oh, that's cool,' Joe commented, with usual nonchalance dousing the impact of his words.

'This is why books excite me,' she jabbed the cover with a forefinger. 'We'll tie this in to the festival; local history, literary references, bringing the two together. Tourists already come to this town for the pretty architecture. Throw in a little local history, courtesy of the quirky bookshop – it'll help put us on the map.'

'And encourage people to read more.'

'That's the hope. After your next meeting with the committee we can have another planning session and incorporate some more ideas.'

With the unwitting reminder of the new addition to the weekly festival meetings, Joe's face fell.

'Sorry,' she said, wincing in realisation.

Chapter Twenty

Caroline and Ethan tried to talk me out of it this morning. But I know what I have to do and nothing they say will make any difference. I timed slipping out of the house, waiting until old Mrs McCarthy left with her basket, shop bound as she is every morning at 9.30. If she saw me go, she'd be straight on the phone to my mother.

My parents had left for the day. I hoisted my backpack onto my shoulder and exited via the back door. Just in case. Yet, crossing the road to the path opposite, there stood Caroline, arms crossed, her right leg sticking outwards in a defiant pose.

'You can't just give up your future for him,' she spat.

I laughed at that. My future is him. There is no point otherwise. She rolled her eyes at me. That was the moment that really infuriated me. What does she know of love? Eighteen and yet to be kissed! Believe me, I know all her secrets. I've been a good friend not to spill them. Caroline has been jealous of this relationship the entire three months I have been with him.

I was preparing to stalk away, but as I turned, Ethan joined us. He heard our raised voices, and ever the mediator he couldn't resist finding out what was going on. His presence silenced me for a moment. Steady, sure Ethan. The nicest boy you'd ever hope to meet. It was easy to stand up Caroline's tirade, but not when faced with Ethan's surprise.

I told them I was going. I told them it was for the best. Ethan warned me not to throw away the opportunity; I had been talking of college since we started high school. I'd be the first woman in my family to go. I wanted to ignore his words. It was true. And I had wanted it for so long. But that was before I met him....

'You're not to tell anyone,' I said, staring at them both, hoping to remind them of their loyalty to me. 'We're just going for a drive to talk it through. I'll be back later, I promise. You are NOT to say a word of what we're planning.'

There was a lie in there. But as I said it, I knew I must honour my vow to my friends. We wouldn't run away today, we'd have to wait just a little longer. I hoped the faint waver in my voice was unnoticeable. I hoped a lot of things. Caroline frowned and strode away, her hair slapping against her back in fury.

Ethan stood a while, just watching me, with a faint but weary look on his face. I didn't meet his gaze. It was loaded with questions. I didn't have all the answers I knew he'd expect.

All I can do is act on my feelings for once. Act on what I know is true. Otherwise, what does it all mean anyway?

Chapter Twenty One

2014

Evelyn's manicured nails glided effortlessly over the fabric of the dress. It hung, tailored for her dimensions, perfectly enhancing her figure. The intricate stitching of miniscule flowers trailed down from the Georgian style bodice, all the way to the hem. The skirt puffed out a touch, leaving enough volume to lift the dress from simple to elegant.

Evelyn's hair was draped into a bun, her natural curls falling gracefully around her face, a few adorning her neck. She wore a white gold necklace of her mother's, a simple single pearl at its centrepiece.

Today was the day. She had shared almost five years with Ishmael and now they were to make a commitment for the rest of their lives. She grinned at herself in the full-length mirror. Their relationship wasn't always perfect, but she loved him. Their lives had intertwined like the boughs of an ancient tree, the roots of which were buried and hidden far into the ground. In that moment it didn't matter that their work life kept them busy, tired and at times frustrated with each other. It didn't matter that his issues with his family jarred against the attachment she shared with her own parents.

She took a steadying breath. She was choosing Ishmael, despite those things. She chose him over any other; for one simple reason. She believed in their relationship. She believed in their shared humour. How a joke turned into a secret smile between them. She believed in their intimacy. How with his expression he conveyed his feelings without ever needing to utter a word. She believed in the plans they made together. She believed in the sense of belonging, sometimes striking at the oddest moments, like last Thursday when they put down the marriage prep and started watching a film instead. Lying next to him on the sofa, his handsome profile enhanced by the flickering light of the television screen, Evelyn knew it was here with him that she belonged.

The door clicked open behind her. Helen entered the room, wearing a cappuccino coloured dress and cream suit jacket. Her thinning auburn hair was held up in a matching bun to Evelyn's. Helen's eyes filled, viewing her daughter, made up and ready to walk down the aisle.

'Wow,' she breathed. 'Ishmael is a very lucky man.'

Evelyn gave a cheeky grin. 'He sure is,' she said with a laugh.

'Dad and I are thrilled for you both.' Helen took Evelyn's hands in hers. 'We can't wait to see what the future holds for you.'

The unspoken question mark hung in the air. Evelyn's grin dropped. Helen's cancer was being treated and the prognosis lengthened as she responded well. However, Helen was not cured. She was not in remission. Tell-tale signs of her illness were becoming more obvious; the thinning hair, the slimmer figure and her skin's faint greyish tone. Her face was drawn, gaunt even.

Helen gave her knowing look and shook her head. 'No, Evelyn. Today is your day. There is no room for sadness. Right,' she added, pulling herself together. 'We need to get you in the car if you're going to arrive fashionably late and not horribly late. Oh, wait until your father sees you. I can guarantee you'll make him cry.'

Helen hooked an arm through Evelyn's. 'Ready?'

She beamed. 'Oh yes.'

*

The ceremony was held in a local manor house, just a few miles outside of Taverton. Having viewed a slew of gaudy hotel venues in London, securing a Suffolk venue took precedence. With its rolling lawns, landscaped gardens and endless fields beyond, the country estate was incomparable. They'd booked one of the smaller, elegant rooms and there they stood on their wedding day, holding hands before the registrar, framed by the grand bay window.

Copper chandelier sconces adorned the plain cream walls, a larger central chandelier hanging from the ornate ceiling above. An entire wall of bookshelves was filled with leather bound tomes. This feature had sold the room to Evelyn. It was as if this room had been made for her.

Exchanging their vows, they nervously beamed at one another. Ishmael wore a traditional morning suit, attire that he seemed uncomfortable in, but had been insistent on. His family were also dressed up to the nines and Evelyn felt a little sorry for her father having to resort to his own wedding suit, after several decades of hiding away in his wardrobe.

Caren and Aimee, her two bridesmaids, wore russet red dresses, also in a simple Georgian design to compliment Evelyn's dress. Caren's jet black hair was pinned up, whereas Aimee's strawberry blonde hair fell down in waves across her freckled shoulders. She'd just flown in from three months in Australia and her skin was sun-blushed and clashed a little against the colour of the dress.

Adrian acted as best man and Ishmael's parents and brother sat in the front row, his mother immensely proud while his father was as tight lipped as usual. Ishmael's voice broke over the vows but he got through it with Evelyn's nods of encouragement. She had to steady herself not to rush her own, taking deep breaths with each line of repetition.

As the registrar announced that they were now husband and wife, they grinned at each other. Delight spread through her as she gazed into his eyes. Holding her hand, he rubbed his thumb against hers and they stepped out into the aisle.

The rest of the day was a blur. All the months of planning disappeared into a Technicolor swirl of laughter, music, food, and swathes of flowers. Their first dance, Adrian's slap of congratulations on Ishmael's back, Caren unconsciously rubbing her stomach; she'd announced their first pregnancy just a few weeks before, Aimee flirting with one of Ishmael's cousins, Ethan and Helen's happy smiles. It all jumbled into a hazy collection of memories.

But one moment stood out in sharp focus and it was the one Evelyn wished to forget. As the speeches ended and the empty plates were gathered by the catering staff, Benesh pulled Ishmael aside. A discreet handshake between them left behind an envelope in Ishmael's grip.

The two men talked in earnest, away from the hubbub of the room, out of earshot. It was the utter fury on Ishmael's face that alerted her that all was not well. The happy, newly wed glow faded fast. Anxiety permeated her body. What was going on?

In an effort to control his voice, Ishmael's expression was nevertheless apoplectic. Ania joined them as she attempted to calm them both down. Evelyn felt detached and excluded from the situation.

Would she always feel like that around his family? And did that come from his parents, or rather from Ishmael himself?

The small group broke up and Ishmael returned to her side, his body shaking from suppressed rage. Taking his hand, she led him away, out into the corridor away from partying guests and up to their honeymoon suite.

The room looked beautiful. Rose petals spread across the embroidered duvet cover and champagne flutes awaited the arrival of a chilled bottle. The four poster bed was a decadent treat and it stood proud against the backdrop of timbered walls. Evelyn felt a pang of sadness that their first visit to the room was under less than romantic circumstances.

'What is going on?' she asked. Her voice sounded breathless.

Ishmael opened his mouth to explain and shut it tight again. Instead, handing her the offending envelope from inside his suit pocket, he told her to open it.

She pulled out a cheque and balked. 'Is this? Ishmael, what is this?'

The amount written on the cheque was obscene. Evelyn's hands shook as realisation dawned.

'It's my parents' wedding gift,' he spat. 'There's enough for a deposit on a flat... in London.'

The words sunk in as she sank down on the bed.

'That is... incredibly generous.'

'It's insulting,' Ishmael said in anger. He moved away from her, his entire body language incredulous, agitated.

The cheque hung between her fingers.

'Why is it insulting?'

He glared at her then and she wished she'd kept quiet. All the simmering issues with his family suddenly seemed too close to the surface. She wished she understood.

'My whole life they have tried to control everything. Where I went to school, what I studied. They paid for my degree upfront, without giving me the chance to pay for it myself.'

'A lot of students would have appreciated not having a loan around their necks.'

He swallowed, trying to control his anger. 'The issue here is that I didn't get the choice. Everything has been predetermined, with money to soften the blow. I didn't even want to be an engineer,' he added, ignoring Evelyn's eyes widening in shock.

'I don't even know *what* I wanted to do, as I was never given the freedom to figure it out. Meeting you, getting away to London, was all about trying to get some control back.'

He kneeled down and took her hands. 'And now, they want me to be shackled to them for life. There's no way I can pay this much back. There's no way I can afford to buy a property otherwise.'

Tears stung her eyes as she contemplated his words.

'Did you…' she asked, choking over her words. 'Did you ever love me, or am I just a point to be made?'

His eyes widened in shock. 'Don't ever think that,' he pleaded, shaking his head vigorously. 'Of course, I love you. You know that.'

'You don't say it very often.'

'You know I'm not great with words, Evie. I do love you. You've never been about making a point. Just… well… you and I did help to show them that I could make my own decisions. That I could choose to be with a woman they had no say so over.'

At the expression on her face, he fell silent.

'I'm messing this up,' he said after a moment's pause. 'You are not the argument here. The issue is them throwing money at me.'

'But they're not controlling you – you've already made your decisions. This is a gift, a wedding gift. That is all.'

'No, it is never just a gift.' He stood up, his face livid again.

Upset and confused, Evelyn gripped the cheque, her vision blurred with hot tears. 'Do you know how many people our age need their parents' help to get on the property ladder? Pretty much all of them,' she answered for him.

'Are you saying I should accept it? Just give in?'

'Have you even asked them if it's just a gift?'

Her frustration grew. If he'd been open and honest at the beginning of their relationship, she wouldn't have to waste so much energy trying to work out what his problem was.

'Or are you just assuming the worst? You know that if my parents were able to, they'd have helped us with a deposit too? Maybe this is a gift, because they love you and they want to help us get settled?'

His glare seared right through her. She held her nerve. Ishmael was hurting. She saw that. Silence swirled around them, the only sound a light ticking from the alarm clock on the mantelpiece. His shoulders drooped as he sat down beside her. He leant forward, clasping his fists together and groaned.

'I'm never going to be free of this, am I?'

'Free of what, Ishmael?'

'You don't understand.'

'No, I don't,' she admitted.

'Other than the occasional run in with your sister, your family is close. My family have always had expectations. Both my brother and I have had to live a particular way, a way that suited my father. He believes throwing money around makes it okay, makes it acceptable. But it's all about appearances. That's all.'

'We're a family now. We're husband and wife. If you want to change your career, then do that. I'll support you while you retrain.'

'You expect us to survive on your salary alone?' Ishmael gave a cynical laugh.

'Well, perhaps if we hadn't run off to London to chase after your career, I'd have had more choice too.'

She regretted the words as soon as they'd left her mouth. They were true. However, five years had passed. She'd had plenty of opportunity to get her own career on track. She couldn't blame Ishmael any more than she could blame herself. Besides, her job wasn't terrible. It just wasn't what she had imagined.

'Right, so my options are to retrain, while my wife resents me for the situation she ended up in. Or, I accept my father's cheque, knowing that the property it buys us keeps me enslaved to my current career. Because that is the point Evelyn - he has written a cheque based on my salary, so starting a career from scratch becomes impossible.'

'Difficult, but not impossible,' she said, trailing off at the expression on his face.

He laughed, but it held no humour. 'What a great start to married life!'

He turned from Evelyn as his words hit their mark. Surrounded by the rose petals on the bed, she struggled to stop the tears falling. He was right. *What* a great start to married life.

Chapter Twenty Two

2014

The buzzing heat saturated the sun bleached wooden planks of the beach hut. A swirl of salty air cut through the brooding humidity, cascading over hypnotic white sand and licking the edges of the decking. Evelyn lay in a deck chair, book in hand, curling her toes toward the enticing respite of a gentle breeze.

The turquoise sea stretched beyond her vision, decorated with sailing boats and day trippers. The sky, beautifully clear and endless an hour ago, now sported the purple bruise of storm clouds. From her limited experience, having been in the Maldives for a few days, Evelyn knew within a couple of hours the sea would churn and the tropical rain would beat down with intensity, striking the dry dusty ground like a drum. At least the storm would break the oppressive humidity.

Ishmael lay on his own deck chair beside her, sun hat pulled over his face, his slow breathing indicating that he had fallen asleep. Following the fraught hours after the wedding, stressed about the cheque which now lay at the bottom of his suitcase, it was a relief to see him begin to enjoy their honeymoon. He'd been silent for hours after the reception. She'd attempted to ascribe his mood to the exhaustion of the day, marred by the subsequent eleven hour flight, and hour and half boat journey. But in truth, Ishmael was fighting his inner demons.

Rather than being the focus of her husband's affection, he'd barely touched her. It wasn't the start to the honeymoon she'd dreamed of. The beautiful weather, the idyllic island and incredible food all played a part in helping him unwind. But it was the two-hour conversation the night before that finally broke the deadlock.

Ishmael had paced from one side of the hut to the other, his thoughts spilling out in increasing verbosity, while Evelyn listened. The sky darkened outside amid the gentle breaking of waves against the shore. The heat of the day had subsided, the night-time air rich with floral undertones and the crisp freshness of the sea. He talked in circles, but he *was* talking. He needed to process. Ishmael did this so rarely, that she realised the importance of letting it play out. She didn't interrupt, despite the growing desire to shake him.

She wondered where that stoic, secure, Ishmael had gone. The one she knew at university; his characteristics that had attracted her to him in the first place. While everyone else had tried to fit in, Ishmael stood out as his own man. Yet, had all this been an illusion? He seemed to care too much about what his parents thought. He fretted over their expectations.

For the first time in their entire relationship, she wondered what she had stumbled into. It was easier in London. Their lives were their own. But there was something bigger going on, which she struggled to understand, a power play which she had no desire to be part of.

Eventually Ishmael ran out of steam, sitting down on the bed next to her. She took his hand, absentmindedly stroking it with her thumb. She said the one thing she knew Ishmael wanted, and needed, to hear in that moment.

'Whatever you decide to do about the cheque, I will support you.'

His body relaxed, the bed slumping under the weight. For the first time in two days he stared deeply into her eyes.

'Thank you.' He lay back on the bed, his emotions spent.

They'd retired to bed that night in each other's arms, Evelyn tenderly curling his dark hair around her finger as he slept.

They spent the next day on the beach, chatting, laughing, reading, their honeymoon far closer to what she'd imagined it would be. She considered his sleeping frame in the deck chair. She loved him so much. Despite the collective disappointments; the life in London that she would swap for the countryside at any opportunity, the job which paid the bills rather than filled her with enthusiasm, the husband that she thought she knew, but was beginning to realise that she didn't. She still loved him. She had still chosen him. She always would.

*

'I've made a decision.'

He clasped her hand in his as they walked across the beach. It was their last evening on the island. A week of snorkelling, sunshine, swimming, sunbathing and cocktails were soon to slip into their memories, with the chartered boat due to take them to the airport in the morning.

The sun set around them as they walked. The sky, a violent dash of pink, lightening the surrounding cerulean to a lilac hue, took her breath away. She squeezed his hand in encouragement, as they wound their way through the palm trees and down towards the breakers. Small crabs scurried across the beach into the shadows. The weather glorious again, the sea had reverted from an angry swell back to a calm ripple. Water lapped over their bare feet, drenching the luminescent sand beneath and retreating as quickly as it arrived.

'Go on,' she said.

Ishmael took a deep breath, his eye line fixed on the horizon. 'I'm going to accept the money.'

Evelyn was so shocked she almost let go of his hand. This was not the answer she'd expected.

'My dad is not stupid,' he explained. 'He knows, as we do, that there's no way we can ever afford to buy a place in London. I want to believe it's just a gift, I really do. But I know the way his mind works.'

'Then why accept it?'

'Because…' Ishmael paused, a frown etched into his forehead. 'Evelyn…' he tried again, his face haunted. 'He's won. I can't out manoeuvre him. Not without leaving us in an impossible situation.'

'We can do anything, Ishmael. We can make it without his help. As you said before, moving to London was about that; making it on our own.'

He shook his head. 'No. We'll stay in a one bed flat, until a child arrives, forcing us to squeeze into a two bed place, or we have to leave London. Fine… we'll make our own plan, just like the rest of the country. But we'll always be the ones who turned down the cheque. In his eyes, I'll always be the son who threw his offer back in his face. I will be the son who rejected his own father. Because *that* is what it is about, Evelyn, that's all it was *ever* about.'

He let go of her hand, exhaling violently, and walked away. All his new bride could do was watch him retreat, waves lapping over her bare toes, soaking through the hem of her white summer dress.

Chapter Twenty Three

2019

Ethan rotated the silk flowers over in his hand. It was the second time in as many weeks that he'd disturbed them from their box. He kept returning. He still remembered buying them all those years ago. The memory was so vivid, it stung; all the associated feelings that went with the simple gifts, gifts he had bought, not knowing, just hoping. A gift that signalled friendship and comfort, but hidden within the desire of wanting so much more, but never dreaming it would be.

They'd had thirty-five years together. Now, Helen was dead and all that was left were her scattered belongings, a crumpled shoe box, journal entries he struggled to read and a palm of silk flowers.

He squeezed his forehead between his forefinger and thumb and shook his head, as if the act itself would dislodge his thoughts. He only had himself to blame and sitting pondering it all in a darkened kitchen would not solve anything. It would not bring her back and it would not quench the growing disquiet that the pages stirred.

Placing the silk flowers into the shoe box on the table, Ethan pushed his chair back and stood. Aimee had texted through the details of her flight. She'd be arriving in just over a week and he had a house to get ready.

*

Having hauled a full bin bag into the wheelie bin, he took a brief moment to admire the garden. Midway through June, the bushes and plants were a magnificent riot of colour, vivid purples, deep reds, intense yellows, all boastful in their beauty. The sun shone down with great beams of warmth, penetrating the heavy laden branches of the trees above, thick with their deep green leaves, and down onto the lawn below. A momentary, mundane, thought crossed his mind that Aimee would at least arrive home to some decent weather.

'Afternoon Ethan,' Gordon called across, as he walked his two black Labradors down the lane past the cottage. 'Having a clear out?' He nodded his grey cap toward the overflowing bin.

'Aimee is home the Monday after next. Thought I'd tackle her room. It… well… it hasn't been dealt with since she moved out.'

'Didn't she leave home years ago?'

'She officially moved out after Helen got ill. She was back and forth with her travels before that. Sorting out her room fell down the list of priorities, to be honest.'

Gordon nodded sympathetically.

'I've kept most things as they are. Aimee will go spare if I get rid of anything she deems important. I just tidied up a bit.'

The dogs strained against their harnesses, keen to resume their walk. 'It's time you and I had a pint down the pub. It's been a while,' Gordon said. 'Come and join me.'

Glancing back at the cottage; the secrets, unresolved questions, and cupboards full of his late wife's possessions, the pub seemed like the perfect respite.

'I'll get my wallet.'

*

'You see, the problem with a permit is that it's handing over the control,' Gordon said, downing the last third of his pint and gesticulating with his free hand. His white hair bobbed on top of his animated head. 'There's no freedom anymore. No 'being your own man' and making your own choices. Everything is on the grid these days.'

Ethan nodded into his own pint. Gordon had strong views on many things and for once it was a welcome distraction. So far, they'd covered the topics of the local housing development, inheritance tax, and the rumours of a new parking permit system along the high street. The dogs rested at their feet, exhausted by their run through the meadow, the men having taken a circuitous route to the pub. Well known by the landlady, Gordon's dogs were as welcome inside as her Great Dane.

'So, where's Evelyn today? Not working in that bookshop on a Saturday, surely?'

'Well, she often has to do Saturday shifts. It's a small business after all. But no, she's not working today. She's in London, visiting a friend.'

'Not the husband?' Gordon enquired, his head tilted in interest.

Ethan knew better than to encourage him. He was a friend and they'd chat about many things, but Evelyn's marriage was off limits. He saw her quiet pain, a mixture of entangled emotions that he was unable to decipher, and recognised her need for privacy.

'No,' he replied, standing up. 'Are you ready for another pint, Gordon?'

They drank their pints and put the world to rights. Half an hour later they walked back through Taverton. As the house loomed closer, Ethan knew he was going to have to face facts. Unless the pages proved otherwise, he might never know Helen's true intentions. He might never understand her real reasons for agreeing to marry him. He might never know if she had completely loved him.

The shoe box had been a surprise. He hadn't known about it, had somehow never come across it in over thirty years of marriage. Now, he realised she had kept secrets. Most of the contents were harmless; letters from pen friends, trivial diary entries, reflections and day dreams, and poetry, many pages of poetry. It was the written musings in between that caught his attention, journal entries that revealed her deepest feelings for the man who came close to ruining her life. There was nothing Ethan hadn't already known, he was present during those years after all, but a betraying fear raised questions. The worry being, of course, that he might not get the answers he hoped for.

They reached Ethan's cottage. 'Thanks Gordon. It was good to catch up.'

'Anytime,' Gordon replied, hoisting his cap a little up his forehead in acknowledgement. 'You know... I've not said anything, after all a man's grief is his own private business. But I believe it'll do you good to get out from that house and spend time with your friends. It's been months since we last had a pint.'

Not missing the irony, following on from very similar conversations with Evelyn and her own isolation, Ethan grimaced. Perhaps father and daughter were alike in more ways than he thought.

'You're not wrong, Gordon. Perhaps it's time for a change for all of us.'

*

Her mind roving through the events of the afternoon, Evelyn slipped into the house unnoticed. The evenings were getting longer, the twilight holding off until late. A faint bluish tinge lit the edges of the horizon, where the sun hung, brushing the landscape beneath.

It was quarter to eleven and there was no sign of Ethan. The hall light had been left on, but the rest of the house was cloaked in darkness, and the only sound was the distant rumble of the washing machine finishing off a load.

She removed her heeled boots, relieved to free her aching feet from their sweaty confines. The day was warmer than expected, but she'd already left for London before regretting her shoe choice. Swinging her light khaki jacket over a spare coat hook, she entered the kitchen, flicking on the light and pouring herself some water into a clean glass from the drying rack. Sinking into one of the kitchen chairs, she closed her eyes.

She'd missed this: spending her weekend catching up with friends, no other agenda but to hang out, drinking cocktails and laughing over shared memories. In London almost every weekend had been like that. Bar the occasional errand or hour spent cleaning the flat, and of course any weekend away visiting family, most of their spare time was spent with friends.

How much had been lost, how much needed to recover, never ceased to amaze her. Two lives that had entwined with one another, to then have to separate into individual entities, took its toll. There was no way to avoid leaving a smudge, an imprint, a fingerprint on each other.

Randall poked his head around the door, giving Evelyn a rare meow in greeting. He stared at her a second, his out-of-character friendliness swiftly replaced with an expression of indifference. She grinned.

'It's taken a year and a half, but you're begrudgingly accepting that I'm back, aren't you?'

He lifted his head at the question, gave a final sniff of distaste and stalked across the kitchen, studying his empty bowl in misplaced hope. Evelyn laughed and downed the rest of her water. She glanced at the clock above the door. It was five minutes to eleven, but she didn't feel tired in the least. Everything about the day had rejuvenated her. The conversation, the time spent with her best friend, even the journey into London had been exhilarating. Wondering why she'd ever considered it a good idea to isolate to the extent she had, she shook her head in consternation. All the fears she'd clung onto, worrying what her friends would say, worrying that they would take sides, all paled into faint embarrassment. She knew, deep down, that Caren would never play games, so why had she allowed herself to indulge in the fear of it?

Perhaps she was coming out of the fog. Maybe she was healing and accepting the mess left behind her. Or maybe, Evelyn reasoned, she had just become desperate and lonely enough to face her own failures.

Galvanised by her thoughts, she opened the fridge. After the busyness of the day and the long commute home she was peckish. Taking out a chunk of cheese and a joint of locally cured ham, she cut slices of each, grabbed the remaining end of a cucumber and a whole tomato and added them onto the plate. She took her rustic supper to the living room.

Curtains drawn, the living room was cast in complete darkness. She flicked on a lamp, and settled across the suede sofa, pulling up the red checked throw over her legs. The silence was a welcome companion. It helped her unwind. It helped her process her thoughts as she felt a lick of calm envelop her. So things hadn't worked out how she wanted. It hurt - there was no hiding from that. She accepted, upon hearing the news that Ishmael was dating, that she still had feelings for him. But that was understandable; they were together for nine years, married for almost four. It wasn't surprising that she might still harbour some affection towards him.

No matter what signs were there prior, no matter what cracks opened and deepened over the years, the split had still been a violent shock. Every decision they'd made, no matter how much she acquiesced, was blunt and sudden. Nineteen months on, she was only starting to process it.

She was safe in Taverton. Her life had tripped over a hurdle, obscuring the route ahead for a time. But she had her family, and furthermore, she had the bookshop. It was hers, bought and paid for. She wouldn't be making the same mistakes she'd made in her personal life. She'd fight for the business. It *would* be a success. One big mistake didn't need to dictate the path for the rest of her life.

Finishing the food, Evelyn settled across the sofa, staring into the unlit fireplace for a while and collating her thoughts. It would be a while before she'd be able to sleep. An owl screeched outside, alerting her to the late hour. She slid from the sofa. Switching off the lamp and taking the plate through to the kitchen, she made her way up the darkened stairs.

Chapter Twenty Four

Joe glanced at Lucie as she replenished the stock on the central table. Lost in concentration she failed to notice his attention.

Sheepish, he drew his gaze away and gave himself a mental talking to. They'd worked together for two weekends in a row now and it had given them the chance to talk beyond the pleasantries. Lucie never shared much about her life outside work, but they'd happily discussed their favourite television shows and books, current events, the upcoming book events Evelyn was planning. They had quite a lot in common and this added fuel to his crush. It was easier to pretend he didn't have feelings when he had known so little about her.

When they weren't working together she flowed into his thoughts. Just a few days ago on his way to work, his peripheral vision caught sight of a handbag in a shop window and it reminded him of one of Lucie's. In an instant he was assailed with visions of her, imagining what she might be doing and how she might be spending her day.

Embarrassed by the memory, Joe left the shop floor for the printer in the backroom. They were printing out batches of letters to be posted out to local businesses and the regional radio show, to try and drum up some interest in the festival. Emails had already been sent out, but Evelyn also insisted on formal letters too. As with everything to do with the business she had both digital and physical backups. He guessed her work in archives had taught her the importance of a paper trail.

After weeks of deferring to his opinion over the upcoming event, Evelyn returned from a weekend off full of energy and ideas. Since then, they'd put together an even longer list of what needed to be done in the weeks ahead. In all honesty Joe was grateful for the input. It also meant he had ammunition when it came to the festival meetings. And ammunition against Mrs Longhorn's scattergun approach to anyone with a different opinion to her own.

Shuddering, admittedly intimidated by the elderly woman, he could at least rattle off a dozen solid ideas for promotion. Even Betty didn't see much wrong with asking the local radio station for an interview.

Evelyn had ordered banners with the bookshop's name and details printed across, as well as matching bookmarks to hand out, and had spent several hours the previous week advertising on social media. There was still a lot to do and many ideas they'd had to put on hold due to budget constraints, but they seemed to be gaining interest. Several customers that week had commented that they had found Taverton Tales through social media, much to Evelyn's delight. She'd also secured another upcoming book launch for a local author, who'd agreed to sell their books at a special price for the festival weekend.

Her sudden buzz of excitement and passion lifted the atmosphere of the shop and became infectious. Even Lucie, someone who completed her shift with a lack of fanfare, caught the wave of enthusiasm, putting her name down to help staff the book launch and talking excitedly about the festival.

'Joe,' Lucie called from the shop front.

'Yep,' he replied, popping his head around the doorframe and craning his neck in her direction.

She held the shop phone in her hand, cheeks red and flushed, panic etched into her face. He left the back room immediately.

'Is everything all right? Of course it's not,' he said, answering his own question. 'You're terrified.'

'Not terrified so much, just... well maybe a little... I need to go. But you'll be on your own in the shop... and I don't know how long I'll be... oh, I've made such a mess of this!'

'What is a mess?'

'I... can't explain. I know I can't just run off without an explanation. It's just so complicated. I've made it so complicated.' She gave a little sob.

Alarmed, he nodded. 'You must go, if it's urgent.'

'Thank you. I'll phone you if I'm going to be a while.'

'Lucie, there's only a couple of hours until closing. Go. Don't worry about things here. I can manage.'

She gave him a relieved and grateful nod, grabbed her bag from the back room and ran from the shop. His gaze followed her retreating figure, long after the door had swung closed behind her.

*

The new morning was crisp and fresh, the hint of warmth was yet to arrive in the subtle hum in the air and the whisper of a possible escalating breeze danced through the tops of the trees. Joe stalked down the high street, pausing at the bookshop, waving to Evelyn inside. It was Monday, his day off in lieu of working the Saturday shift. Lucie was due in today. He wondered if she would be.

Curiosity getting the better of him, he pushed the door open and stepped inside. Evelyn was opening the first of several boxes that had arrived from the suppliers. Two customers browsed on opposite sides of the shop; one amongst the science fiction novels, the other with their nose in a history book.

'Can't get enough of the place?' Evelyn asked, distracted with a pile of Stephen King novels. She scanned them all into the computer's database.

'I wanted to ask about Lucie,' Joe lowered his voice. 'I was a bit worried after she ran off on Saturday. I see she's not in yet,' he added, noting the time on the clock. It was ten past ten.

'She'll be in at lunch time. She had a family emergency.'

'Oh,' Joe replied, worrying at his jaw.

'That's all she told me. She's not one for big explanations.'

'No, she's not.'

'Joe, go and enjoy your day off.' She hoisted the books off the desk, glancing at her watch before lifting the next pile.

Realisation hit him. 'Ah, your sister's flying in today, right?'

'Yes,' she said in heavy exhale. 'Yes, she is.'

Deciding to leave it there, Joe bid goodbye and left the shop. He lifted his head to the brightening sky, the last clouds skittering across his vision, as the blue intensified in their absence. It was going to be a beautiful day. Forcing his hands deep into his pockets he crossed the high street and headed towards the café. He needed a full English breakfast before contemplating the day ahead.

Ordering an enormous plate of sausages, bacon, beans, hash browns, egg and mushrooms, he sat down at the chrome table with its white Formica top, his mind mulling over his last conversation with Lucie. In her panic she'd talked about making a mess of things. He wished he understood what she'd meant. As their relationship was purely professional, he couldn't even describe himself as a friend, but he did at least have her mobile number for work reasons. After spending the entire Sunday wondering if he should send a short text, just to enquire whether everything was okay, he had almost driven himself to frustration. See-sawing between not believing it appropriate to invade her personal space, even by text message, and feeling like a terrible work colleague for not contacting her, he'd had to resort to watching a marathon of superhero films for distraction.

Would she accuse him of being uncaring for not sending a message? It was a risk that he'd have to take. He would have to wait a full week to see her again, when they next shared a shift. It would be a long week.

*

Evelyn unlocked the front door, a shot of apprehension greeting her as she entered the darkened porch. She'd tried to prepare herself for Aimee's visit, her thoughts running through the possible conversations they may have, the inevitable questions that would be raised about her failed marriage. Over the last few days, busy at work and with planning, she'd managed to achieve a reasonable state of composure. Now she was faced with her sister's arrival that composure was under threat.

She heard voices in the kitchen and Aimee's distinctive tinkle of laughter wafting through the ether. She scolded herself for allowing thoughts of her younger sister to get the better of her, and pushed open the door.

Ethan leant with his back against the sink, arms folded and relaxed, deep laughter lines highlighting his joyful expression. No matter his previous reticence, it was clear that he was delighted to have his youngest home.

Aimee sat at the kitchen table, staring at Evelyn, sporting the faintest smirk. Her reddish golden hair hung loose and fell almost the entire length of her back. She wore a short sleeved purple vest and light blue denim jeans. A threaded belt adorned her waist. Raising her hands behind her head, she arched an eyebrow.

'I'm home,' she said. There was a hint of challenge in her tone.

'I see,' Evelyn replied, noticing that she was still holding the door knob. Her fist had tightened around it and she had to concentrate to uncoil herself and let go.

116

She noticed her father's relaxed demeanour flicker, his eyes wary. She knew it pained him to see his girls at odds, for no good reason other than their difference in personalities. She decided to make an effort.

'Welcome.'

A pause fell on the room. Time seemed suspended for a brief, charged moment. It was broken by Aimee's creeping grin. She jumped from the chair and strode over to Evelyn, grabbing her and embracing her in a bone bruising hug.

Evelyn gasped with surprise. Ethan appeared as stunned as she. Then he cracked his own grin, lighting his entire face, breaking into relieved and unguarded laughter.

*

'I couldn't just stand there and let this pillock kill himself, all for a selfie,' Aimee exclaimed, in between mouthfuls of Chinese takeaway. 'So I yelled at him, grabbed him back from the edge and called him an idiot.'

Ethan frowned with consternation. 'He might have pulled you over.'

'Dad,' Aimee replied with irritation. '*That* is not the point of the story.'

'Then what is?' His forkful of food was paused between his plate and mouth.

'Well... if you'd let me finish. So, I shout at him and tell him what an idiot he is, and then we get talking. Turns out he's still a prat, but he's following me round the hostel like a lost lamb for weeks. Anyway... as it happens I realise I quite like him after all. Liam and I have been dating for the last six months. But he had to go back to New Zealand as his visa ran out. So, now... we'll see. I haven't made any decisions yet.'

Ethan risked a glance at Evelyn as they both tried to process the influx of information.

'You've not mentioned him on the telephone,' he said, remembering his forkful of food and putting it in his mouth.

Aimee replied with a shrug. 'As I said, I haven't decided yet. I'm only twenty-seven. I'm not in any rush.'

She pushed her fork around her plate, scooping up the remnants of her Kung Pow chicken. 'I thought it was time to head home for a while. I need to work out what I want. He's not keen to live in the UK, so I also need to figure out where I want to live.'

'Leave the UK for good, you mean?' Ethan asked, concerned.

'Travelling is fun, but I can't do it forever. Working in bars at night and hanging out on the beach all day is amazing,' she said with a contented exhale. 'But at some point you have to move on. Most of the others at the hostel are in their early twenties. I'm considered *old* by their standards. Old! I never felt it until my last birthday. Then I realised, all my friends were heading back home and settling down. I'm getting left behind.'

Evelyn pushed her own food around her plate as she listened. She and Aimee had made almost opposite choices in life. She'd settled young, marrying her first love. At twenty-seven years old she was already someone's wife. Aimee had done the opposite, throwing responsibility out of the window and jumping on a plane. She had been the source of her parents' worry for years; a young female travelling alone, or in small groups of strangers, often dropping out of contact for weeks at a time, sometimes to reappear with no warning at the front door. Aimee would vow to settle, and get a local job for a few months, before getting itchy feet again.

Her flightiness had angered Helen, who used to accuse her youngest of being irresponsible. They'd all be concerned for Aimee's safety, especially when there was a gap in communication. Since Helen's passing she'd had travelled in Greece, before holding down a bar job and enjoying the Mediterranean lifestyle. It couldn't last forever, though, surely?

Now it seemed that both of them had reached a crossroads. Different decisions, different lifestyle choices, yet both at a standstill and wondering where to go from here.

Ethan exhaled. 'Well, you're welcome here for as long as you need, until you figure it out.'

'Oh don't worry,' Aimee scoffed. 'I won't be here as long as Evelyn!'

She raised her head sharply. Less than sixty minutes, she thought in indignation. Sixty minutes was all it had taken for Aimee's first gibe. Actually, she reasoned, that was quite good going for her sister.

'I won't be here for much longer.' Evelyn was making plans now; for the business, her finances, her future.

'Both my daughters are welcome here as long as they need,' Ethan reiterated, standing up with his now empty plate, signalling the end of the current conversation. 'There's ice cream in the freezer, if anyone wants?'

'Is it toffee flavoured?' Aimee questioned.

'Of course, what else would I buy for my baby's return but her favourite ice cream?'

Aimee grinned in satisfaction. She looked like a seven year old girl again, eyes lit up, big beam across her face, sun-kissed freckles decorating the bridge of her nose. 'Thank you, Daddy,' she replied, with a feigned innocence.

Evelyn rolled her eyes.

*

'That seemed to go well,' Ethan whispered to Evelyn. They stood at the top of the stairs saying goodnight. Night time shadows fell through the house as one by one Ethan had switched the lights off on the way up. Aimee was in the shower; her faint singing heard from the landing even behind shut doors.

'Hmm,' Evelyn offered. The rest of the evening had been pleasant, perhaps too pleasant. Other than the one obvious poke regarding her living situation, Aimee had been well behaved. But Evelyn couldn't shake the feeling that a storm was brewing.

'Maybe we shouldn't jump to conclusions. She's growing up, after all. Maybe she's maturing; becoming more considerate, even. Maybe this Liam is good for her.'

Evelyn nodded in acquiescence, not wanting to pour negativity over her father's happiness at having his family back under one roof. Now was not the time.

She leaned over and kissed his cheek. 'Night, Dad.'

'Sleep well, honey,' he replied, squeezing her arm.

She left him standing in the darkened landing, strips of moonlight cutting through the gloom from the large window above the stairs, illuminating the carpet around his feet. She pushed the bedroom door shut behind her and sank onto the bed. There was silence other than a distant muffled sound of doors opening and closing. There wouldn't be a lot of peace in the coming weeks, not with another person in the house. She would have to take her opportunities where she could. Closing her eyes, she ran through the events of the evening. Seeing Aimee again drew a mixture of emotions and encouraged a peculiar concoction of memories. But she was too tired to unpack them all now.

Distracted she headed to the chest of drawers and undressed, pulling on a clean pair of pyjamas. Leaving the bedroom, she headed down the hall to the now empty bathroom. Pausing on the way, she knocked on Aimee's door.

'Dad?'

'No, it's Evelyn.'

'Oh... come in.'

She pushed open the door. Aimee sat cross-legged on the single bed, the bedside lamp highlighting a pile of photographs scattered across violent pink bed linen, the only spare and clean duvet cover Ethan had found and a throwback from the girl's childhood. A small cardboard box lay, empty, beside them.

'I found these under the bed,' Aimee explained, running a hand over the photographs. There were dozens, all charting various stages of their upbringing; pictures of Helen holding each of them at different ages, a teenage Aimee squeezing the life out of an unimpressed Randall, ball games in the garden. There was a photo of Ethan standing next to a young Evelyn and Aimee, as they paddled in a stream in some forest somewhere. Glancing away she experienced a jolt, as her eyes scanned over a familiar figure. A photograph which was partially hidden by the one in front, the background dark having been snapped on a night out, showed Evelyn with her arms around Ishmael as he grinned towards the lens.

She remembered that evening. It wasn't long after she'd joined him in London. They'd treated themselves to a night out, having been so careful not to spend too much amid the cost of London life and paying back student loans. It was a simple meal in a restaurant chain, nothing fancy, but Evelyn felt so happy; positive for the first time about the future they were creating together. All fear had gone. They were doing it; they were making a life for themselves. She remembered asking a stranger to take the photo. She'd sent her parents a digital copy the next day, not knowing that they had had it printed. She hadn't even done that.

A heavy ache settled in her chest. She turned away.

'I know,' Aimee said in a small voice, tucking a still wet lock of hair behind her ear. 'It's hard to see photos of Mum.'

Bereft that her late mother wasn't even the reason for her distress Evelyn bowed her head to stop the tears that threatened.

'Yes,' she whispered. She pulled herself together. 'Goodnight, Aimee. It's nice to have you home.'

'Hmm,' Aimee murmured, her attention already back to the photographs splayed out over the bed.

Evelyn smiled. Aimee hadn't changed all that much.

'Night,' she repeated, pulling the door open and slipping through, softly clicking it shut behind her.

Chapter Twenty Five

It's time. We're going. We're going to drive and see where the wind carries us. He is tired of it all; tired of the world telling him what to do. He has his reasons, so do I. My reasons are him. It will always be him.

Last night we drove for over an hour, through the narrow country lanes and all the way to the coast. He drives fast, but it's exhilarating. I feel like we can achieve anything when we drive, to just go and see where we end up. I laughed in excitement. Laurence turned his head and laughed with me.

'Imagine,' he shouted over the roar of the engine. 'Imagine what we can do. What we can achieve without all these rules, without them all looking over our shoulders.'

My fears for our future all melted away in that instant. He does want to be with me! As soon as we arrived at the beach, he pulled me out of the car and into his arms. I was weak beneath his kisses. My God, I can see nothing but him. He is in every thought, every time I close my eyes and there he is. I cannot comprehend a life where we are not together. I love him with all my being.

So we are to go, to run, to live life how we want. He is going to clear his savings. His family are rich. He has enough. We won't even need to consider jobs, not for some time. We can just be.

I do worry for my parents. It will be a shock for them. But I cannot be away from him for years. I cannot bear all that enforced time apart. Why should I punish myself? This way we can be together now. We can figure out the rest as we go. They might not like it, but they will in time accept it. After all I am the only one of my female friends planning to go to college. Most are to go straight into the workplace. Two are heading to secretarial school. Caroline wants to be a nanny.

Mum and Dad will have to accept the change in direction. But I know that they will be angry at first, they will try to persuade me against him. I just know they will. I can't allow that to happen, so I will avoid it instead.

All will be fine and well in the end.

Chapter Twenty Six

2019

Joe's thumb hovered over the Send button. He'd spent three days mulling over the pros and cons of sending Lucie a text message. A decision that he wouldn't have even contemplated for longer than the briefest second, had the message been to anyone else, had become a gigantic mountain of proportions.

'This is ridiculous,' hissed Joe, pushing the button and flinging the phone down on the arm rest next to him.

He knew he tended to overanalyse and this week had raised the bar for his more neurotic tendencies. Deciding that a casual yet polite message was acceptable from a work colleague, he'd composed a two lined text. But as soon as the decision was made, he second guessed himself. What if she found the interaction inappropriate? What if something terrible had happened and his text message brought it all back to the surface and distressed her?

'Shut up!' he groaned at his racing thoughts.

It was done now. He grabbed up the latest novel from a sci-fi series he was ploughing through and immersed himself in the pages. He had to restrain himself from picking up the phone and rechecking the message.

It was seared into his memory anyway.

Hi Lucie, just checking that you are all right after Saturday? Let me know if you need anything, Joe.

That was it. Light, polite, without probing for too much information. He'd circumnavigated the trap of whether to end with an emoji or even a cross for a kiss. Leaving it as 'Joe', there was little room for misinterpretation. Or so he hoped.

Ignoring the phone and trying to prevent himself straining his ears for the sound of a beep, Joe went to put the kettle on. Slipping the phone onto the bookshelf on the way to the kitchen, he knew it would dilute the chances of checking it by the smallest, but still significant degree.

Engrossed in the pages of his book, as the kettle boiled, he relaxed. He'd be twenty-six soon. He was a little too old to be wrapped up by teenage-like uncertainty of how to address, speak to, or message a woman. Or at least he thought he ought to be. It didn't help that the rules seemed to be constantly changing.

But his intentions were good. He was worried about Lucie. He wished he knew more about her, so he understood what she might have faced this last week. And yes, he admitted to himself that he did *like* her. But he also wasn't an idiot. Joe knew that she did not feel the same way. But that didn't stop his concern for her, nor prevent his desire for a friendship, if nothing else. He'd still become her friend and he'd choose to be happy with that.

The kettle clicked off and the room was plunged into a sudden silence. He poured the water into a mug and doused the tea bag inside. Resisting the urge to check his phone, he collapsed onto the cream sofa bed, which had seen better days, and sipped his tea. Still distracted, he tried to keep his attention on the novel.

He shifted in his seat to shake his nervous energy. This was agony. He groaned. How easily he'd slipped into a pathetic state. He needed to get on top of his crush.

The phone broke the charged silence with a shrill cry and he jumped in his seat, narrowly avoiding the spill of hot tea. Joe reached the phone and registered with a plummeting disappointment Evelyn's name across the screen.

'Yes, boss.'

*

'Evening Joe, I'm sorry to call you at home.' Her voice lowered so as not to disturb Aimee and Ethan, who were wading through old photographs of Helen.

Ever since Aimee's arrival, all she'd wanted to do was reminisce about the years gone by. Evelyn watched her father as he pored over the images on the table. He had taken the request to get the photo albums out with good humour, but she recognised the strain in his countenance. She knew this was hard for him. The weeks spent sorting through Helen's belongings had already proved that.

'Hello? Evelyn, are you still there?' Joe's voice cut into her thoughts.

'Sorry,' she said, moving away from the kitchen and down the hall towards the living room. 'I need to ask you a big favour. Would you be free to help host the author event next week? I will be there too of course, and Lucie will be behind the till. We've already sold all the tickets and I'm still getting calls, so let's open it up – make it an even bigger event. But I'll need all hands on deck, if that's okay?'

'Sure. I had nothing else planned anyway.'

'Thanks Joe. It's exciting that this is taking off. This is just the start. We can do so much with the bookshop.'

'Yes,' Joe replied. He sounded distracted.

'Okay,' Evelyn paused. 'I won't disturb you any longer. Have a good evening, Joe.'

*

'You too,' he replied, as he disconnected.

Knowing it would torment him otherwise Joe stared at the phone in disgust, before holding down the side button. With a satisfying click the screen went black. Slipping the phone into a drawer in the kitchen, he returned to his book and to the less mentally anguishing backdrop of interplanetary warfare.

*

'Any plans for the weekend?' Ethan asked as he topped up Aimee and Evelyn's cups of tea.

'Not particularly,' Aimee muttered in reply, her chin in her hand.

'I thought you'd want to catch up with some friends.'

'None of my close friends live locally. That's the problem with making friends when you're overseas. They live all over. I want to go visit Beks and Josh up in Nottingham. I haven't seen them in a year. I might go and visit Olivia in Cornwall too. It depends on how long my money lasts. I'll need to get a job soon.'

'All my school friends have moved away,' Aimee continued, preventing an open mouthed Ethan from questioning Aimee's finances, job prospects and general future plans. 'Nas is in London. Laura and Nicky never moved back here after university.'

127

She paused, her last words hanging in the air. 'I'm not quite sure where I fit in, actually.'

He closed his mouth, deciding against questioning her. Were they all at a crossroads in their lives?

'Shall we take the tea outside?' he asked instead. 'It's a lovely day out there.'

They followed him out into the garden. The sun was blinding in intensity and Evelyn held a hand to her forehead to guard her eyes. Ethan led them towards his workshop, stopping halfway there and pulling the tarpaulin off the outdoor table and chairs hidden beneath.

The trees surrounding the perimeter of the garden threw a refreshing shade across the table, and rustled gently above them in the warm breeze. They sat down in companionable silence for a few minutes, watching the birds hopping between the foliage and enjoying the distant sounds of insects in the fields beyond.

'I thought maybe we could do something together this weekend?' Aimee said, breaking the peace.

Ethan raised his eyebrows. 'I'm free.'

'I have to work Saturday,' Evelyn said, taking a sip of her tea.

'Oh,' Aimee said, in obvious disappointment.

'Don't worry,' he reassured. 'We can go out and do something, just the two of us. It'll be great. We've not done that for years.'

Aimee perked up. Evelyn gave a little cough of discomfort. The truth was she had Sunday and Monday free. Some of the time would be used for mandatory shop admin, but she did usually take some time out for herself too. Her issue was selfish; did she want to give up that personal time to share it with Aimee? She knew she'd feel guilty if she didn't.

'I can spare a few hours on Sunday,' she admitted. 'But, I do have paperwork to do, so I can't take a whole day off,' she added as a caveat.

'Well, Aimee and I can go out on Saturday as planned. You can make your own plans together.'

Aimee nodded with a little uncertainty, as if unconvinced that Evelyn wanted to spend time with her. Great, she thought. Now she felt even guiltier.

Raising her gaze from above the rim of her drink, she added. 'It'll be brilliant.'

*

'Would you shut up for just one minute?' Evelyn exclaimed, pulling the car into a passing place and letting the engine run.

She thumbed through the road atlas, her Sat-Nav forgotten in its inexplicable tendency to try to get her to cross entire fields or blocked byways to get back to the main road. Suggesting a drive out into the deep Suffolk countryside, to find a picturesque pub for lunch, had seemed such a good idea an hour ago.

Arguing over which music to play in the car, and then over the general direction they were heading, and it wasn't long before Evelyn lost track of where they were and wished she'd just taken Aimee to Taverton Inn instead.

'You need to head towards the spire,' Aimee shrugged, pointing out the ancient church in the distance, visible by the tip poking above the woodland.

Evelyn glared at her. 'You've said that for the last five minutes, but this road is not going in that direction is it?' she hissed, failing to keep calm. 'You can see that the road bends ahead to the right, not the left.'

'Give the map to me. I'm good at reading maps.'

Evelyn sighed and shut her eyes, her head falling back against the head rest. Aimee slipped the atlas off her sister's lap and fell into silence as she perused it.

'Here! We're here,' she announced, pointing her forefinger to a tiny lane, so insignificant that it wasn't even colour coded.

'How can you tell?'

'The church spire is here on the map, north-west, and where the road then bends, you can see exactly where we are. We need to go back the way we came, and turn right...' she paused. 'Just there. We'll be back on the main road in a few minutes.'

Evelyn looked at her. 'I didn't know you read maps.'

'I've spent most of my twenties travelling.'

'Well, that'll do it,' Evelyn said in amusement. 'Right, let's get back on track. I am starving.'

Checking her mirrors, she pulled the car out of the passing place and used the narrow lane to turn around. Aimee navigated and within a few minutes they were driving towards the junction that led to the main road. Heading for the spire, they entered a miniscule village, with less than twenty houses lining the street as well as the obligatory country public house. Parking outside the church, they walked over the road and into the pub, surprised to see it packed with patrons all tucking into heaped plates of traditional Sunday roast.

'This is great,' Aimee said happily. 'I haven't had a Sunday roast in years!'

Exhausted by the exertions of simply getting there, Evelyn slipped into one of the last free tables and passed a couple of twenty pound notes to Aimee.

'Would you mind ordering for me? A glass of their house white is fine.'

Aimee was already distracted by the rustic farm house decor that adorned the pub. 'It's so *quaint*,' she said, with a mischievous grin. 'It's like I've gone back in time.'

'This is deep farming country,' Evelyn replied, weary. 'Besides, it's considered rustic chic these days. You've been away far too long.'

Aimee laughed and headed for the bar. Evelyn placed her chin in her hand, her elbow resting on the cherry-black table beneath. What was it that caused such exhaustion in her after spending any length of time with her sister? Maybe because Aimee had always seemed so much younger; four years separated them in age, and noticeably in maturity too. It didn't help that Evelyn was more serious. Aimee had a flair for the dramatic and an attitude of taking life as it came. This had led to some interesting life choices; such as the six months she spent on a Kibbutz.

Evelyn watched Aimee in contemplation. In all honesty she missed her. She missed the light relief of a character who never took life too seriously. She missed her smart and quick remarks and the humour beneath them. Despite Aimee's acidic tongue; a tongue that was often used as a weapon, Evelyn still missed the woman behind it. Their family was fragmented enough following Helen's death. Living overseas left its own void.

What Evelyn didn't miss was her sister's uncanny ability to highlight where everyone else was going wrong in their lives, with little, if any reflection on her own. The fact that Aimee hadn't yet displayed those characteristics since arriving home was unnerving. Evelyn suspected it was still coming, and realised part of her exhaustion was trying to be prepared for the attack. The worst part was that Aimee was never deliberately malicious. She just didn't engage the filter that most people used to avoid offending others. Consideration wasn't high up on her lists of priorities.

Curious about the absence of her sister's impulsive trait, she wondered at the reason for the change. Aimee stood at the bar with her back to Evelyn. Her body language was relaxed as she chatted to the landlady. She threw her head back and laughed at some comment and Evelyn smiled.

'That woman is hilarious,' Aimee said a minute later, placing their drinks on the table. She nodded towards the landlady. 'I bet she has a few tales to tell, what with running this place,' she added, sipping her Pimms and lemonade.

'Making friends with the locals?'

Aimee shrugged and fell quiet.

'So, how long will you be with us? Just to get an idea, of course,' Evelyn asked, noting Aimee's immediate tension at the question.

'I... don't know.' Her gaze drifted over the confines of the pub.

'You mentioned that you might need to get a job?'

'Yes, yes...' Aimee replied distractedly, taking a long drawn out drink.

They fell into silence for a while. Finding common ground between them wasn't always easy.

'So, what about you, are you divorced yet?'

The word 'divorce' itself, and the insensitivity behind the question, hit Evelyn in the gut. It was almost like a physical blow.

'No, not yet,' she said, keeping her gaze fixed on her glass of wine.

'Why not? It's not like you have children or a fortune to fight over.'

Two strikes in as many seconds. Aimee was returning to her usual self. Evelyn swallowed hard. The dream of having a family with Ishmael had had to die a long time ago.

'We have to be separated for two years. Neither of us cheated and there was no abuse. It'll be two years in September. Then we can apply for a divorce.'

Perhaps it was the upcoming deadline, the inevitable countdown of when they could divorce, that was causing all her recent uncertainty. Adding Ishmael's rumoured girlfriend into the mix, it was little surprise that Evelyn felt the way she did. There was a finality approaching. She hadn't spoken to Ishmael in a long time; when they had it was to deal with the flat sale, then the subsequent division and collection of their belongings. All that had happened many months ago. Now, there seemed a quickening of pace, an official march towards the end. It scared her, and she wondered, selfishly perhaps, whether she was ready. Either that or maybe she wasn't over him, not quite yet, not totally.

'Tell me about Liam,' she asked, keen to change the subject.

Aimee shifted in her chair, her lips twitching. 'I like him. He's different. Maybe it's just because he was raised in a different country,' she added with a shrug. 'But he sees things in a different way. It

131

challenges me. Apart from the stupidity with the selfie, he's a pretty cool guy. He gave me this before I left.'

She held out her wrist and showed Evelyn a delicate silver chain. Cocooned within some spiralled silver wire was a small triangular piece of jade; Aimee's favourite gemstone. It dangled against her still tanned skin.

'It's very pretty,' Evelyn said, touching the jade with her forefinger. 'And it's very 'you'. He must know you well already.'

'We have lived in each other's pockets for the past six months. He knows me better than anyone.' A wistful air spread over Aimee's face.

It was in that moment that Evelyn realised. It all made sense. Aimee's softened attitude, her uncharacteristic sensitivity - at least for the most part. Aimee was in love.

Why then the talk of having not made a decision, her insistence that it was early days, the talk of settling here with a job when Liam had expressed a desire to not live in the UK?

'Tell me a little about him. What does he like? What is his personality like?'

Aimee pushed her forefinger across the tacky surface of the table.

'He's just a guy, you know? He likes surfing and swimming. He likes action films and books.'

Their conversation was interrupted by the arrival of their roast dinners. The plates were piled high with slices of lamb, wedges of roast potatoes, honey glazed carrots and parsnips, steamed broccoli and fresh peas. Individual miniature jugs of gravy and a shared container of condiments were placed on the table beside them.

'How's Dad doing?' Aimee asked, as she scooped up a forkful of meat and potatoes, complete with a liberal soaking of thick gravy.

'You spent all day with him yesterday. You probably know better than me.'

'That's not what I meant. You've been living with him for over a year. How's he doing without Mum around?'

She remembered her argument with Ethan in the street, right before his phone rang announcing Aimee's impending return. Both were guilty of not sharing their innermost feelings. They had settled into a comfortable routine of co-existing, neither one opening up to the other. But for a long time it was what they each needed.

'You know that he's been sorting through Mum's belongings?' She sliced her knife through the meat.

'Didn't he start six weeks ago? What's taking him so long?'

Evelyn took a deep breath. 'Oh, I don't know. Perhaps getting rid of the love of your life's things is hard to do?' she answered with sarcasm. Sometimes her sister was a real irritant.

'I suppose you know all about that?'

Evelyn stuttered over a choking laugh. Aimee's words stung, but they weren't untrue.

'No, Ishmael was quick enough to remove his stuff. I took longer to sort mine.'

She noticed Aimee had stopped eating, her fork hovering in front of her mouth. 'What happened to you two? You seemed so in love.'

'Well, they say that nearly one in every two marriages…' Evelyn began, before shaking her head. They were both skirting around the real issues; Aimee and her relationship, Evelyn and her lack thereof.

'Ishmael has spent most of his adult life trying to prove himself. I saw the real him behind closed doors. But he was always striving at work and with his family. Towards the end, I can't honestly say that I knew who my husband was, what was real and what wasn't. He seemed so confident when we met; so at ease with himself. I didn't realise at the time that that was just the unguarded Ishmael. I got to see that version of him less and less.'

Aimee's forehead creased in confusion. Evelyn realised that explaining the complexities of her marriage, over the relative triviality of Sunday lunch, might prove impossible. The truth was that there had been many small imperfections which had grown, melded and entwined over time. Add a reluctance to change or to receive help and it had resulted in the recipe for a broken relationship.

'You were too young to get married,' Aimee interjected, nodding as she did, as if having figured out the entire conundrum. 'You should have waited longer.'

'Mum and Dad married younger than I did,' Evelyn pointed out, cross that Aimee assumed to know the full reasons for her marital decline, ignoring the information she had just shared.

'It was different back then,' Aimee said, discounting Evelyn's comment with a flick of her wrist.

'Ishmael and I were together for five years before we married. I knew that our relationship wasn't perfect, yet I still chose to marry him. This has nothing to do with age, which goes nowhere near the true reasons why my marriage is dead.'

Her voice, having risen to a crescendo, attracted the attention of the customers at the next table. Composing herself, she picked up her fork and stabbed it into a roast potato. Aimee didn't respond to the outburst which antagonised Evelyn further and she angrily stuffed the potato into her mouth.

She knew she was no longer close to her sister and hadn't been for years. But where had Aimee been during her separation? Where had she been during those long tear sodden nights, when Evelyn had felt so alone and confused and broken?

Aimee had been gallivanting around Australia, and then Greece, spending her days in temporary jobs and skipping onto a plane before the roots of settling down took hold beneath her feet. Evelyn took a deep breath as she chewed. As angry as she was, she couldn't expect Aimee to abandon her own life to console her through hers.

A phone call or an actual hug would have been nice though.

'I am sorry about you and Ishmael,' Aimee said, breaking into the stew of Evelyn's emotions. 'I liked him.'

Evelyn's reaction was as violent as it was sudden. Before she recognised what was happening, the tears arrived in a torrent. She swallowed painfully as the sobs consumed her. Aimee stuffed her paper napkin into Evelyn's hand. She stood up. Several customers were staring in her direction and she added mortifying embarrassment to the list of emotions cascading through her.

'I need a minute.'

Her face now a mess of hot salty tears, she dashed from the pub.

Five minutes later, Aimee casually sauntered to the car, where Evelyn sat with one leg out of the car door the other crumpled beneath her on the seat. Her shoulders hunched, but tears ceased, she exhaled.

'Feeling better?' Aimee asked, with a typical nonchalance that made Evelyn snort.

'Oh, I haven't felt this good in days,' she replied, in a sardonic tone.

'Good. Your food is getting cold by the way.'

Aimee leant against the open car door as if she hadn't a care in the world, and Evelyn managed a smile. Life had a funny way of seeming dramatic, burdensome and ridiculous all at the same time.

'Are you coming back in?'

Evelyn paused before answering. 'Sure.'

Chapter Twenty Seven

Lucie bustled into the bookshop, jacket over her arm, bag slung over her shoulder. It was already too warm for the jacket, but she was running late and didn't want to cause further delays by taking it home. Joe appearing a little flustered at her arrival, nodding towards her in welcome. His gaze instantly fell from hers.

'Thank you for the text message. I'm so sorry I didn't reply. I meant to. But the weekend has been so busy that I forgot,' she said.

'I hope that things have settled down now?'

'Yes. Everything is fine.'

He studied her for a brief moment. 'Good.'

'Yes,' she repeated, before noticing the heat rise in her cheeks. She felt an inexplicable embarrassment. 'It was just a family thing…'

'You don't have to explain.'

'I know. I just thought seeing as I hadn't remembered to reply to your text….' She left the comment hanging.

She didn't like the sudden stifled atmosphere. She had always enjoyed Joe's company, the stories he told, and his in depth knowledge of the books surrounding them. He was easy to talk to. She never felt awkward around him. It was one reason why she enjoyed the job. Home life was so busy and so complicated at times that the simplicity and sheer enjoyment of a shift in the bookshop was a welcome tonic.

'Why don't you hold the fort for a few minutes and I'll make us both a cup of tea?' he offered.

Lucie slipped in front of the till and logged on. 'That sounds great.'

Joe left her to tend to the shop and headed to the kitchenette. 'I need to update the website today,' he called back. 'Do you want to write another blog piece?'

'Oh, I suppose I could. I enjoyed that encyclopaedia Evelyn left out. You know - the one about Suffolk?'

'I wouldn't have thought you were into non-fiction,' he said, poking his head around the door frame.

'I like the stories. It's full of little anecdotes. I know they're true, but some of them read like fiction.'

'It might be a good idea to blog about it.' Joe moved back into the shop while waiting for the kettle to boil. 'With the festival coming up, we can use the stories to create interest in the town. Evelyn's already posting snippets onto social media, but we haven't done anything on the website yet.'

Lucie grinned at him with enthusiasm. Aware of the slight blush creeping across his cheeks, she withdrew her gaze. 'Yes, I'd like to do that. I'll have a read through and choose a story to include.'

They glanced at each other, for a moment longer than necessary, before he ducked back into the kitchen area to finish making the tea. A small smile escaped her lips.

*

'And this is my pride and joy,' Evelyn exclaimed, pushing open the bookshop door and letting Aimee through in front of her.

'Ooh, *very* quirky. I like it. There's almost something Byronic about the place.'

'What, you mean the lack of consistent lighting, giving the place a moody and atmospheric glow?' Evelyn asked in amusement. 'Or perhaps it's the architecture? It was probably built around his time. How do you know about Byron, anyway?'

'I read,' Aimee answered with a shrug and moved further into the bookshop.

Behind the desk, Joe was packaging up an order to be posted out for a small extra cost. He acknowledged them with a brief 'Hi'. Aimee clocked him for a second, before raising her eyebrow at Evelyn, the insinuation clear.

'No,' Evelyn said, with emphasis. 'Not even close.'

'But he's cute,' Aimee whispered. 'Well, nerdy cute, but still cute.'

'Then you ask him out.' She straightened a book on the display table.

'I have Liam.'

'Oh yes. Perhaps if you mentioned him more, I might remember you have a boyfriend.'

Aimee glared at her, before turning her attention to browse the shelves. Evelyn approached Joe.

'Where's Lucie? On her lunch break already?'

'No, she's in the office. I asked her to blog for the website. We had a thought earlier,' he said, explaining their idea regarding the local encyclopaedia.

'Good plan. Anything that raises the profile is a winner. We need people to seek the bookshop out. Try and link the stories to Taverton's own history. Reel them in, so to speak.'

'Yes, Captain,' he replied, with a quick salute. 'Is that your sister?'

Evelyn nodded and folded her arms. Bringing Aimee to Taverton Tales was an attempt to prove that her life wasn't a total mess post-breakup, especially after the ugly crying incident at the pub yesterday. It was to demonstrate that she had other very important and exciting things in her life. Aimee had a strange tendency to inspire the competitive dormant side of Evelyn's personality.

'It's a little pokey, but I suppose that's what you want for a bookshop?' Aimee commented, sidling up to the desk. 'You want it to have character, right?'

Joe reached out his hand to introduce himself. She shook it with enthusiasm then lost interest in favour of the attractive notebook covers displayed next to the till. Evelyn shrugged at Joe.

'Was there anything in particular that you came in for?' he asked. 'Something you need me to do perhaps?'

'No, I am just showing Aimee around. But while I am here... anything I need to know?'

'Just delays with the online orders again. They were meant to arrive today, but the email said it'll be at least tomorrow now.'

'How are we supposed to compete with online retailers when we have nonsense like this to deal with? I'm trying to make this place a success,' she added, lowering her voice so Aimee wouldn't hear. It wouldn't help to persuade her sister that Evelyn's life wasn't a complete joke, if she knew the real struggles of the business.

'It'll be all right,' he offered. 'Sales and customers are up.'

'Thanks Joe. I really hope so.'

'What do you two have planned for the rest of your day?'

'Oh, not a lot,' Aimee answered, distracted by a purple suede notebook. Flipping it over and pulling a disgusted face at the price sticker, she placed it back in its display case.

'We're going for a coffee soon,' Evelyn interjected. She still wasn't quite sure how her Monday had also been commandeered by Aimee, but it had. Rather than stress about it, she was trying to be philosophical. It wasn't often that her sister was home after all.

'Hi,' Lucie said, giving a small wave as she exited the office. She stood next to Joe at the till.

'Morning Lucie, I heard about the blog piece. I'll read it later, but well done on the initiative. Perhaps you can post more regularly? I'll post the blog links to social media and that'll bring more traffic our way.'

'Okay,' she said, despite appearing unsure.

'You'll need to blog once a week,' Evelyn suggested, gauging Lucie's reticence. 'I will pay you for that extra time. You can do it from home, if you like.'

'I'd like that,' Lucie conceded. 'I just hope I'll have time....'

'You pick the days. Do it at the pace you're comfortable with. I'll pay you per post. We can discuss the details of how much.'

Evelyn just stopped short of crossing her fingers behind her back. She hoped she could afford the extra pay, but reasoned it wouldn't be much and the extra website traffic would balance it out. Witnessing Lucie's reaction, the sense of pride that her writing was good enough and that she was being given an extra responsibility, was worth paying the extra pounds for.

Joe beamed with pride at Lucie and Aimee guffawed beside Evelyn.

'Right,' Evelyn stated, sensing her sister was about to cause a scene of some kind. 'We're going to the tearooms.'

She hooked her arm through Aimee's and gave a perfunctory goodbye to her colleagues. Aimee giggled as they left the shop.

'It seems that neither of us would stand a chance with Joe, even if we were interested.' She sounded pleased with her deduction skills. 'He is besotted with that blonde girl.'

'Her name is Lucie.'

'I think that she quite likes him too.'

This did surprise Evelyn. 'What gives you that idea? Lucie is very quiet. She arrives at the shop, does her job and goes home again.'

'Perhaps she's only like that with you,' Aimee scoffed. 'They have a connection. You can see it when they look at each other. It's pretty obvious,' she added.

Boredom descended over Aimee's features. 'Come on,' she implored, pulling Evelyn's arm. 'You promised me a coffee.'

Chapter Twenty Eight

My throat is parched. I can barely sit up for the pain. Mother brought my notebook and pen at my insistence, although I saw the disapproval beneath her concern. They think I should be resting. I am already stuck in this bed. I won't be going anywhere for a long time. The doctor has made that clear.

They won't tell me much. Just that he is all right. That we are both lucky it wasn't worse. I am stuck here. I can't walk. I would have started college today. Not that we were planning for that anymore, but that isn't even a possibility now – not even as a backup plan.

Caroline visited yesterday but I got tired of her pandering, not to mention the faint accusation behind her glare, as if she imagines this is my fault! Ethan also visited. He brought me a blue silk flower, which was sweet.

Oh, but I want to be free of this hospital bed! I want to see Laurence. Why won't they let me see him? My father said that the police have been investigating. I don't know why. It was just a road accident. Just a silly accident after a silly argument, that is all. How were we to know that the bend was coming? We were so keen to get away. I was so anxious about the consequences that in that moment it didn't seem a good idea at all. My reluctance caused the argument, which in turn caused Laurence to lose focus on the road. Perhaps this is my fault after all?

I have had pains in my legs all day today. The doctor says it is a good sign. It might mean I am getting some sensation back. It might mean... oh, perhaps there might be some hope after all. I am not sure I care much. He has been discharged. He hasn't visited. Why hasn't he visited?

The police were here today. I have managed to walk a little way. My mother cried with relief. I just cried. The police say his family have dropped the charges against the car. I thought it was his, but it belonged to his father. He also stole their money. He had told me that it was given to him as an early inheritance. That wasn't true. But his family won't press charges against him for those things, of which I am grateful.

I can understand the lies. He wanted to get away. He wanted us to be free. I am sure he never meant to hurt anyone in the process. The police say he is to be investigated for reckless driving. I want to defend him, but they shake off my concerns about the argument. They keep bringing it back to the speed. I have always known that Laurence drove too fast, though I don't dare admit it out loud. He is in enough trouble already.

He still hasn't visited. Apparently it is not a good idea, because of the investigation. I am pleased it is not because he has fallen out of love with me. That is my biggest fear. I could not bear for that to ever happen.

Chapter Twenty Nine

The crumpled edges of the paper revealed its age. Ethan contemplated the contents. Beneath him the table was covered, loose pages spread out in neat piles and in chronological order, as far as he'd been able to work out. Without dates to confirm, he'd had to guess the timeline of some of the entries. It helped that he had been around at the time they were written, even just in the background, hovering in silence, ever hopeful.

He'd delayed the task for over a month, but now he studied the pages, resolute and determined. Whatever he and Helen had, it was real to him. Their marriage was a happy one. They had loved each other. But he couldn't stop his thoughts wandering; wondering if he had loved her more than she'd loved him. After all, he was no Laurence Scott.

With reverence he placed the sheet of paper on the table alongside the others. The girls would be home soon and he wanted the journal entries to be packed away, well out of sight, before then. Realising he wouldn't have time to piece it all together in the time he had left, he gathered the pages, taking care to keep them collated, and lay them inside the battered shoe box. Perhaps the largest mystery was why Helen had kept them. Her clutter across the house hinted that she hadn't liked to throw anything away, but this didn't reassure him. He knew too much about her past.

He'd never describe himself as a weak man. He had known the depth of Helen's feelings towards Laurence, but he had wanted to be with her despite that. It was a choice many would have walked away from. But it had always felt like the correct one to him.

Replacing the lid, Ethan returned the shoe box to its position above the kitchen cupboards. He pushed it as far back as he could reach, so the cardboard walls and lid were no longer visible.

Water cascaded from the tap into the empty kettle, and he waited while it boiled, removing a forest-green handmade mug from the cupboard, and placing it on the work surface beneath. Helen had made it during her pottery phase; another hobby that had been and gone.

Popping an Earl Grey teabag inside, he stared at the mug for a while. Its sides were rough and uneven, yet Helen had insisted on keeping it. It was an achievement and Helen always liked to remind everyone of their achievements, including herself. It was what had made her a natural teacher and was perhaps another hint why the journal pages had remained in her possession for so many years.

A brief flicker of a memory danced through his mind: Helen, cradling the same mug, laughing as she relayed something ridiculous one of her pupils had said to the class. He didn't remember the details of the conversation, but could recall the gentle creases around her bright blue eyes, as she was consumed by the humour of the anecdote. Her light pink lips opened in unguarded delight as her delicate laugh emanated around the kitchen.

The ease at which she'd shared her daily life with him, the countless times they had laughed over something amusing that had tickled one or the other, that's what relationships were made from. That's what gave them their roots, their foundations. The little things, that really mattered.

A heavy crackle of tyres upon gravel alerted him to his daughters' arrival. Ethan removed another two mugs from the cupboard. The click of the front door gave way to a cacophony of noise, shattering the contemplative silence. Their voices were raised in argument.

'I'm just saying that you need to get out there more.' Aimee whined, a characteristic when she felt she was losing the fight. 'You've never experienced the world. You married too young....'

'Will you just drop it?' Evelyn sounded weary.

'Not until you admit it... oh, hi Dad,' Aimee said, rounding the kitchen door and spotting her father standing next to the now boiling kettle.

'Good day?' He asked, with a tilt of a grin.

Evelyn's expression deflated. She sat down at the kitchen table. 'Any post?'

'No, no post. Anyone want a cup of tea?'

Aimee screwed her nose up. 'I'll pass. I'm going to go and have a shower.'

'It's half past four,' Evelyn commented in consternation. Her chin rested in her hand, her expression grim.

'Yes, I know,' Aimee replied, a snap in her voice. 'I didn't get a chance earlier.'

'Right,' Ethan said, cutting through the tension. 'Evelyn, do *you* want a cup of tea?' The atmosphere in the room had grown ugly. He didn't know what had happened, but he had no intention to stoke it further.

'No… yes, thanks, I would.'

Aimee glared at Evelyn and stalked out of the kitchen, her heavy footfalls on the stairs echoing through the ceiling. Ethan poured their drinks in silence. He heard Evelyn groan behind him as he crossed over to the fridge and reached inside for the milk.

'It was a bad day then?' He handed Evelyn her mug.

'It started off well.'

'Then she said something offensive?'

Evelyn lifted her eyebrows in response.

'That's my Aimee,' he said, between sips. 'She doesn't mean to be rude.'

'That makes it worse. She thinks she has it all figured out. She knows what each of us are doing wrong and yet try and get anything out of her about her own life….'

Ethan had noticed that. Aimee wasn't being forthcoming about the reason behind her visit, and he wasn't buying her vague explanation about figuring out what she wanted – that had never been her style. But neither was being transparent about what she was going to be doing next, he reasoned. However, even questions about her boyfriend were fended off and guarded with a veil of secrecy. Something more was going on there.

'You seem to be holding your own.'

'She wasn't winning. I'm not going to be pushed around by my little sister.'

'Good for you,' Ethan said, with a laugh. 'Before we know it, she'll be off again and we'll find that we miss those constant remarks about our lifestyle choices.'

'For all we know, she's here for the long term.'

They looked across at each other sharply. Evelyn sank her gaze into her mug, hiding her horrified expression from Ethan's view.

*

'Come through, it'll be fun,' Caren insisted, her voice distant and electronic due to the bad connection. Evelyn was hovering in the back garden, trying to establish a decent mobile phone signal. 'I haven't had a birthday party in years, not since the kids arrived. Adrian's parents have offered to have them for the night, so I intend to make the most of it.'

'I'm also getting caterers in,' Caren added persuasively.

'Yes, that sounds great.' Inside her mind was screaming the obvious question. Would Ishmael be there?

'Evelyn?'

She watched a solitary black bird make its way across the grass in search of food. Momentarily jealous by the ease and simplicity of its life, she remembered that in spring they were often bullied, and even killed, by the jackdaws that circled their nests. Nature was cruel to both animal and human.

The oak tree at the far end of the garden stirred in the summer breeze, the leaves rustling in harmony. She matched a deep breath to the rhythm. She mustn't keep hiding. She knew that. One day she'd have to face the past.

'He won't be there,' Caren's voice penetrated Evelyn's thoughts, guessing the reason for her silence.

'Okay,' she whispered, not trusting herself to try and say anything more.

'No, I want an evening with no drama, or complications. Just lots of food and drink and laughter, no annoying ex-husbands causing issues.'

'In that case I'd better be there.'

'London is poorer without you.'

Evelyn's brief inspection of the garden and through the gaps in the foliage to the fields beyond told her, in an instant, all she needed to know.

'I think I am where I need to be.'

Saying their goodbyes, she disconnected the call. With little else to focus upon, aside from the bookshop's paperwork waiting on the desk in her bedroom, she strode around the side of the house and out through the old wooden gate. It led her down the paved path to the lane. To the right, another one hundred metres or so down, she veered onto the public footpath that would take her through the fields beyond the house.

It was a beautiful day. The sun had already reached its apex and was beginning its gradual descent towards the horizon, but with the promise of light for several more hours. The long June evenings were blissful and she looked forward to relaxing in the garden later, wine glass in hand and lathered in a liberal dash of insect repellent.

But for now she walked. The warm air was like a comforting blanket across her skin. The purr of insects made for a harmonious soundtrack. She thought of her childhood years and the many afternoons spent running across these fields with her friends. Most had left Taverton now. Those that remained she was no longer close to; inevitable perhaps with the years in London in between.

She breathed in the fresh country air and her body relaxed. The last couple of months had been confusing. As she'd put down plans to improve the bookshop, her personal life combusted. Feelings that lay dormant now worked their way to the surface; her marriage, thoughts of Mum, Ishmael, her sister's return.

She stared up at the clear blue sky, noting the whispers of cloud in the far distance, the curvature of the vast open space above. Standing below, a minute figure surrounded by fields, with no one else in sight, Evelyn felt very small. It was a good sensation; a reminder that the world still spun, even when life wasn't going the way she'd hoped and planned.

A stile led to the meadows beyond. Wild flowers punctuated the rolling grassland, and she climbed over the wooden divide and onto the pale green scrub beneath her feet. The house stood behind her in the distance. Her bedroom window and the corner of the roof were just visible through the trees.

Evelyn sat down on the cushiony grass and soaked up the atmosphere. She drew her knees up, placing her chin on top. She watched two butterflies dancing around one another as they rose from a nearby hedge and drifted into the sky above. Leaves rustled to her right, a squirrel emerging from behind one tree trunk and running to another. Birds squawked overhead; perhaps thirty, maybe more, swooping in unison in a figure of eight, before continuing their journey. The sun baked overhead, her skin embracing the warmth.

Here was peace. The air was still with the exception of the sounds of nature. The atmosphere was charged, yet natural. Everything around her belonged, there was nothing out of keeping.

For the first time in ages she felt relaxed. And for the first time, in years, perhaps even decades, she dropped her head, and between cracked words and spent emotion, she prayed. She wasn't even sure who she was praying to, what she believed, if anything. But she was beyond trying to understand her feelings. It was a small act, and she sniffed back the threat of tears once she was done. A spreading sense of comfort enveloped her.

Pulling her thoughts together, she pushed up off the ground, straightened her clothing and let free a long, drawn out exhale. Bereft at having to leave the peaceful surroundings, she headed back towards the house.

Chapter Thirty

July hit the streets of Taverton with a wave of intense heat. The shop, cramped in space and with low ceilings, became an unpleasant environment to work. Evelyn sent Joe off to the old fashioned hardware store up the hill with instructions to purchase several electric fans, but he arrived back with one, the very last of their stock. It did little to dispel the stifling air.

In the midst of this Evelyn prepared for the upcoming festival. Four weeks stood between them and the event and she still needed to consider the applications of local authors who wished to advertise on the bookshop's stall. Joe had created clues for a book related treasure hunt, which would take place along the high street and finish in the shop. And the design for the storytelling flyers had been emailed to the printers, which she hoped would launch in early September.

She'd booked in a promotional slot for an interview at the local radio station and Lucie blogged each week on the website, relaying local anecdotes and tying in promotions to the upcoming event. Unrelated to the festival, they had another book launch party at the end of the week. Joe and Lucie were in charge of the logistics. All this was on top of serving customers, fulfilling the basics of running a business and Evelyn's own plans as she sought to etch out a distinctive brand. The positive signs that the bookshop's outlook was improving gave her a much needed boost of confidence.

She returned to the shop floor from the back room. With arms piled high with paperwork and files she used her elbow to flick on the kettle on her way through. Spotting Joe and Lucie, heads bowed towards each other as they jotted down notes for the launch party, she wondered if Aimee was right. They did seem to be in sync with one another. Even their movements were mirrored. Neither seemed to notice, however, and Evelyn wasn't sure what she'd feel should they start to date. If it went south, she might lose both members of staff.

'How about moving the chairs in the opposite direction this time?' suggested Lucie. 'During the reading the author can be framed by the window instead of just standing in front of the till. I have some fairy lights I can bring in. We'll drape those around the window. It'll be really pretty when it starts to get dark.'

'I like that idea,' Evelyn confirmed, as she passed.

Joe smiled at Lucie in encouragement and Evelyn noticed the ever so slightest blush reach the younger woman's cheeks. Yes, Aimee was right.

The empty shop awoke as if from a slumber with the splintering peal of the bell above the door. All three were greeted with the hunched figure of Betty Longhorn shuffling towards the desk. Joe's face paled, Lucie didn't seem fazed at all, and Evelyn adopted her usual professional stance.

'Morning, Mrs Longhorn...'

'This heat is abominable,' Betty chipped in, fixing her beady dark eyes upon them. 'But I supposed you young'uns don't feel it like I do.'

A flushed and dishevelled Joe contradicted her claim.

'What can we do for you?' Evelyn asked.

'I need a word with this Joe here,' the old woman replied, shifting her blouse, the fabric irritating her skin in the heat. 'It's the festival. See there's too many furreners in the committee, don't know the area so well do they? We need to stick together, boy.'

Lucie's eyes widened. Guessing the cause for the reaction, Evelyn leant in and whispered.

'She means people who aren't from Suffolk. It's old fashioned slang.'

It didn't sound quite as reassuring as she'd hoped.

'But, Mrs Longhorn, they do have experience planning festivals,' Joe explained, the crack in his voice betraying his anxiety at questioning her viewpoint. 'Felix Watson worked on a committee in London, which organised huge events. And, Robert Lancaster has lived here over ten years now, so he's pretty much a local now.'

Betty glared at him. 'In his second home,' she said incredulously.

Joe opened his mouth, shut it again, and shrugged helplessly at Evelyn and Lucie. 'What did you have in mind Mrs Longhorn?'

'When I make a suggestion, I need you to back me up. We need a united front.'

Joe stared at her. 'I… but I like their ideas. They're good.'

He fell into silence, the effort of standing his ground displayed across his features. Evelyn squeezed his arm in reassurance.

Betty considered him for a long moment and expelled a deep disappointed sigh. Moving away from the desk with a shake of the head, an act which seemed to use her entire stooped body, she turned her back to him.

'I read that Pride and Prejudice,' she murmured, as she shuffled towards the door.

'And did you enjoy it?' Evelyn asked, crossing the shop floor to open the door for the elderly woman.

Betty lifted her head, her watery eyes reaching the curious gaze of Evelyn's own bright blue irises. 'That Mr Darcy,' she huffed, shifting her attention towards Joe. 'They still made men like that in my day. Not so much anymore.'

With that she slowly placed one foot in front of the other, exiting the bookshop confines. Evelyn shut the door behind her and faced the shop floor, witnessing the beet-red cheeks of her colleague as he contemplated the potential consequences of standing up to Betty Longhorn.

'Well done, Joe,' she said with a laugh.

*

He stole a glimpse in Lucie's direction, flinching as he did so. He needed to stop. This crush was getting unbearable. He felt powerless by his increasing feelings. She was so poised. Quiet, but secure. He was an embarrassed, bloated mess in her presence. Add the altercation with Betty Longhorn into the equation and he wasn't having the most confident of days.

Lucie bustled past, her arms filled of books, blowing away a stray hair as it tickled her face. Her eyes met his and she plonked the books down at the desk.

'You mustn't let her get to you.'

It took him a second to connect her words with the subject of conversation.

'Betty's just a bit gruff,' he said.

'I think the school boy in you is still scared witless by her.'

'Hey!' He fell silent at the realisation that she was right.

149

They grinned at the absurdity of it all. Lucie broke the eye contact first, scooping up the books and heading over to the shelves. The moment passed. Joe ducked his head to focus on the folder sprawled open on the desk; in it the long anticipated police checks that allowed them to launch the children's storytelling hour, and the various lists of ideas on how they were to promote and run the events. He had been rehearsing reading books in front of the mirror.

Perusing the notes allowed him to gloss over the moment he and Lucie had just shared. He was fatigued with the endless train of thought, the constant urge to analyse her every word, and the fretting that followed him around like a heavy cloak.

'Will Evelyn be back in tomorrow?' Her question punctuated his contemplation.

'Yeah, she's only taken this afternoon off.'

Evelyn was heading into London for some friend's birthday party. Joe hadn't paid attention to the details.

'I thought she might be heading out with her sister,' Lucie mused. 'They have a strange relationship, don't you think?'

'I… haven't really thought about it. No different, I guess, to me and my brother. We were always squabbling. We get on okay now, but I wouldn't say we were close.'

'Evelyn just seems a bit on edge when her sister is around.'

'It happens. Do you have siblings?'

'No, it's just me and my mum.' Lucie paused, catching Joe's attention. She shut her mouth in haste, as if preventing herself for saying anything further.

Joe studied her with curiosity.

*

Plates clattered in the background as caterers passed around trendy hors d'oeuvres and platters serving flutes of champagne. Evelyn absentmindedly took a flute, shaking her head as the waitress offered her a mini-roast dinner in a bite-size Yorkshire pudding. The living room was already crowded. So much for the 'just a few friends' Caren had promised.

Attractive charcoal grey walls contrasted against the white washed bookshelves, the bronze light fittings, and enormous bay windows at the front, open French doors at the back. It was a large space, two separate rooms knocked into one, and it was expensively decorated. She hadn't been to their house in a while and she noticed small changes, such as the new calico sofa suite and art work she didn't recognise. Music trilled in the background, emanating from the vast impressive sound system which took up half an ash wall unit. The song was unidentifiable above the chatter, but the melody was pleasant and calmed her.

Caren was in the far corner of the room, laughing and throwing her hand over her companion in mirth, dressed to the nines in a deep forest-green dress which hugged every curve of her body. No expense had been spared. Not the food, drink, nor Caren's body had avoided the cheque book, or the extravagance, for what was the simple occasion of a birthday party. She'd explained upon Evelyn's arrival that she planned to ignore her fortieth in two years, so her last two birthdays of her thirties would be celebrated in style.

Evelyn scanned the room, wondering how much money the private caterers, décor and stylish lighting had set them back. She didn't even remember the last time she'd been able to shout her father a takeaway, without him slipping a ten pound note into her palm to contribute towards his share.

She couldn't blame Caren and Adrian though. They worked hard, had two children, and rarely had the chance to stop. When had they last had the chance to watch the horizon fizz in the twilight sky as the sun dipped? When had they the chance to visit Evelyn in Suffolk; to take in the jaw dropping awe of endless, stupendous skies and mirror like rivers and former mill ponds and gorgeous coastline that the area was famous for? Why not then, use their money to entertain and to become the social hub in their friendship circle? It was the preference of one lifestyle against another, neither proving better except to the personality it suited most. Eight years in London had taught Evelyn that.

Sipping champagne she caught Adrian's eye and they shared a knowing smile. He adored witnessing his wife being the centre of attention. Evelyn moved through the room, navigating between the other guests, and joined him. He clinked his glass against hers in greeting.

'It's good to see you. You look well.'

'It's wonderful to be here,' she said, taking another sip and surveying the room. 'I'm not sure I recognise everyone.'

'Well, Farrah and Daniel couldn't make it.' Adrian counted on his fingers as he scrolled through the list. 'And I'm sure you've heard that Libby moved to New York for her job. David and Hannah… well we've not been in touch for a while. In fact we've not seen or heard a thing from them since Christmas. Have you?'

'No, I lost touch with a few people,' she said, clearing her throat.

They watched the buzzing crowd for a couple of minutes, relishing the comfort of a fellow introvert, happy to observe the goings on without too much pressure to participate. Evelyn examined Adrian in her peripheral vision, noting that he hadn't got away unscathed by Caren's indulgent display. His aubergine collared shirt had been pressed. He wore brand new tan leather shoes that she was convinced had just been removed from the box. Expensive smelling cologne wafted from his direction. Not too much, just enough to be subtle. Even his dark short hair appeared coiffed, though there was little to work with. It was a far cry from the sportswear he wore at weekends, whether training for another half marathon or playing squash at the gym.

Evelyn herself had spent an entire hour trying to get her wayward curls into something deliberate and purposeful and perhaps even neat. Running out of time before needing to catch the train, she'd grabbed an older, but barely worn sapphire wrap-around dress. Teaming it with a couple of long silver necklaces and delicate small hoop earrings, she made up for the lack of bling by applying some bright red lipstick. Against her dark features, the ribbon of colour lifted the ensemble. Satisfied, she'd grabbed her go-to black heels and blue sequinned clutch off the bed, and a heavy black cardigan that she'd wear if the air grew cold on the way home.

On the train journey over, Evelyn decided that she needed to address the elephant in the room. Ishmael. And what he was doing in Suffolk all those weeks ago. She'd been watching both her inbox and post box for evidence that he wanted a divorce. She saw no other reason why he may have visited, if indeed it had been him at all.

But she knew that hair, those greying flecks and the pattern they chose, the shape of his face, that salmon pink shirt that he'd had for years. Even from a distance, the stance, the slope of his gait was unmistakable. It must have been him.

But why the visit, and why the subsequent silence? If he wanted to finalise the divorce, after all the two year mark was fast approaching, then why not even an email or two in preparation? Was she expected to sit, wringing her hands, waiting for months for the heavy drop of unannounced divorce papers onto the hall floor? Despite selling the flat and splitting the funds, were there still things to discuss? Or would it be complete radio silence, perhaps even announcing an engagement to his new girlfriend, to all their friends, before having the decency to let her know too?

For all Ishmael was, he wasn't spiteful and he wasn't cruel. From the gasping pain in his eyes during their last fight, and even weeks later as they discussed the sale of the flat that he'd always resented, there was no malice; instead an air of sentimentality and regret.

But perhaps their time apart had changed his perspective. Would he blame her, just as he blamed his parents? Or would he understand the part he had played?

Arriving at Caren and Adrian's attractive town house, she'd been ushered in by a talkative and animated Caren, the living room door opening onto the elaborate scene, and Evelyn had yet to find a moment to ask questions.

Realising now that Adrian would be the best bet, she faced him in his silent contemplation. Taking a large gulp of champagne to bolster her courage she was shocked to find the near empty flute being refilled by a waiter, hovering beside her with an open magnum.

Adrian noticed, raising his eyebrows in amusement. 'It's a good thing that Caren doesn't want a fortieth party. There'll be no budget left, if she organises another one of these next year.'

Evelyn chuckled. 'Adrian.'

'Hmm,' he replied, nodding over at a guest who'd called out 'all right Ade?' on his way past.

'I...' the words stuck in her throat. She was almost too scared of what the answer may be to even ask in the first place. 'Do you... do you happen to know if... if Ishmael took any time off work in May?'

The puzzlement on his face alerted her to just how stupid the question sounded. It was so random. 'Sorry, I know it sounds strange. I just wondered if you knew.'

'I don't believe we even saw each other in May. I've been working on a different project. Hang on.' Adrian mentally calculated. 'We went to a friend's fortieth and he was there. Late April, maybe early May. And he and I went out for a curry in June, but....' He paused as if trying to piece together her reasoning. 'I don't get what's so important about May?'

She closed her eyes. She was going to have to be frank.

'Do you know if he came through to Suffolk in May?' She prepared to adorn the question with further detail, but stopped sharply at the admission on his face. He knew. She stared at him as his expression registered shock, mingled with a dash of guilt. Adrian pointed in the direction of the hallway.

'Shall we chat?' he asked with all appearances of nonchalance threatened by the reddening tips of his ears.

Evelyn nodded, following him through the crowd. Her head pounded with the combination of people's chatter, the music punctuating through the house, and the sheer fear and adrenaline of what Adrian might be about to divulge. She was glad she'd avoided the hors d'oeuvres, having bought a sneaky Pret-A-Manger sandwich at the tube station earlier. She wasn't sure her rolling stomach could handle her sudden surge of emotions.

Out in the hallway, he signalled to the right and they walked down the darkened hallway to what Evelyn knew opened up into the utility room. He flicked the light on before ushering her in.

He left the door ajar. The optics wouldn't be good if they were found in a closed room together. His concern for the little things briefly amused her, before the crashing dread of what he might have to say brought her back to the present.

'Well, it's… you see…' he began, stuttering his words and running a nervous hand across his brow. 'I didn't know… not at the time. I just….

'Perhaps breathe,' she instructed. He caught her eye, stopped, and gave a short laugh.

'It's no big secret. I just hadn't realised you knew.'

'I saw him.'

'Oh… that would do it.'

Despite her nerves, she smiled.

'Why was he there, Adrian?'

'That's not my place to say.'

Evelyn closed her eyes and took a controlled breath. Was everything going to be smoke and mirrors? Would she ever get a straight answer from anyone?

'But you knew he was coming?'

'No, I knew *afterwards*. He told me when we went out for the curry.'

'Does Caren know?'

'Oh, God no, of course she doesn't!'

The creak of the door had them both spinning on their heels. Caren stood in the doorway, her half empty flute of champagne tipping precariously as she craned her neck to peer in. 'I told you no surprises Adrian. That's why I planned it all myself,' she entered, tripping on the lino. She looked a little tipsy. 'I don't like surprises.'

Registering Evelyn's presence, Caren cocked her head to one side. 'What is going on?'

'Really, it's nothing,' Evelyn stuttered. 'I know it looks bad.'

Caren laughed. 'What… did you think… oh, believe me, darling, you two are the least likely people to be getting up to adulterous mischief! No, I meant concocting some birthday surprise, despite strict instructions not to.'

'There's no surprise honey,' Adrian said, in a soothing tone.

'I heard you say,' Caren pointed a finger against her husband's chest and leant into him. 'Hmm, you smell nice. Anyway, you said that of course I don't know. Don't know what?'

Keen to get some solid answers, Evelyn backed her friend up. 'You can tell her Adrian. We want to hear it.'

He gave a defeated grimace. 'Evelyn was asking me about Ishmael. She thought she saw him in Suffolk….' He tailed off. 'She wanted to know if I knew.'

Caren studied her husband for a moment. 'Let me guess. You did know.'

'Afterwards, I promise.'

'Why didn't you tell me?' Caren's voice was shrill and indignant.

'Well, quite possibly because of your reaction and the fact that you would have shared the information with Evelyn. I was told in confidence.'

Evelyn and Caren swapped glances. 'Ha, you've broken that confidence now,' Caren pointed out, with a hint of triumph. 'So, why did he come to Suffolk? What did he say? And what happened when *you* saw him? She added, addressing Evelyn.

'We didn't speak,' Evelyn replied, her arms folded, her nervous energy spent. 'I just glimpsed him in the distance. I didn't even know if it was him at first. But, something niggled that it was.'

'Adrian?' Caren swivelled back to her husband.

He shook his head. 'I'm sorry, I can't break his confidence. He had his reasons.'

Evelyn's stomach lurched as a pang of anxiety shot through her. What was going on? 'What *can* you tell me?' she forced, her voice breaking.

Caren's expression crumpled, and faced her husband, flushed and angry. 'Adrian! You men can't play these games! It's not fair.'

'No-one's playing games.'

'Then answer her questions!'

'Listen, I don't want to spoil your birthday,' Evelyn said, a sudden urge to leave the room enveloping her.

'He needs to answer. If Adrian won't, then we'll phone Ishmael.'

'No!' Evelyn's response was deep and guttural and they all froze in the seconds that followed.

'You'll have to speak to him at some point,' Caren said, her voice softening. 'You know that, don't you?'

'Not now. Not like this,' Evelyn said, shaking her head. 'Let's just go and enjoy your birthday. Please.' She pleaded.

Adrian cleared his throat. 'Yes, that's a good idea. We have the cake to light.'

Caren was far from impressed. 'That's a convenient excuse.'

'You paid for it. And designed it, I might add. It would be ridiculous to get all tangled up in this and forget the reason why we're here tonight.'

His placating tone worked. Caren held Evelyn's hand and nodded, leading her back toward the living room. Adrian shared one last look with Evelyn, before they re-entered the room. It was the look of sheer dejected sympathy.

Chapter Thirty One

'Who's up for the beach today?' Aimee mumbled through a mouthful of cornflakes. 'I miss the beach.' The spoon rang against the side of the porcelain bowl. She raised her gaze. 'Well?'

Ethan had noticed Evelyn's red-rimmed eyes and the heavy bruises beneath evident of broken sleep. Did Aimee not see the signs? Evelyn was in no state for a jovial day out, even if he did believe it would be good for her. For two days she'd avoided engaging them, her line of vision stooped to the carpet beneath her feet when she did venture from her room. He had no doubt her behaviour stemmed from the last visit to London. She'd arrived home, quiet and contemplative, worked in the bookshop for a few days, then barricaded herself in her bedroom for the last two.

He was surprised to see her enter the kitchen this morning and make a cup of tea in silence. He hoped this meant she was thawing from whatever had left her in shock.

Aimee looked between them. 'Just me then? Dad, can I borrow the car?'

'My insurance isn't inexhaustible. It'll cover you another few days and that's all.'

'You could extend it,' she said, smiling sweetly.

'Sure. I'll get a quote for another month and forward you my bank details.'

The grin left her face. 'I'd better use the car while I can then.'

'Want to talk about it?' Ethan offered, after Aimee had sauntered out of the room. He already knew the answer.

'Nope,' Evelyn replied, following her sister's footsteps from the kitchen.

*

The wall blurred alarmingly, snapping her back into the present. Not even realising that she'd been staring at the grubby white surface, she fought to refocus her attention to the staff schedule lying half completed on the desk. Over the summer their shifts changed, seesawing between covering each other's leave and having all hands on deck over the festival period. Planning who worked when descended into a complicated maths puzzle. It had been amplified greatly by the sleep deprivation. She was exhausted. She hadn't slept more than four hours a night since the party.

Every evening without fail, with her head nestled against the pillow and the bedside lamp switched off, the all-consuming thoughts would arrive. Unanswered questions circled, painful memories of the conversation under the stark light of the utility room all stirred her from sleep and into an enforced wakefulness.

She'd spent two days of solitude in her bedroom, snatching pockets of slumber, none of it enough to quell the exhaustion flooding her limbs.

Being at work was painful, her muscles heavy and lethargic, her brain fuzzy. She hid in the back office, while Joe served the customers out front. An empty can of cola sat on the right of the desk. She knew she should have bought two cans. She needed the energy.

Tempted to close her eyes and let the gentle melody of Joe's friendly chatter and the electronic chattering of the receipts printing draw her into a siesta, she instead forced herself out of the chair and grabbed her purse from the desk.

'Joe? I need to pop out for five minutes.' She passed him on her way through the shop. 'I'm going to grab an espresso. Do you want anything?'

'No, I'm good.'

She pulled open the door, relishing the wash of fresh air as it awakened her. Striding up to the church she scrolled through her phone messages from the last few days, reminding herself of their contents. The bench in the small park caught her attention and she sat down to read.

'I can't believe he kept that secret. I'm fuming!'

'What is Ishmael playing at? Why the hell was he in Suffolk?'

'I wish I'd said something to him now, when he turned up with that woman!'
All from Caren, with Evelyn's own confused replies in between, the two women had built a wall of solidarity with each other. The men in their lives had secrets, and all they had in defence was the ability to dissect the minuscule information offered. But it was all speculation.
'Perhaps Ishmael wanted to talk and lost his nerve?'
'It's almost two years... we can divorce soon... maybe...'
'But he's never even mentioned it!'
'He might be serious about her....'
'If that's the case, I'll go round there now and give him a piece of my mind.'
'He's allowed to date, Caren....'
Even though the conversation had gone around in circles, Evelyn was grateful for the regular contact. The last five days had been some of the loneliest of her life. Sleepless nights, watching the shadows play around the dimensions of her bedroom, led to grey fatigued days. Avoiding eye contact with her dad and sister layered the burden of guilt. And she was far from happy to be barely cognisant at work. Physically she might be present, but emotionally she couldn't focus. A lull hung heavy in her thoughts, giving the impression that she was walking through a dream, gazing down on them all but not included in any conversation. She needed sleep. She needed peace. A new life would be handy too, she thought cynically.

She wrestled to bend her thoughts on what she was able to control. The festival was three weeks away. It had to be successful. The aim was to drive enough traffic towards the shop that they wouldn't be forgotten again in the colder, quieter months.

The summer holidays were close. Lucie had booked a week's leave early on. Both Joe and Evelyn were saving their leave for after the festival. With Joe on the festival committee, they had the leeway to do as much as they wanted during the three day event; the book treasure hunt, the local author stand with Q&A sessions, special offers and prizes, a local history corner to attract both tourists and locals. Ethan had offered to lend them his office's barista machine and he and Gordon were going to bring along a sofa to create a snug coffee and reading area. A soft launch of the children's reading hour would get the word out, and Evelyn hoped they could secure a regular audience for September when it would become a weekly occurrence.

She needed to stay focused on what was important right now. Yet again, she was reminded of her good fortune of having Joe on board. His advice had saved her from slipping up on many occasions. She'd give him a pay rise as soon as the bookshop sales increased enough. He could launch his own bookshop one day. He couldn't work in her bookshop forever. There were few opportunities for promotion. Unless he took over the business from her one day, she thought.

She fiddled with the zip of her purse, extracting a few pound coins, and made her way back down into town. She required a double espresso if she had any chance of finishing the rest of her shift.

*

'I want something gripping. But not depressing. I don't mind gory, just not 'they killed a dog' gory. And a strong female lead would be great,' Aimee added, leaning on the counter and fiddling with the bookmarks.

Joe thought for a second or two, heading over to where the thriller novels were located. He withdrew four titles and passed them across to Aimee for perusal.

'That was quick,' she said, flipping each book over and studying their blurbs. Her large pink shoulder bag bashed against her hip. She lifted it onto the counter with a thud. A lurid green and purple striped towel rolled out towards Joe.

The bell above the door rang. 'What are you doing here?' Evelyn asked, from behind them.

'I wanted to buy a book. Thought the bookshop was a good a place to start,' Aimee replied, sarcasm dripping from her words.

The two sisters observed each other for a moment. Evelyn crossed the shop floor, coffee cup in hand, disappearing into the back room.

Joe raised an eyebrow. Aimee shrugged, returning her attention to the novels. Silence fell over the shop.

'I thought you were going to the beach?' Evelyn had reappeared, leaning against the back room door frame.

Joe noticed her hollow eyes and pale skin. Her body language was tense and harassed. The females in his life all seemed to have a cross to bear. He wasn't sure he was ready to ask why.

Aimee's eyes narrowed at the question. 'I wanted a book to read for the beach. I thought I ought to support my sister's business in the process.'

Evelyn nodded. 'Thanks.' She disappeared into the back room again.

*

160

She flung the empty takeaway coffee cup in the small bin behind the desk and concentrated on trying to log what needed doing. But her mind just wasn't in it. Either the espresso had yet to hit the spot, or today was going to be a complete lost cause.

'I'll take this one,' she heard Aimee say through the open door. The beep of the till and the mechanical printing of the receipt punctuated Evelyn's tired thoughts. She groaned in defeat at the messy desk. There was no way she could concentrate.

'Will you be home in time for dinner?' she asked, poking her head through the door frame, her voice sounding heavy even to her own ears. It was her turn to cook tonight. She had no idea how she'd find the energy, even if she had only planned omelettes and salad.

'Oh don't worry about me. I'll pick up some fish and chips.'

'You seem flush. I thought after your reaction to Dad's suggestion about the car insurance that you were running out of money.'

'I have a little in my savings.'

'Wouldn't it be best to keep it? You don't have a job lined up yet.'

Aimee wrinkled her nose in disgust. 'You're not Dad,' she said, with a barely controlled hiss. 'Don't even try to give me advice.' Grabbing the towel and shoving it into the cumbersome bag, she marched from the shop, her face darkened in anger.

Joe averted his gaze. Evelyn appreciated the gesture. She didn't know where to begin explaining the strained relationship she shared with her sister.

'Joe,' she said, as a wave of exhaustion, mingled with sadness, washed through her. 'I know this is a massive favour to ask, but do you mind finishing up here by yourself? It's only three hours until closing.'

He considered her for the briefest of moments. 'Take all the time you need.'

*

The house was cool and, thankfully, empty. Evelyn slid her sandals off her feet, massaging the aching arches, and climbed the stairs. At this time of the afternoon the house was cast in shadow, the sun hidden behind the tall mature trees that lined the back of the property. Considering how fatigued she already felt, the natural gloom boded well for an afternoon nap.

At the top of the stairs, she placed her phone on the small half-moon table under the single paned window. Its only other companion was a vase, one of her mother's favourites, which Evelyn filled with wild flowers from the garden or the lane.

She wanted no distractions. Just for the silence to envelop her and pull her into an uninterrupted slumber, for all the thoughts and responsibilities to melt away for a few hours into a happy void of nothingness. She didn't want to dwell on the issues with Aimee. As if there hadn't already been enough swirling around her mind. Aimee's secrecy and unanswered questions, her flippancy surrounding money and the topic of Liam - all threatened to pull Evelyn in. Right now, she couldn't afford to get involved. She needed to sort her own mess out first.

She threw herself onto the bed, not even having the energy to draw the curtains first, closing her heavy eyelids against the woken and alert world around her. She welcomed nothing but nothingness. She needed sleep.

Chapter Thirty Two

Ethan and Caroline visit me every week. Each time he comes, Ethan brings a silk flower. Their visits are a nice relief from my daily recovery. Walking to the bathroom wears me out. But the doctor says that I am making progress and that there is hope that my injuries will not be permanent. But my life has already changed. I cannot see Laurence. He has been charged with reckless driving. That is why he cannot come to the hospital, because of the court case. At least I know it is not because he doesn't love me anymore. He is simply not allowed.

His name is like a dirty word around here. My friends and family spit his name as if he is the devil himself. They don't know him like I do and it breaks my heart. They will never accept Laurence now. How I wish sometimes, that our attempt to escape that night had been successful. There is now no chance for my parents' blessing. I do not even know if and when I can see him. I do not know if anyone will ever let us be together after this.

My legs are getting stronger. I can walk the entire length of the wards and back without getting tired. There is talk that I may be able to go home soon. But I don't know what I am going home to. My college course started over two months ago. It is not even an option anymore. Mum and Dad say that I can try again next year. But I have little to plan for now.

Ethan said I will be home for Christmas. I do love Christmas. He visited me again yesterday, bringing a couple of books for me to read. I am pleased. I have been bored for days. The novels my mother brought along last week were devoured in hours. There is little else to do here. Writing poetry is depressing now all my thoughts are on the upcoming court case and the news that Laurence's family are moving out of town to avoid the scandal. I cannot conjure up words that aren't already laced by sadness, so I do not bother.

I worry that he will move with his family once this is all over. Will we ever be reconciled? Not hearing from him is worse than the pain, the recovery and boredom. I do not know how he feels about me. Doubts creep into my mind and I hate myself for it. We had a future planned together, and now I betray him with thoughts that he will forget me, that he will tire of waiting.

And the thought that he might go to prison – well, it is too horrid to contemplate. Our lives are in tatters.

Chapter Thirty Three

2015

Reaching across Ishmael, Evelyn felt his entire body tense. She knew he hated it when she did that, a habit that developed in the small confines of their London flat, never having adequate space when more than one was in any room at the same time. Her fingers tightened over the spine of the book and she withdrew herself from his vicinity.

He gave an apologetic grimace, his focus remaining on the laptop in front of him. As he was working on a presentation for a big client, Evelyn tried to be sensitive for his need for silence. She just hated feeling as if she was walking on egg shells while she gave him space to concentrate. Once the presentation was complete, he'd return to the Ishmael she knew and loved.

It was unfair to place the blame all at his feet. His job demanded a lot. It was a stressful high level environment and Evelyn understood his irritation at any unnecessary noise or distraction. Besides, she reminded herself, she'd caused an argument a few days ago because she'd been left to do all the housework. Even now, the shrillness of her reaction made her cringe. It was so over the top, so unreasonable. His expression of shock, his jaw tightening to suppress irritation, stuck with her. They were both taking their frustrations out on one another.

She wanted some normality again. Come summer they would visit family, spend their leave in the countryside, relax on the beach. They'd fly off for a few days to a nice resort in the Mediterranean. All the stress of reaching deadlines and finishing projects would melt away, as they sipped refreshing drinks around a sparkling pool, searched for idyllic bays and soaked up the local historical attractions. She longed for that break from busy life. She longed for when they'd reconnect as a couple.

She left the room, heading for the bedroom and removing her phone from her pocket. She dialled the number that was so familiar she still entered it manually. It rang for a long while, but she'd learned to be patient.

'Hello?' The voice was little more than a whisper these days.

'Hi Mum. How did the chemo go?'

*

The room fell into darkness, save for the lurid flashes of the television screen. The hour was late. Evelyn had no idea what the film was about. She'd zoned out about twenty minutes ago, checking her phone regularly instead.

Ishmael's presentation would have been over and done with hours ago, the team enjoying their usual trip down the pub afterwards. He'd be home soon enough. Being teetotal, he was often one of the first to leave. She yawned, stretching her limbs across the length of the sofa. If she wasn't careful she'd fall asleep and miss congratulating him. That's if the presentation had gone well, of course.

The metallic scrape of the key connecting with the lock roused her. The gentle thud of shoes fell to the carpet below. A plastic scrunching combined with the smooth slide of material being shrugged off his shoulders preceded a brief silence, and then Ishmael emerged from the hallway.

'It went well,' he said, a tired, lopsided expression on his face, his work suit crumpled. A bunch of red roses hung heavily in his right hand, the cellophane crinkling as he handed them over. 'They're a peace offering. I know I have been a pain to live with the last few weeks.'

Roses were her favourite. It was always the little details with Ishmael. It always had been.

'Thank you. They're beautiful. I'm so pleased the presentation went well.'

She took her spare hand in his and drew into his embrace. His lips met hers and they stayed like that for one heady minute. He pulled back, stooping to nestle his head in the crook of her neck, his breathing deep, tired.

'You're exhausted.' Her chin rested on top of his dark hair. 'Can I make you a cup of tea first or straight to bed?'

'Sleep,' he replied, muffled.

'Go. I'll sort the flowers out.'

He groaned with spent energy. Lifting his head, he cupped her chin in his hand, staring into her blue eyes with an expression of longing.

'I love you Evelyn. I know I don't deserve you.'

'Don't talk like that! Of course you do. We both do... deserve each other, I mean.'

He smiled, his eyelids drooping with the effort. 'You're the best choice I ever made.'

He left her in the living room, crashing onto the bed without undressing. She took the roses to the kitchen, preparing them and displaying them in a clean vase on the kitchen table. She peered in to the bedroom. Ishmael still wore his white shirt and boxers, his mouth open and already snoring. She watched him in silence.

*

'Here's to the Benson project!' Adrian shouted in triumph, lifting his drink in salute. Caren, Evelyn and Ishmael raised their own glasses amongst the group of friends and colleagues. A loud cheering resounded across the room.

Evelyn grinned at Ishmael. His team had secured the project with the promise of a large profit share. Ishmael was now the company golden boy and he took the news with a typical stoicism. But Evelyn knew the tell-tale signs. It was in the flustered expression in his eyes at being the centre of attention, which dissipated as people approached to congratulate him. It was in the slight dip of his shoulders, reminiscent of that first date back in the pub when they were students. She'd assumed it a sign of nonchalance, of not caring what others thought. Now she knew him better, she realised it was a way of hiding his insecurities behind an emotional fence. The tension in his shoulders gave it away.

She squeezed him arm in encouragement, whispering 'I love you,' into his ear. He faced her as she passed, their eyes locking for a brief moment.

'Adrian's like a peacock, loving all the praise!' Caren guffawed in Evelyn's ear, breaking her concentration. Ishmael nodded his assent, giving her one last glance before melting into the congratulatory crowd.

The pang of his sudden absence was interrupted with Caren's high pitched cackle.

'He'll be riding on this one for weeks,' she laughed. 'Are you prepared for the late nights and deadlines?'

'No, not at all,' Evelyn replied, her heart sinking at the thought. Even her dreams of balmy summer holidays couldn't dislodge the reality of what was coming. Each new project widened the wedge between them a little more. His recent affection would succumb to the demands of work.

'Come over for dinner next Friday night,' she offered. 'You can bring Matilda if you like,' she added, referencing Adrian and Caren's toddler. 'We'll have something simple, like pasta. Something she'll enjoy.'

'Half of it will end up on your wall.'

'I don't mind.'

'I bet Ishmael will.' They both knew he liked a tidy, clean flat.

'He loves children,' Evelyn stated in his defence. It was true, he did. They'd talked of when to start a family. He was perhaps keener than she, now his job was well established. Her career still left a lot to be desired. Working in an archive office was fine, but it didn't set her world alight. Spending her spare hours browsing second hand and independent bookshops had become her secret hobby. It didn't fit the clean sharp lines of their modernistic lifestyle. It was her little indulgence, a place where she felt herself. She'd love to own a bookshop one day.

'That would be great,' Caren enthused. 'You have no idea how the invitations have dried up since Matilda was born. We're not in vogue anymore,' she surveyed her husband, as he gave a boozy cheer from the corner, surrounded by work colleagues. 'Were we ever?' she laughed.

'You always will be to me,' Evelyn slipped her arm around Caren's waist, drawing her in for a side hug. 'I miss having you round.'

'We need to make it a regular thing. I'll be around more after...' Caren paused, her drink hovering at her mouth.

'Oh, do you have a new job lined up?' Evelyn knew Caren hated having to go back to work full time after her maternity leave. Caren had admitted searching for part time jobs online, in the evenings.

'Not exactly...' She downed the rest of the pale liquid and studied the empty flute for a second. 'We weren't going to say anything just yet. But seeing as you're my best friend, and we're already celebrating... we're going to have another baby.'

Evelyn's eyes widened. 'Caren, that's brilliant! Isn't it? Or is it a bit soon?' Matilda was twelve months old and Caren had only been back at work for six.

'Well, it's a little sooner than planned. But we wanted a two year gap between them anyway.'

Evelyn eyed the empty champagne flute in her friend's hand, not knowing whether to draw attention to it. She'd seen her consume the one glass, but surely Caren knew it wasn't a good idea? Caren followed Evelyn's gaze and grinned.

'Sparkling grape juice,' she whispered. 'It throws everyone off the scent. Although the stuff is revoltingly disappointing,' she added with a grimace.

Evelyn hugged her again. 'I'm so happy for you both.'

She was. She truly was. She swallowed down the instantaneous sinking in her gut, and the crashing wave of concern that her own journey into parenthood may not be so simple. There was still plenty of time. She and Ishmael needed to overcome a few hurdles first, like any couple. That's all.

*

The crispness of the dawn air drew Evelyn closer to Ishmael's warmth. Not wanting to open her eyes, the heaviness of sleep still enveloping her body, she nestled into his arms, falling asleep again within seconds.

The next thing she heard was the piercing screech of the alarm. It sent her nerves into alert mode, her body still fighting against it, but failing. Ishmael stirred beside her. Eyes still focusing in the semi-darkness she turned over to face him. He was already sitting up, his body angled from hers, as he swung his legs over the side of the bed and prised himself up.

'Morning,' she managed, her voice husky with sleep.

'I need to get into the office.'

And so it began, she thought. The celebration had finished not even twelve hours ago. The excitement and intimacy and comfort of her husband's attention when they returned to the flat, and now it was all back to business. Cold, perfunctory and factual; Ishmael was already focusing on the job ahead and he would do what was necessary to complete it. It was who he was. It didn't make him a bad person. He was just, yet again, trying to prove himself. To who, she often wondered.

She considered speaking up. With her silence, how could he be expected to know how she felt? He wasn't unreasonable. He wasn't abusive. But he could be neglectful, without being aware. Their marriage was equal. He would want to hear her concerns and thoughts too.

Instead she watched him walk across the room and enter the bathroom. She allowed her fear for their future to be drowned out by the cascade of the shower. It was easier to listen to the melody of water resounding against the glass, the harmony as it trickled toward the shower base and into the drain below. It was easier to focus on that, than to address the issues that weighed their marriage down. It was easier to carry on pretending that all was fine.

But they were neither stupid nor naïve. They would pay for the brushing under the carpet; she knew they would. It would catch up with them. The problem was she no longer identified when it had started feeling wrong. Perhaps if she'd, they'd, paid more attention they'd know the origin of the issue, and it could have been dealt with it at the time. But they had been circling for a while. Something wasn't right.

She loved him. Oh how her heart still craved him. She'd chosen him. He had chosen her. Last night with the physical closeness, the flowers the week before, showed, indeed proved, that there was still love and affection between them. In those pockets of happiness she forgot. She forgot that they had bigger problems that were not being dealt with. She pretended that this was normal; that this is what marriage *was*, that it wasn't always about heady emotion. It wasn't always butterflies and shots of electricity through her nervous system. It was about making a decision. It was choosing to develop companionship and friendship. It was about liking each other as much as it was about love.

She'd thought they'd mastered those things. But now she viewed others and their relationships. Adrian and Caren, Dave and Hannah, Mum and Dad; none of them were perfect, they all had their little issues, but those were an aside, not a regular presence. It wasn't holding them back, leaving them awake at night worrying for the future. At least she didn't think that it did. But then you never really knew, did you?

Perhaps this was as good as it was ever going to be. And for the sake of being with the man she loved, could she live with that knowledge for the rest of their lives? On stronger days, she believed so. She wanted to. She was no quitter. She had chosen him and he was still the one who left her breathless. Perhaps that was enough, and all that was needed?

She sank beneath the covers, focusing on the dull torrent of water, allowing her mind to empty of all the worries, all the concerns. They'd get through this. They were strong enough. She knew they were.

Chapter Thirty Four

2019

'It's time we had a chat.'

Ethan leant over the kitchen table. A brief flicker of alarm crossed Aimee's features, quickly veiled behind a teasing grin.

'That sounds serious.'

'Yes.'

Ethan pulled a spare chair from the table and sat down. He noted her eyes flicker across at her dormant phone. A mug of tea stood forgotten next to her right elbow. A novel lay face down in front of her crossed arms. Wearing an old red woollen jumper, she appeared more vulnerable than she was. The clothing was far larger than her slight frame and Ethan wondered if it belonged to the elusive Liam.

'You've been home for a while now. And...' he held up his hand as she tried to answer. 'You are more than welcome here. I just wondered if you could shed light on your plans.'

Diplomatic, discreet, Ethan posed the enquiry carefully. Still her nostrils flared. No matter how delicate he'd been, she still managed to take offence. It must be exhausting, he pondered, the constant reacting to everything that is said to you. To always expect the worst, always be on the defence.

He remembered a younger version of Helen, with auburn hair and freckles across the bridge of the nose. She had been a quiet child, like Evelyn, but the fieriness of her teen years balanced that out. That hot temper had subsided with maturity. She'd gained a sense of belonging.

Perhaps that was what Aimee missed, a sense of belonging? Was that why she seemed in fight or flight mode all the time?

And yet, he wondered. Who said anything had to be missing? Perhaps this is who Aimee was, and who she always would be. A combination of the two personalities of her parents, mixed in with her own unique qualities and experiences. He hoped it wouldn't get her into too much trouble. That she wouldn't wound and be wounded along the way.

'I've said I'll get a job,' she spat, her voice stabbing into his thoughts.

'It's not about the money.'

'Sounds like it to me.'

She picked up her mug of tea, contemplating the contents and slamming it back down to the wooden table. The pale calico liquid splashed over the side and Aimee issued an expletive, her eyebrows knitted together in frustration.

Ethan inclined in his chair, studying her.

'What is it about my question that offends you?'

'You just... I don't... I'm trying, okay?' She fiddled with the frayed sleeve of her jumper.

'Aimee, you came home at short notice and with a mystery boyfriend somewhere over yonder. You haven't opened up since you've been back. Did something happen in Greece that you had to get away from?'

'No,' she snorted. 'Don't be ridiculous.'

'Then why are you here?

'Maybe I just want to spend time with my family,' she said, her voice breaking in anger.

'There's nothing wrong with that.' He placed his hand over hers. It twitched beneath his palm, but she didn't pull away.

'I'm just asking for some clarity. I want to understand. If you can't talk to me about it, then speak with Evelyn. She knows what it is like to be at a crossroads.'

'Is that what you think? That I am at a crossroads?'

'Your phone is attached to you. You check the screen two dozen times a day; and that's just when I am around to spot you. Is it Liam? Are you waiting for him to get in touch? Have you not heard from him? Or are you waiting on a decision?'

Aimee pulled her hand free. 'You think I'm going to talk to my dad about this?'

The chair scraped against the lino as she stood. Slipping her phone in her pocket, she snatched up the book. Ethan noticed she was leaving him to mop up the mess she'd made with her drink.

'Then talk to Evelyn,' he repeated, his voice raised to be heard over the slamming shut of the kitchen door.

*

'It's halloumi, try it,' Lucie said, waving the tub of salad in Joe's direction.

He crinkled his nose in disgust. 'I'll stick to my ham sandwich, thanks.'

'I can't believe you haven't tried halloumi. I wonder if Taverton is in some sort of time warp sometimes.'

'Oi!' Joe replied, not really annoyed, as he was enjoying the verbal tussle between them. Evelyn had called in sick for the second day in a row. Lucie agreed to cover some of the hours so he wasn't alone in the shop for two days running. There hadn't been many customers, so there'd been plenty of time to talk.

'I'm sorry,' she said, laughing. 'I know it's a lovely place, but Taverton is like another world sometimes.'

'We do have halloumi here. I just don't like it the sound of it.'

'You're funny,' she said.

Funny in a 'you're a little weird but harmless' kind of way, or funny in a 'you're hilarious and I want to marry you' kind of way, he wondered. He berated himself. They were friends now, proper friends. He was not going to allow his ridiculous, embarrassing crush obstruct that.

'Do you mind if I go off for a bit?'

'No,' he said, despite feeling the opposite. 'It is your lunch break. I'm surprised you stayed in the shop.' He was fishing, he knew it, but it was unusual for Lucie to stick around during her breaks. She usually dashed off as soon as her hour started.

'Well, I like chatting to you.' She peered up at him then, her cheeks reddening. A swooping in his gut, which felt a lot like hope, almost tipped him off balance. He suppressed the reaction.

She went to the back room to collect her bag. He busied his hands, neatening the pile of free promotional bookmarks positioned beside the till. He cleared his throat and tried to concentrate on the hovering pedestrian outside. It appeared that she was experiencing an inner

175

debate of whether to enter the bookshop or not. The bookseller in him willed her to give in.

'I'll be back in half an hour,' Lucie called out, passing him with a brief wave. She pulled her hair back into a ponytail as she approached the door. She often did that, he noted. It was endearing.

As she exited the shop, the uncertain pedestrian made a decision, grabbing the handle after Lucie's retreat and entering the bookshop with a peal of the bell.

'Good afternoon,' Joe greeted them, his thoughts still on the retreating figure of the woman he was falling for.

*

The late July sky was a vivid blue, untainted by clouds and the occasional bird gliding by. The garden now a riot of colour, from the pink speckled foxgloves, to the ornate forget-me-nots which spilled over the rockery, had been Helen's pride and joy. She hadn't been a natural gardener at all, that fell to Ethan and in recent years to Evelyn. But she'd enjoyed the artistic side; the chance to create unusual sculptures and centre pieces. Anything that was different and drew the eye, such as the rockery and the small orchard she'd asked Ethan to plant. There were fairy doors, old and decrepit now, that were placed in the garden when Evelyn and Aimee were small, long before they were trendy. Mosaic pictures and glass folk art decorated the corners of the mossy cracked patio. Small pebbles and shells, collected from many beach visits, decorated random areas of the garden – some between pots, others in small piles around the trunks of the trees.

Some items had overgrown, or fallen apart over the years, like the little rustic house Helen had begged Ethan to build for hibernating visitors. Or the rope swing that hung from the birch tree at the far end of the garden, a ratty thing caked in dirt and grime and no longer of use to two teenage girls more interested in the outside world than the insular comforting one their parents had created.

Evelyn sat on the grass, her knees drawn to her chest. The breeze through the tree tops led the leaves in a melodic whisper. The blades of grass in the shade of the trees were a deep, thriving green, whereas the remainder of the garden displayed the tell-tale patches of a dry, scorched, summer. Her fingers reached out and clasped the rim of the coffee mug at her side. It rested at a precarious angle on the grass and she lifted it to her lips.

She breathed in the aroma. The last week it was little things like this that brought a sense of peace. It was small, but she would take it. The shop was a distraction, but it wasn't peaceful. Lucie had taken her week's summer leave and Evelyn had no choice but to drag herself into work. She was at least sleeping again, but the heaviness hadn't eased. She wondered if she was depressed or whether she was just grieving. The two weren't mutually exclusive, she knew, but the timing of it all made her question her reaction. Their separation was just shy of two years. A conclusion was coming, whether she liked it or not.

And that was the crux of it all. She didn't know whether she liked it or not. She'd thought the steps she'd carved out were leading her to independence, leading them both to resolution; the sale of the flat, moving home, buying a business. She didn't need Ishmael anymore. But that didn't answer the question of whether she still *wanted* him.

An all too familiar sheen of tears obscured her vision and she shook her head, as if willing them away. She was thirty-one. Her marriage had been over a while. She needed to face reality and deal with it. With the bookshop turning a slow financial corner, there was nothing stopping her future from being a positive one. She'd had solid blocks of time, months even, where there'd been no thought of her husband and the life they'd once shared. Perhaps it was a natural process; to go over what had happened, as the time approached when they could divorce? Why did it still hurt though? Was that normal too?

'Thought I'd find you out here,' Aimee's voice smashed into her quiet contemplation. Evelyn swallowed the spike of resentment her sister's presence invoked. It wasn't Aimee herself, but the thought of making conversation when all she wanted was to be alone with her thoughts.

Aimee sat down next to her, holding her own mug of coffee between both hands. Evelyn noted she was wearing that jumper again; the red one her father had pointed out. It was at least five degrees too hot for it.

'It's so beautiful out here, isn't it? When I am overseas this garden is the one thing I miss the most.'

'Not your family, then?' Evelyn asked, teasingly.

Aimee stuck her tongue out at her. Evelyn raised her eyebrows. Aimee really was childish at times. And she, Evelyn, could be too serious, too quiet and too passive. She sniffed as the tears threatened again.

'It reminds me of Mum. I find I can't remember her features as much, not without checking photographs. At least here I feel close to her. It reminds me of who she was.'

This was such an explicit admission that Evelyn paused, her coffee mug halfway back to her lips. Aimee was not the sentimental type. She never usually opened up.

'Is this because Dad told you to talk to me?' Evelyn asked, regretting her words in an instant. Aimee's open expression closed down like a shutter and she pursed her mouth as she looked away from her sister.

'I'm sorry,' Evelyn said, scrambling. 'He told me that you might want to chat sometime. He was trying to help. And, I'm being insensitive. I'm an idiot, ignore me.'

'Well, it was actually.' Aimee sniffed in derision. 'Because of what Dad said, I mean. But I didn't want to. We've never been close.'

'We were once. You might not remember that far back.'

'All I remember is that I adored my big sister. But she just ignored me,' Aimee said, the accusation in her voice as clear as the sky. 'I gave up.'

'Is that what you think?'

'That's how it was. You weren't interested. It's fine. We were four years apart. We never had much in common anyway. Besides, you went off to university, and then it was all about Ishmael. You made it clear that he was now your family.'

'What? That's not how it was!'

'It was Evelyn. He was your world.'

Was that true? How quickly she had followed him to London, even though she hadn't wanted to live there. How decisions were made for his career, but never for hers. But that's what a relationship was, right? Making choices and making compromises. But at five months in, had that been normal? Why hadn't she spoken up and said something? Was that where they'd gone wrong?

'We got married – we were each other's family. That is how it works,' she replied, defensive.

'I'm not calling you out for it. You did ask.'

Evelyn felt a sudden drag of fatigue. She didn't have the energy for an argument. She'd pushed too Aimee fast, which had resulted in her usual deflection tactics. They weren't going to get anywhere. Not today.

'I need to get to work. If you want to talk, you know where I am,' she offered, putting her hands against the spongy grass and pushing upright.

178

Aimee nodded, her gaze set on the swishing trees.

*

Ethan placed the lid onto the shoe box, smoothing it under his palm. All of the pages had been sorted into chronological order. The contents revealed little, except the months that she had waxed lyrical over Laurence Scott. She'd had no compunctions about sharing her feelings about *him*.

The act of keeping the journal pages suggested how important that time of her life had been. Ethan was just a passing mention. No that wasn't fair, he reassessed. He was always there in the background. Helen had stopped writing the journals after he'd made his promise. There was enough there to demonstrate that she'd been fond of him, that there had been a connection between them. And Ethan believed, in the years that followed, that Helen's love for him had burrowed deep. So what then had he hoped to achieve? A hint, a sense, that what she felt for him was as exhilarating as her love for Laurence? That Ethan hadn't been a second choice?

They had been happy. He knew Helen had loved him. Then, why didn't that knowledge settle his fears? They'd had thirty-five years of marriage, two children, a loving home and a multitude of memories. That should be evidence enough. He hated that the journal entries now led him to question their unity and the depth of her affection.

As a teenage boy, Ethan had already been so sure of his love for Helen. His heart would skip a beat at how her hair fell across her face and how she would blow it away, annoyance knitting her brow. He still recalled the visceral punch to his gut when she stared at him with those piercing blue-green eyes. He'd been in awe of her, at times even scared of her. She had a side to her, so like Aimee, a side that wasn't afraid to show what she thought. But she had a quiet side too, a contemplative side, like Evelyn. She thought deeply, loved her poetry and art, and expected so much of a world that so often failed to deliver.

She'd changed a lot after they got together. Had he stifled her personality, no matter how unintentional? Had she amended herself to better suit him? He had never thought so. Helen matured, her accident being the starting point. But if he had been second best, wouldn't it then figure that she might change herself to fit in to her new circumstances? With an ache of sorrow, he hoped she hadn't.

'Oh, for goodness sake,' Ethan expressed, pacing the kitchen, throwing accusing glances back toward the shoe box. Instead of resolution, he'd succeeded in adding more doubts to the list.

Helen had been happy. They'd been happy. He never saw even a hint that she regretted her decision. She wasn't so good an actress that she could have hidden the truth from him for three decades. It wasn't in her personality to hide her feelings.

But reading the pages of her love for that man, and her subsequent devastation, had not helped. Not one little bit.

Chapter Thirty Five

'Fine, you want to hear it, I'm here to talk!' Aimee declared at the top of her voice, bursting through the bookshop door, ignoring the bemused customer beside her.

Evelyn met her sister's gaze with an expression of disbelief. What on earth possessed Aimee to think that now was the right time, in the middle of the bookshop, halfway through Evelyn's shift? Joe bit his lip and shrugged at her.

'Let's go to my office.' She held out her arm to direct Aimee through. 'Right,' she added to Joe with a steadying breath. 'I'll be back soon.'

She shut the door behind her. Aimee sat on the grey office chair, swivelling it with her legs. She'd placed her massive leather bag on the desk, right on top of the posters for the festival, crumpling the pile on the one corner. Evelyn crossed her arms.

'That was quite an entrance.'

'I knew if I didn't come now, then I... well, wouldn't.'

'So is this going to be a vague, throw me a morsel, type of conversation? Or are you going to tell me what's been going on?'

'It's no major mystery,' Aimee said, a flicker of annoyance dancing across the bridge of her nose. She swivelled to face the desk and studied the contents for a brief moment.

'Well it is to Dad and me.'

'You make it sound like you're planning to settle in that house for the rest of your life.'

Her comment rankled and Evelyn took a deep breath. Deflection, always deflection, but the worst part was Aimee knew which button to press.

'Dad enlisted me because you weren't talking.'

It was Aimee's turn to squirm, but Evelyn held her ground.

'You've come here to tell me. So, do that, talk to me. You've said yourself it is no big deal.'

Aimee balked, losing her nerve, and held her silence. Running a fingertip across the edge of the desk, she avoided eye contact. Evelyn sat down against the half sized filing cabinet, making herself level with her sister.

'It can't be worse than my pathetic life,' she joked.

Aimee's lips twitched in amusement.

'I'm... I knew I'd have to tell you eventually, but I've been putting it off.'

'Tell us what?'

'Oh Evelyn, I wanted to tell you and Dad together. I know I've been secretive, but I was hoping you'd just be pleased I was home and not ask too many questions.'

'Just start from the beginning.'

'I'm... I'm planning to move to New Zealand. To be with Liam, in case you hadn't guessed.'

'But...' Evelyn stuttered, her mind running over all the recent conversations she'd had with her sister. 'You said you weren't sure about him, that you were too young to worry about settling yet.'

'I know. Part of coming back to England was to spend time thinking about our plans. He knows I needed to consider everything, and to break the news to you and Dad.'

'Is that why you've been sentimental about those photographs of Mum?' Evelyn wondered aloud.

'I don't get to say goodbye in person, so....' Aimee bit her lip. She seemed so vulnerable that Evelyn couldn't feel mad about the secrecy.

'So, you're planning to run away with a guy we've never even met, not even on a video call?' She emitted a sharp laugh. 'You realise that you criticised Ishmael and I for heading off to London together. And now you're doing the same thing... just on a much grander scale.'

Aimee had the decency to wince.

'It's okay. I'm not annoyed.' Evelyn stood, stretching her legs. 'I'm making a coffee. Do you want a hot drink? We can talk more in a few minutes.'

'If you're busy, I can come back...'

'No, you stay where you are. We need to work out how to best tell Dad.'

*

'You have aphids on your roses.'

'Right, thank you Janice, I'll take a look later,' Ethan replied, the car door open in his hand, having paused at the sound of footsteps approaching across the gravel.

Janice peered around with a beady expression, nodding towards the house.

'Are your daughters not at home today?'

Ethan shut the car door, his other arm holding an open cardboard box containing some old paperbacks of Helen's. Evelyn and Aimee had already helped themselves to the ones they wanted. The rest were going to a charity shop the other side of town. He took a deep breath. It would have to wait until later.

'No, they are both out. I haven't seen you in a while Janice. Have you been keeping well?'

'I didn't want to interfere, you know, while your youngest was home.'

So even the neighbour, who'd perhaps met Aimee once, knew enough to keep a low profile? He could imagine Aimee's comments if she'd seen Janice popping in with baked goods every week.

'How is the baking?' he asked, for want of anything else to say.

'It's been a little hot for baking. But I'm sure as the weather cools I'll be able to drop off the odd treat. Is your daughter home for long? I just ask, as a friendly neighbour, you understand?'

'You'd be better off asking her that. I have no idea how long Aimee will be staying.' He hovered for a brief second, before turning towards the house. The crunch of Janice's footsteps followed.

'Must be nice having a full house again,' she persisted.

'Almost full,' Ethan replied as Helen's beaming smile came to mind.

'Oh yes, of course.'

'Is there something specific you wanted to discuss?'

The box was gathering weight with every passing second.

'I just saw you and thought I would say hello.'

'Right.' Ethan contemplated leaving it at that, but her jittery body language hinted at a misplaced hope. He had no intention of leading this woman on.

'Janice, I'm sure you mean well,' he started, but got no further as Janice withdrew.

'Oh no, I won't be bothering you,' she said, removing her gaze from the house. 'I'm just checking in, as good neighbours should.'

'And I appreciate that.'

'Gordon checks in on me from time to time, and I'm sure you would too, if not for your daughters taking up all your time,' she added, her sentence ending on a chilly note.

'They're a welcome distraction. You know that if you have any problems you just need to phone either Gordon or myself.'

'I'm not sure I have your mobile phone number.'

'But you have my landline. If you need help when I am at work, there is a contact number on the company website.'

'Yes, I best let you get on then.' She peeked at the box, curious.

'Books,' he said, leaning down to place it on the floor. 'You're welcome to have a scratch around. They'll be going to charity otherwise.'

Janice craned her neck, reminding Ethan of an emu as she leant down, her back curved liked a bow. He was tempted to leave her to it, but didn't want to appear rude.

'There are plenty of novels in there. And some craft books too. Helen liked her crafts.'

'Oh they're Helen's books are they?' Janice asked, snatching her hand back. Ethan swallowed down his annoyance. Did she think she would catch cancer from a paperback? A sudden swooping pang of grief hit him. He knew Janice wasn't trying to be cruel, just insensitive, but it still jarred. He viewed the box with a grimace. It had been a fresh attempt to finish the job he'd started. The job that now seemed endless. Was every little step going to include a setback? He pulled himself together. He was going to take this box to the charity shop and he was going to do it now. No more delays. Picking it up again, he started towards the car, calling back to Janice as he did.

'I'm heading out now. It was nice to chat.'

Sliding the box into the boot of the car, Ethan slammed the door shut and approached the driver's side. He gave a short wave, adding a well-meaning chuckle at Janice's confused expression as he reversed out of the drive and the car pulled away.

*

Ethan viewed the cupboard with grim satisfaction. The shelves were neat, ordered and poignantly lacking Helen's belongings. It was one cupboard, just one, but it was done. He still needed to finish clearing out the under-stairs cupboard and Helen's wardrobe, now void of clothing, but still containing piles of paperwork and photographs, bags of makeup and ancient bottles of perfume. It would all need to be sorted out.

The shoe box of journal entries had dominated his time and thoughts. Picking away for clues drained him, to the point that the physical exertion of removing her possessions became overwhelming. He shut the cupboard doors, placing a hand on the smooth white slats as they met the frame. Downstairs a burst of noise erupted through the porch. The girls were home.

Taking another second for himself, Ethan allowed the wave of disruption wash over him, staying in his quiet corner on the upstairs landing.

'Hello Randall, you mangy old boy,' Aimee exclaimed.

'I don't know how you do it. He never comes to me. You've been away for as long as I've been back *and* you insult him, and still he's all over you. I get nothing but an upturned nose.'

'Randall's always loved me more.'

'That's not true!'

'I just have a way with animals, that's all.'

Evelyn's snort of derision was loud enough to carry up the stairs. 'Dad, are you home?' she called. 'You are going to have to tell him.' He heard Evelyn's hiss in her sister's direction.

'I'm upstairs.'

'Okay. I'm putting the kettle on. Will you join us?' She shouted.

'A few minutes,' he replied, the cool surface of the cupboard door still resting beneath his palm. Rearranging the shelves was a victorious task, but it left him exhausted. Would this ever get easier?

He pulled his hand away, running it through his hair in habit. Stepping back he entered the main bedroom, pushing the door to, while his eyes fell on the shoe box. It rested on top of the bed with the lid off. He wondered if he was torturing himself by hanging on to it. The journals revealed nothing that Ethan didn't already know. Helen had been obsessed, as only a teenage girl could be. Anyone who knew her back then saw her passion, saw how she became beguiled with the archetypal bad boy. Ethan had waited his turn, patiently, achingly. And he had won her best years.

Frustrated with himself and the nagging presence of needing to let go, he threw the lid across the bedroom. It spiralled down to the old cream carpet, which had yellowed around the edges with age. Sinking onto the cushioned mattress he glared at the lid. A plain, nondescript item, harmless and weak, and yet it held so much power over his thoughts. He smirked. Helen would tell him to snap out of it. Oh, how he missed her.

But now was not the time for self-pity. The grief would simmer as it always did, but his girls were home and like parents everywhere, even when their children were grown up, he readjusted his mask to fit their needs.

*

'You had such a crush on him when you were younger.'

'I did not!' Evelyn retorted, her cheeks blazing red with embarrassment. She slammed the cups down on the work surface, harder than planned. Aimee knew how to wind her up.

'You did. You wrote down your name with his surname. I remember reading it.'

'Aimee!' She swivelled around, her embarrassment switching to anger. 'Where did you read that? Did you go through my diary?'

'We were just kids,' Aimee shrugged, as if that excused her indiscretion.

'That is not the point. My diary was private. All my things were private. What were you even doing in my room?'

'This was half our life time ago.' Aimee played with the wooden fruit bowl in the middle of the kitchen table. She eyed Evelyn with veiled bemusement. 'How can you still care about things like that?'

'Easy, when you're the one on the receiving end,' Evelyn replied, lifting the boiled kettle, while trying to mask the alarming sudden prickle of tears. Her emotions were on edge. Hearing no smart comeback, she glanced over her shoulder, seeing the expression of fear spread across her sister's face as the kitchen door creaked open.

'I'll have Earl Grey, please,' Ethan announced as he entered the room. Aimee shifted in her seat, alert and anxious. He noticed, catching Evelyn's eye and raising an eyebrow. Her heart went out to her father. He had no idea what was coming.

'Sure,' she said, replacing her father's tea bag and pouring water into the cups.

'Is everything all right, Aimee?' He took a seat opposite and studied her.

'Yep,' she replied, unconvincingly.

'The upstairs cupboard is finished. I've repurposed the shelves. The bottom one is for reference books, the middle for paper and stationery, and the top one has all the photographs in boxes. Try and keep it tidy, at least for a while.'

'Mum used to keep all sorts in there,' Aimee reminisced. 'I remember coming across her soap collection. She loved that orange blossom one.'

'Helped yourself, did you?' Evelyn remarked, annoyed with herself for being catty. 'Ha ha,' Aimee said, with a roll of her eyes.

'Glad to see that you two are getting on as well as ever,' Ethan quipped, accepting his cup from Evelyn with a thank you.

'There are a lot of memories here. When I think about it I can still smell the orange blossom soap. And do you remember Mum's candle phase?' Aimee snorted in recollection. 'We had weird wonky candles for months!'

Evelyn smiled and raised her cup to her lips. She leaned against the kitchen counter, leaving space for Ethan and Aimee to talk at the table.

'I think I still have an unused one stashed in a box somewhere,' she said. 'It was that horrible pointy purple one she made for my birthday. I felt guilty for months for never using it.'

'A blessing in disguise,' Ethan added. 'The wicks never burned properly and the candles would collapse to the side. One nearly set fire to the flowers on the mantelpiece. Mum stopped making them after that.'

'Why did it take so long to sort out Mum's things?' Aimee asked, her tone sensitive for once.

'I should have done it ages ago. Grief does funny things to you.'

Grief certainly does, Evelyn thought.

'I needed to come here and see this place again.'

She lifted her head at Aimee's words. She'd begun to wonder if her sister would back off from telling Ethan.

'It's your home Aimee, and always will be. Both of you girls are welcome any time. Your Mum would want that too.'

'I know. But I came back for a reason, Dad.'

'Go on,' he said with caution.

'I knew a while ago, but I still needed to be here and know for sure. Because, it's a big decision and it'll affect us all.'

'What will?'

'I'm moving to New Zealand to be with Liam. That stuff I said when I first moved back about not being sure… well, I don't know why I said it. Maybe just to avoid having to tell the truth, or maybe I just wasn't ready to say it? But, we plan to get married. I know it's quick,' she added, seeing Ethan's expression. 'But we won't marry straight away. I can visit for six months without a visa, which will give us time to make further plans and I can get to know his family and we can decide what we want. Then we'll come back here for a bit and he can get to know you while I apply for a permanent visa. So, that's… that's what we've decided.'

Aimee's expression was alert and despite covering it quickly, Evelyn saw a flicker of fear pass over her features.

'I…' Ethan stopped and cleared his throat. 'Then what was all this talk about getting a job?'

'I wasn't deliberately lying. I just didn't know how to raise the subject, and it felt easier to let you think that I didn't expect you to pay my way. I do have enough savings to last while I'm there on holiday.'

'You have enough to last you six months, all from working in a bar in Greece?' Ethan asked, sceptical.

'I've been writing travel articles, actually.'

'Really?' Evelyn injected in surprise.

'Yes. I have been working as a freelance travel journalist for a while. It's a good way to supplement my income, and let's face it seasonal bar work is not a long term goal. I write for blogs and some magazines too. I enjoy it. I want to write a series of travel books, but they're a while off yet.'

Evelyn laughed in surprise. 'Well, let me know, and we'll be sure to stock them.'

Aimee hid a grin. 'Daddy, I know it's shocking to hear all this. But I am not as hazardous as I appear. I do have plans. And I can be sensible.'

'This is a lot of information to take in,' he responded, shaking his head. 'At least we'd met Ishmael before Evelyn ran off to London with him.'

'Liam will come over to meet you all. It'll be in the spring, when it begins to warm up. He won't want to come in winter. I'll head over to New Zealand around September time, in their spring, and then we'll enjoy the best of both climates. Sorry…' Aimee said, stopping at Ethan's expression. 'I know that's not the point. But we have discussed this in detail. We're not making plans without thinking it through.'

'I've not even seen or heard you on the phone to him while you've been here.'

'I wait until you and Evelyn are out. I was scared I'd forget I hadn't told you yet, and something would slip out and you would hear.'

Suddenly sorting the upstairs cupboard seemed trivial.

'I just wanted to wait for the right time.'

'Can I then ask that you phone and video call him when we're around from now on? The quicker we can get used to each other, the better I feel about you running off to the other side of the world. At least he won't be a complete stranger to us by the time you leave. As a father I am very uncomfortable with the idea of having never met him.'

'I'm not a child anymore, Dad.'

'No, you're not. I won't try and stop you going Aimee. That's your choice. But I want to get to know the man you're planning to marry, who for all I know might be a con man or worse.' He lifted his hand, as Aimee attempted a retort. She fell silent.

'It's my duty as a dad to check these things.'

'Did you check up on Ishmael?' Aimee said, her eyes flashing. Evelyn tensed, wondering what her point was.

'Yes, in fact I did. I even travelled up to meet his parents before she moved to London with him.'

'Did you?' Evelyn asked with surprise. She hadn't known that.

'Yes. I think they had concerns, as we did, although we all agreed that you were in love and seemed well suited. It was just the timing that alarmed us. But we didn't stop them, Aimee,' Ethan added, his attention back on his youngest. 'And I won't stop you. However, if I discover he has a criminal record for drug smuggling, be sure that I won't stay silent. And you'll be in my prayers, for certain.'

'You'll like him Daddy.'

'I really hope so.'

Chapter Thirty Six

The start of the summer holidays brought a flurry of new customers to the shop. Young families, locals and tourists, were drawn in by the range of children's books in the window display. Interspersed with buckets and spades, real sand across the display surface, and a blue sheet hanging behind for the sea, all the current favourite children's authors had their latest titles on show.

The sudden influx of younger customers gave Evelyn and her staff a chance to promote the children's story corner, due to start in September. Following an impromptu performance by Joe, at the encouragement of the parents, he mentioned to Evelyn the idea of offering a second, later session, so that primary aged children could attend after school.

He and Lucie handed out promotional stickers and ran the parents' purchases through the till. He noted how at ease Lucie was with the children, wondering if she'd be interested in joining in with the storytelling sessions. It would mean extending her shifts though and he was not sure whether Lucie or Evelyn would be open to the suggestion.

Evelyn hovered behind them, phone in hand. She looked distracted. He hoped she was okay. She had seemed pale and withdrawn over the last few weeks and prone to small talk about the business, never straying into anything personal. The last couple of shifts the old Evelyn appeared to be returning. But today she again appeared fretful and stressed.

'You're good with the kids,' Joe said to Lucie as his boss moved out of his eye line.

She seemed thrilled with his compliment.

'Thank you, Joe.'

'I want to try another of those Austen books,' a reedy voice said, punctuating his thoughts. He turned with a heavy heart to the familiar source. Betty Longhorn, all five foot two inches of her, glared back at him, her rheumy eyes challenging.

'I liked that prejudice one. What else can you recommend?'

Evelyn was the resident Austen expert, but she'd moved back into the recesses of the shop, phone against her ear.

'Well there's Northanger Abbey, or perhaps Persuasion? And of course, Sense and Sensibility, which is popular. Do you remember the film?'

Mrs Longhorn gave an expression of not having a clue what he was on about, blended with a heavy air of indifference. Joe bit his lip. 'Why don't I just show you?'

He led Betty Longhorn away from the till area, not noticing that Lucie's gaze didn't leave him as he traversed the entire shop, the elderly pensioner shuffling along behind.

*

'Listen, I've been thinking,' Evelyn whispered down the phone. 'I need some help while Joe is on holiday in a couple of weeks. Lucie can only commit to a few extra shifts. In all honesty, we'll need to use another pair of hands over the festival too. It won't be much, just a couple of hundred pounds between it all, but, it'll help me out and it'll give you something to do.'

Silence met her ear and she wondered if they'd been disconnected. 'Hello?'

'I'm here.'

'Well?'

'Why are you doing this?' Aimee asked.

'Because I have half a dozen shifts I've not been able to find cover for. That's why.'

'I'm surprised you want me anywhere near your shop.'

Evelyn held her tongue, knowing her sister's assessment was accurate. It had taken several days of consideration before plucking up the courage to offer the work to Aimee. It was enough that they were all under the same roof at home, without working together too. The reality was that with the plans she had for the business, there would have to be an expansion of staff. Unfortunately the bookshop didn't earn enough to support another full time member of staff, and with

Aimee twiddling her thumbs until September, it seemed the obvious choice.

'I need help, you need something to do. So do you want the work, or not?'

There was a pause. 'I think I'd quite enjoy it.'

'Great. If you come into the shop one morning next week I'll show you the ropes. I can give you a couple of days of work while you train. The first proper shift will be the week of the festival, which starts on the ninth of August. I need you to know what you're doing before then, as we're expecting the footfall to be massive that weekend.'

'Will I be able to learn everything in time?' Aimee's voice betrayed the slightest crack of uncertainty.

'Have you worked with a till before?'

'Yes.'

'Have you dealt with a full venue, with lots of waiting customers?'

'Of course I have.'

'Then you'll be fine. If anyone wants book recommendations Lucie, Joe or I will be around to step in.'

'I'm a reader too.'

'Well then, you have nothing to fear.'

*

'I'm still annoyed with Adrian.'

'Don't take Ishmael's failings out on your own husband, Caren. Or my failings, while we're on the topic.' She heard her friend huff down the phone line. She'd just arrived home from the shop after an evening of paperwork, and she made her way upstairs to her bedroom, phone nestled under her chin. 'Instead, let's plan our next evening out.'

'Now I can agree with that.'

'It's either going to have to be in the next two weeks, or when I take leave at the end of August. I hope that's okay. I know it can be difficult with the children.'

'Adrian owes me! After the men's behaviour, I think we can slink off for a girl's night out. Indeed, we can dine out on this for a while.'

'Ishmael owes me nothing,' Evelyn said, swallowing down the sadness that thought provoked.

'Well then, Adrian can owe us both.'

She laughed. 'Great. Send me a few dates via text and we'll finalise some plans. I need something to look forward to.'

'Is your sister still driving you up the wall?'

'To be honest, she's just one of many distractions. And her time at home has taught me that we can get on. She's going to be working at the bookshop next week.'

'You're kidding!' Caren snorted.

'I'm just pleased the bookshop is making enough of a profit to employ her. Six months ago that wouldn't have been possible.'

'I'm pleased for you, Evelyn....'

'It's still early days.'

'I know, but it's your dream. I'm pleased it's working out. I must admit, I thought you running back to Suffolk would be a temporary thing. I saw you needed it, and let's face it London was never your home. I just thought a few weeks, or even a few months would be enough to pull your thoughts together. I didn't imagine it would be the start of a whole new chapter.'

'I couldn't go back. Not now.' Suffolk was always where her heart belonged. At least now her heart had made space.

'Well then, I think it's only fair we make some time to come through and visit. I want to see the place my best friend deems better than a life in the capital.'

'You are more than welcome. I'd love to show you around.'

'I will refrain from saying something curt like "that'll take all of five minutes."'

'Is that your way of saying it, while pretending to have not said it?' Evelyn teased.

They both laughed, and she stretched out her legs across the length of her bed, as they began to cramp beneath her. She'd forgotten how long she and Caren could talk.

Chatting on, they made tentative plans for a visit to Suffolk. She wondered if it would happen. She'd never known Caren and Adrian to head out into deep countryside, not even for a romantic weekend away. It was still fun to plan though, and she liked the idea that Caren was at least keen.

The combined interruption of one of Caren's children announcing they'd wet the bed and Ethan's voice calling up from downstairs brought a natural end to their discussion.

'I'd better go,' Caren sighed. 'I can't wait until my life consists of not mopping up a variety of disgusting fluids.'

'I best be off too. We're about to connect to New Zealand and meet Liam for the first time. Or at least 'meet' behind computer screens. It's about eight in the morning there already.'

'Good luck.'

'You too.'

*

'Aimee will be coming in this morning for her training.'

Joe reddened. Evelyn's sister unnerved him. She wasn't like Evelyn; composed, serious at times, never wasteful with her words. Aimee seemed unpredictable in comparison. For some reason his mind then skipped to Lucie as it usually did with little provocation.

'I'm sure she'll do fine,' he replied, pulling his thoughts back to the present.

'Oh, I'm sure she will too. She seems to land on her feet wherever she goes and whatever she does. I don't know how she does it. Dad absolutely loved Liam on the video call. He's being reserved for appearances sake, but I could tell he liked him. Even after Aimee's lies and pretence, she still manages to get away with it.'

Being privy to only the basics of what was occurring in the Storford household, Joe nodded mutely.

'I've got Lucie coming by to do an hour or so of leafleting. If it's quiet and going well with Aimee, then perhaps join her. Join Lucie I mean. The more leaflets we get out there, the better. The festival is getting close.'

Evelyn stepped into the kitchenette to make them both a drink, while Joe, alone on the shop floor neatened the bookmarks on the counter, a grin spreading across his face.

Chapter Thirty Seven

I found out today that the charges have been lessened. The chances of an actual prison sentence are reduced, but not impossible. My heart is lifted at the thought that soon, this might all be in the past and behind us. These long months of recovery, of waiting, my heart almost bursting in the desire to see him again, could soon be a faint and past nightmare.

I am now walking unaided. Caroline and Ethan take turns to walk short distances with me. I appreciate their friendship more these days. They have stuck by my side, while others have peeled away, either embarrassed by my injuries, or put off by the gossip surrounding the court case.

Autumn is sliding into winter now. The trees are almost bare and the chill hurts the bones that are still healing. I think back to those long summer nights, those days in his arms, dreaming about our future together. It will take a while, but I believe we can return to those dreams.

All this will be behind us and can be forgotten. Family and friends may disagree. Their attitude towards him is still hostile. But they don't see what I see. They don't know him like I do. He has made mistakes, I know that, but if I can forgive him, then why can't they!

They will see. They will all see, one day.

The court case began this week. My father didn't want me to attend, but I just had to. Mother supported me as I sat on the cold, solid bench, the hard wood putting pressure on my joints, causing me to give a sharp exclamation of pain. It was worth it though, for the visit afforded me my first chance to see Laurence since the accident. I sat across from him in the public gallery and I did not pull my gaze from him the whole while.

197

He was wearing a smart black suit, and was thinner and taller than I remember. Funny how close we were and how well I knew him, yet months spent apart and the memory has already altered. Laurence had gel in his hair and it was darker as a result, which I didn't like. I preferred his natural hair, free and wild, stroking against his collar and curling at the ends. I willed him to look my direction, but he didn't, not even for a second. My heart sinks even writing this. I had so hoped he would.

Perhaps he had been told not to, but my heart still hurts.

With the lesser charges there was no need for a jury. There was no alcohol present in Laurence's system. No drugs. It is being presented as an unfortunate accident, careless at worse.

The judge will deliberate and decide what action comes next. I could barely breathe as my mother led me away. I cried all the way home.

I am so scared. I cannot imagine how terrible it would be if he had to go to prison.

Laurence has received a suspended sentence and some community service. As long as he doesn't break the law in the next twelve months, then he is safe from prison. Oh how happy this makes me! Things can be normal again. Well, perhaps not as normal as before. My father will still not allow his name to be mentioned under our roof. Mother is a little more sympathetic. I notice her watching me, every time my father rants against the man I love. As if she understands the strength of my feelings, amid the impossibility of it all.

But I don't believe for a second that it is unmanageable. Time will prove a healer. They do not know him like I do. How can they deny, when my whole existence is filled with thoughts of him? They will see. They will learn. They'll have to.

When will he come and see me? I wrote a letter last week, telling him it was okay, telling him that I still loved him and all had been forgiven. I know he never meant to crash the car, he never meant to hurt me. Mistakes happen.

But I have had no answer. Perhaps his parents are preventing contact? I sit here, watching the snowflakes falling outside the window, wondering when this nightmare will end. I will keep writing until he answers. He has to answer eventually.

Chapter Thirty Eight

'You did not!' Lucie squealed. Her entire face lit up and she burst into giggles.

Delighted by her reaction, Joe laughed, amid a mingling sense of relief that she found him funny, that she liked his stupid anecdotes.

'I did,' he replied with a trickle of insecurity. He didn't want to assume anything, but his thoughts were crashing in from all different directions. He had put off pursuing anything in case he'd read her incorrectly. The embarrassment and awkwardness would be unbearable if he got it wrong.

They'd spent the best part of the afternoon handing out leaflets in the now bustling main street. Everyone was out, enjoying the sunshine, visiting local beauty spots, pottering through the various and quirky independent shops. Already signs and posters for the upcoming festival were displayed in shop windows or across the external walls of some of the buildings. Handing out leaflets for their own stall proved a good talking point. An hour of work had lengthened under the weight of questions from passers-by.

The breeze accelerated and Joe's cheeks began to smart with the combination of sun and wind. He hoped he wasn't beetroot red. As the afternoon sun beat down, the pedestrians had trickled away, and left with a small pile of leaflets between them, they chatted as they made their way back to the shop.

He stopped, his remaining leaflets flapping aggressively between his fingers, as the wind picked up pace. It was ridiculous. Every waking thought was consumed by this woman and his uncertainties wouldn't improve unless he did something about it. Going against his introverted instincts, he faced Lucie, who was already glancing up at him, an expression of slight surprise on her face. Swallowing down twenty-six years of being the underdog, Joe decided to take the risk.

'Would you like to get a cup of tea, or coffee, after work?'

'Oh.' She started. He held his nerve, resisting the threatening plummet of his stomach.

'It might be difficult,' she said, a little panicked, with her gaze everywhere but his.

'Don't worry about it,' he injected with speed, trying not to appear devastated.

'No, it's not that I don't want to,' she said, placing a hand on his arm. It seemed to burn through his clothing. 'It's a little awkward, you see? No, of course you don't. Why would you?'

Joe wished he'd stayed in his little bubble and had never risked popping it.

'Just forget about it.'

He pulled himself together, approaching the shop a hundred metres or so away. It was like a beacon of safety.

'I don't want to forget about it,' Lucie replied, keeping up with him, her voice cracking. 'I would like to. It's just a little complicated. I would need some notice, that's all.'

'Really?'

'Yes,' she said with a nervous grin. 'I can organise it for after our next shift, if you like?'

'Yes, I would like that. Very much,' he added, wondering briefly if he was taking his ebullience too far. He didn't want to put her off.

'Brilliant.'

'Brilliant.'

*

'You did well today.' Evelyn said to Aimee as she locked the shop door behind her.

The wind whistled between them as the sisters huddled in the alcove between the bay windows of the bookshop and the boutique next door. It gave a little shelter and Evelyn peered out to the street beyond, witnessing several of her festival leaflets blowing along the road. They were already out of reach.

Joe and Lucie had both seemed giddy and insistent on the success of their afternoon. Evelyn hoped the effort hadn't been in vain, their leaflets dumped or forgotten by the pedestrians they'd spoken to.

'Thanks. Do you think I'll be up to speed by the festival?'

'I don't see why not. We'll be having a staff meeting next week to go over everyone's responsibilities. It would be helpful if you're there.'

'Well, well, my sister the big boss.'

'It doesn't feel like that most of the time.' Evelyn adjusted her shoulder bag as they braved the wind and stepped out into the street.

'Don't put yourself down. You've achieved a lot. It couldn't have been easy starting again. I guess I have that to come.'

'You've started again numerous times, Aimee. You'll be fine.'

'Yes, but this is different. I am starting again with someone else. Everything rides on this being successful. If it doesn't work, I'll be alone on the other side of the world to my family.'

'You're right. That's huge. But Aimee, you are strong. You'll deal with anything that comes your way.'

'Funny, I always thought of you as the strong one.'

Evelyn gave her the side eye.

'It's true!' Aimee stated, noticing her expression. 'You're so steady, so… balanced.'

'You make me sound riveting.'

'It's meant to be a compliment. How you've dealt with everything… I know I haven't been here to witness it, but you've picked yourself up after Ishmael and got on with things.'

Evelyn felt a bubble of hysteria rise up. It expelled itself in a high pitched yelp of indignation. Aimee stopped in surprise.

'Is that what you think? Oh Aimee, if only that was half of the truth. I thought I knew grief after Mum died, but it turns out the grief of not knowing, of not having a conclusion, is even worse.'

'Are you talking about the divorce?'

'I'm talking about it all. Every last messy little bit of it.'

'You should call him,' Aimee said, grabbing Evelyn's arm as her eyes widened. 'I mean it, Evelyn! Have you spoken to him at all during your separation?'

'Not since we sold the flat. We agreed there was nothing left to say. Not until we could divorce, at least.'

'But, isn't that time coming up?'

'You know nothing about it, Aimee.'

'I know I don't. But he was your husband. I know you split and you had your reasons, but it sounds like you're in limbo. Wouldn't it have been easier to just talk it through, so you could move on?'

'I'm beginning to wonder.'

'Wonder what?'

'Oh, pretty much everything. The last few months, I…' She wasn't used to opening up to Aimee, and her argument with Ethan along the same street came to mind. 'I'm not sure my heart is catching up with my head. Come on,' she added, before Aimee interjected. 'Let's get home. This wind is awful.'

*

The tearoom was emptying out, the tourists peeling away in search of restaurants where they'd while away the evening hours. Joe wished he'd picked another venue, one that would be open for more than another half an hour. It was long enough for a cup of tea, which had been their arrangement, but nowhere near long enough for his liking.

Lucie seemed happy though and settled herself at a small two-seater table by the window. She smiled as he joined her. Their shift together in the bookshop had passed without incident and with a steady stream of customers, both of them nervous and anticipating their get together afterwards. It was nice having a few extra shifts with Lucie he thought, as he studied the drinks menu.

'What are you going to have?' She asked, peering over her own menu.

'I think I'll just have a mug of tea,' he replied, his stomach rumbling, giving away his hunger, yet conscious of the tearoom's closing time.

'I'll have the same.'

Joe ordered for them both and sat back down, watching as she secured her hair into a ponytail. Small feather like wisps of blonde hair escaped the hair band and fell across her cheeks.

'I've been looking forward to today. I don't get a chance to get out much. It's either home or the bookshop, or the park.'

She let the sentence hang in the air, withdrawing her gaze from his. He wondered if she meant or even willed him to pry, to ask why not. The comment seemed loaded, as if she wanted to divulge more, but was unsure how to without invitation.

Plucking up the courage, after all it had taken a risk to ask her out in the first place, Joe decided to plunge ahead.

'I know this town doesn't offer a massive social scene, but there are things to do here. There's a popular book club, or a dance studio if that's more your thing. There's a running club too. Taverton has a Facebook page with local events, if you're not sure what to get involved in. Or the village hall has a list on the wall, of what runs when.'

'You're kind Joe, but Taverton is not the problem. I...' she paused, as the waitress placed down a large pot of tea and cups onto the table. Joe thanked the waitress.

'It's rather complicated,' she added with a frown.

He picked up the pot and offered to pour. She nodded. Silence fell between them.

'You don't have to share if you don't want to.'

'You're my friend. I don't have many here yet. It's not that I don't want to... in fact there's no shame in it, it's just that, well I don't know what you meant by asking me here.'

A prickle of heat crossed his cheeks. 'You mean, if I asked you here as more than a friend?'

He couldn't quite believe he was saying the words. But it was done now, and asking her to tea was always going to provoke a conversation around why. Joe noticed, with slight surprise, that she was blushing too.

'Yes, that's what I meant. I feel embarrassed even asking, in case I have the wrong idea.'

'You're not wrong,' he admitted, his heart pounding at being so bold.

Sitting up straighter she placed a hand around her cup of tea. 'I'm glad. The problem is that it makes things more complicated.'

'Why?' His voice lowered in fear of scaring her off an explanation.

Picking up her cup, Lucie sipped the tea. 'The thing is, you need to know everything, even if this never goes further, if we never even go on a proper date. Or perhaps this is a proper date,' she laughed with uncertainty. 'I wouldn't know. I am not very good at this kind of thing.'

'Me neither.'

'You see, you need to know, because you need to weigh up all the information. I don't want to lead you on, but I don't want to lose your friendship either. Promise me that won't have to happen.'

'What did you do? Rob a bank?' Joe laughed at his own joke, before falling silent, wondering if maybe it had been something less ridiculous but equally serious.

'I have a son, Joe.'

It was so far from what he was expecting that at first he lost his ability to respond. Staring at her, he didn't even notice the cup that was in his hand, still hovering halfway between the table and his mouth.

'But... what?' he managed.

'He's nearly two. His name is Sam.'

'Why have you never mentioned him?' Joe asked in confusion. 'You've worked in the bookshop for six months.'

'I know it seems crazy.'

'I just don't understand.'

Lucie peered out of the window for a brief moment. She composed herself.

'I was a teenage mum. That was a big deal in the village I grew up in. I know it sounds unlikely these days, but when you've grown up with these people your whole life and then they judge you for falling pregnant at eighteen... well, it wasn't fun. My mum came up with the idea of moving and having a fresh start. Not too far away, just somewhere big enough where we'd melt into the background for a while. She works part time, so she has Sam on the days that I work.'

'But... Taverton isn't enormous. Why haven't I seen you out and about with him?'

'You work at the bookshop full time. If I take him out, then I avoid walking past in case you, or Evelyn, spot us through the window. That phone call, where I had to run home, that was because he woke up with a high fever and was ill for a few days. I daren't even tell Evelyn the truth, even though I wanted to.'

'But she's your employer.'

'I know. But, you have to understand, Joe. I was always the quiet one growing up. I'd never even had a boyfriend until I was sixteen and he promised me the world and never once delivered. We were together for two years, during which I worked, while he sat unemployed and playing computer games. I ignored my friends and my mum who warned me that he would let me down. Then I found out I was pregnant. And everything fell apart. For someone who had no motivation to ever get a job or make an effort, he got out of my life sharpish. He's never been involved with Sam.'

'But I was left to raise our son. And to put up with the stares and the comments about being a teenage mum and after a free flat, or even being easy for falling pregnant so young, despite having only been in one relationship.'

Lucie paused and took a deep breath.

'I was scared of ruining things here. I was scared I'd be judged again. I was nineteen when Sam was born. I had to learn to be an adult and a mum overnight. Starting again in Taverton was a chance to escape the past. But if people knew the truth, it might ruin that fresh start. I know I would have had to tell you all eventually. But I was home for a long time with Sam and when I started working, it just seemed easier to pretend. No one would expect me to be a mum at twenty-one anyway.'

'You say you're interested in me. I like you too Joe, but you have to know the truth. I'm sorry I didn't say anything, but it didn't seem relevant until I realised where our friendship was heading. I understand if this changes things. My son doesn't have a dad who is interested. I can't even get regular child maintenance payments out of him, despite threating court cases. It's messy and I can't allow anyone into my life unless they can take on Sam too.'

'I know that's heavy. But you see I am not my own free agent. Sam and I come as a pair. I promise it won't affect our friendship if you decide that this doesn't go any further. I won't judge you for that.'

'Wow.'

Joe retreated behind his cup of tea. Of all the courses their conversation could have taken, this one blindsided him. Conscious to not appear judgmental, or even unsupportive, his thoughts raced to settle on a reply. Failing, he took another sip of his drink.

'Joe…'

He put the cup back down onto the saucer. 'I wish you'd told us.'

'It might have affected how you felt.'

'I doubt that,' he said with a short laugh. 'I've liked you since you started at the bookshop. Having a child wouldn't have made a difference.'

'What are you saying, exactly? Just so we're clear.'

Joe cleared his throat, squeezing Lucie's hand. It rested tantalisingly close to his. 'I'm asking you out on a proper date. Perhaps we can have dinner next week, before the festival kicks off?'

Lucie appeared a little shocked, her eyes widening in realisation, before bestowing Joe with the freshest, most beautiful smile, he had ever had the fortune to witness.

Chapter Thirty Nine

2016

Evelyn pressed repeat, placing the phone back to her ear. The last message her mother left had been played more times than she cared to count. The anxiety that it might be deleted by accident haunted her every time she listened to her mother's recorded voice.

Months had passed since her death and many months before that pointed towards the end result with a chilling yet resolute certainty. They focused on making memories together. Aimee returned home from her gallivanting and even Ishmael pulled back on his work requirements to cherish the last few weeks of Helen's life.

Evelyn hated the thought of her father stuck in that big house on his own. He sounded lost whenever she called, as if not even sure of his voice, having for so long weaved and blended his speech and thoughts with that of his wife's. Her heart broke for him. Her heart broke for herself. Mum was gone.

Meanwhile the yawning chasm in her and Ishmael's marriage widened. All seemed fine on the surface. Few would have guessed the truth. Every weekend they hung out with friends and out would come the masks and the pretence. But when the evening was done there was no longer any closeness, no longer even the briefest of glances in each other's direction. She would head to bed, her mouth shut, swallowing the disappointments and the issues, and Ishmael would set up at the kitchen table, folders in hand, paperwork to keep him busy until the early hours.

She'd wake Monday morning, dress in silence, focus on the commute ahead, the flickering of the strip lighting in the basement office the only company. Their tiny, neat flat, previously the respite she could retreat to at the end of the working day, had become colder than her husband's distance. There was nowhere light or warm to retreat to anymore. Everything was stark, barren.

Holding back a sob, Evelyn pressed the repeat button again. This time she listened to half the message before the crushing sense of burden weighed down on her chest. This wasn't healthy, she knew. But with the world around her threatening to implode, there was little left to enjoy but precious memories. She scraped the chair backwards, cringing at the sound, and entered the living room. Maybe, where real life failed, the television would prove a welcome distraction.

*

'I didn't realise it was that bad,' Caren said, taking a bite of croissant and placing it back down onto the white napkin on the table. The café around them buzzed with patrons, who like the two women, had also emerged at the crack of dawn for the ant-like commute across the city.

'Ishmael takes his work seriously and this project has even made Adrian a bit jittery. Things will improve again, surely?'

'You're assuming there's anything left to improve upon.'

Caren raised an eyebrow at that. 'You're the last person I'd expect to be defeatist.'

'I'm trying not to be. I still love him, and I've always believed that that's enough. I'm just not sure he thinks the same way.'

Fiddling with the knotted corner of the croissant, Caren fell into silence. This was so out of character Evelyn took note.

'What?'

'I just wonder what it is you both want. It sounds as if you're living like strangers under the same roof. Do you have goals? Do you make dreams together?'

'We haven't for a while, no,' Evelyn admitted.

'Then start there. Get back on the same page. One of you has skipped ahead a couple of chapters without telling the other. Sort it out.'

Back to her pragmatic, no nonsense advice, Caren picked up the pastry and bit it into it with satisfaction.

'I'm worried we're past that stage.'

'Will it hurt to find out?'

'I guess not.'

'Then sit him down and talk. Marriage doesn't just work without the effort being put in.'

'I'm aware of that.'

'Put it into practise then.'

*

Life carried on and after those initial dark months, Evelyn sensed the pressure to set aside her grief. It was not just the loss of her mother that was the problem, but also the grief that highlighted issues in her marriage. It was no longer enough to just carry on as usual. Both she and Ishmael were miserable. The day was coming when a difficult conversation would have to take place.

They'd been drifting apart for so long, that even Caren's well-meaning advice had little impact. Caren didn't know the half of it. She saw the fun side, the social life, getting out into London and enjoying the sights together. She didn't see the evenings where Evelyn sat alone, with no one to talk to, her husband's energy and attention poured into whatever he was trying to prove this time. Be it work, a potential upcoming promotion, or their finances which he obsessed over as if hoping that telepathically his father would sense that they'd do quite well enough on their own, thank you very much.

Caren didn't feel the suppressed frustration Evelyn felt, wondering whether, and failing, to open her mouth and raise her concerns. The fight for her marriage had slid into a grey soup of routine, ignored conflict and the dying hope of reconciliation. She should have stood up from the first, when the boundaries of the relationship were established. So much had suffered under their lack of communication, under her passivity.

Months had passed since Ishmael last held her. She missed him and yet, part of her was relieved too. Released of his expectations perhaps, or maybe she'd just grown used to her own company. She found it hard to share herself these days.

Some of Caren's advice still resonated. The idea that with work and effort the marriage may stand a chance, gave Evelyn a spark of hope. The tiniest morsel that might, if she wished hard enough, might result in the rebuilding of what they once had. It was this fragment that kept her going, as she made her way home at the end of another long work day. No matter how bad things got, if the love was there, and she did still love him, then there was a chance?

Chapter Forty

2019

The opening morning of the festival was warm and bright; the sun heating the tarmac below, in between the cooling respite of scuttling clouds above. Having woken at the crack of dawn, Evelyn headed into town at seven to open up the shop and prepare. Joe would join her at eight and Ethan had promised to also come through and help with carting the endless paraphernalia they had managed to accumulate over the months of planning.

Their pitch would display the latest titles on promotional offer and the sheets of questions for the 'treasure hunt', and backed with large banners advertising the shop. A second table and chair was reserved for the two local authors giving book readings and each were to host a Q&A session. In the bookshop Lucie and Aimee could assist any customers that found their way inside aided by the treasure hunt questions.

On day two of the festival, there'd be an hour long workshop on creative writing, led by one of the authors from the day before and a first taster session of Joe's storytelling. The coffee machine, borrowed from Ethan's office, would draw the parents in, as well as the sofa he'd brought from home.

Day three planned to be the biggest of all, with the book launch party of a third author and a competition for those who'd followed Lucie's historical blog posts online, the prize being a hamper of books. Evelyn hoped all the effort would help put Taverton Tales on the map.

She peered out of the window. Bunting hung between the lampposts, spreading down the length of the street in pastel swathes. A light warm summer breeze licked the edges of the fabric triangles, lifting them in rhythm. The early morning air buzzed with the potential heat of the day. Already several shop owners manned their tables with the uniform white tablecloths piled high with products or advertising services. She felt a pang of nerves which surprised her. Up until now it had all been planning and organising. But the day was finally here. If she was to make the business a success it was important that this event went well.

She printed off a list with the titles and quantities of the books on display, checked the two floats, one for indoors, one for sales in the street, and collected up jiffy bags full of free promotional bookmarks and leaflets. A knock at the door drew her attention. Joe hopped from foot to foot, hands deep in his pockets, waiting to be let in.

'Thanks,' he said as she opened the door. 'Gosh, this is all a bit exciting, isn't it?'

She smiled fondly.

'I'll get on with setting up the table outside. Then I can start on the coffee machine.'

Despite Joe not being a coffee drinker, and indeed even hating the smell, he had proved the only one able to deal with the temperamental machine. The previous afternoon Evelyn, Aimee and Joe had all struggled to get it working. An urgent call to Ethan hadn't thrown any light on their troubleshooting. His secretary switched the machine on when she started for the day but she was on her summer leave.

Finally Joe got the knack, and set out discovering the perfect volume and strength of the coffee grounds. This was a massive relief to them all, after Evelyn's earlier attempts had tasted more like muddy bath water than aromatic, emotion-inducing heaven in a mug.

'Can you manage the boxes?'

They were stacked full of books, ready for the outside display.

'Sure,' he said with a shrug.

'Just don't hurt yourself, they're heavy.' Evelyn called back, already crossing the shop, her mind on the endless to-do list that would swamp the next few hours. 'Aimee and Lucie should be here in an hour. Let's get done what we can before there are too many cooks.'

*

The picturesque main street, festooned with bunting and decorated with the attractive shop fronts and colourful plasterwork of the timber framed buildings, created a riot of colour that lent itself nicely to the festivities.

A stage further up the street, placed in front of the sage green double doors of the town hall, was being utilised by local singers and dance groups. Taverton's two art galleries were running outdoor art workshops. Even the hardware shop joined in with a wood smith demonstrating simple DIY projects, using local wood and materials, and of course the shop's own range of tools.

Small groups gathered periodically around the bookshop's table, eager to get their hands on free bookmarks or on a sheet of questions for the treasure hunt. The form for the book hamper competition was filling up quickly, much to Evelyn's satisfaction. The first author had already completed their book reading and was now signing copies inside the bookshop. Evelyn hoped Aimee and Lucie were making steady sales. It was proving a little sporadic outside, with so many distractions from nearby pitches drawing potential customers past.

Taking a quick break, Evelyn dashed across the street to the bakery's pitch, which stood parallel to theirs. The cake stands were filled with delicate custard tarts, millionaire's shortbread, almond croissants, and mouth-watering cheese straws, icing dusted doughnuts and a few local specialities, such as the Suffolk harvest cake sliced into wedge sized segments and laden with invocative spices.

Evelyn chose five pastries and watched with growing hunger as they were placed inside a large white paper bag, rustling as the corners twisted over. She let Joe have first choice and then took the remaining pastries into Aimee and Lucie. Ethan had left for work after helping them set up, so Evelyn tucked the bag containing the last cake into her handbag after withdrawing her own. She returned to Joe and they ate, grinning, as they observed the fun around them.

*

'That will be £18.98 then please,' Aimee asked, placing two books into the customer's reusable tote bag and chucking in a couple of freebie bookmarks on top.

The attractive middle aged woman, wearing a cobalt blue scarf which induced her dark eyes to sparkle like the night sky, tapped her card against the screen surface. 'This is a lovely place,' she mused, awaiting the receipt.

213

'Thank you. My sister owns it.'

'We've just moved into a cottage on the outskirts. It's amazing to have an independent bookshop nearby. They seem to be rarer these days.'

'I'll let my sister know. She'll be so pleased to hear you like the place.' Aimee handed the receipt over, giving Lucie a surreptitious nod of satisfaction. It wasn't the first compliment they'd heard this morning.

It hadn't taken a lot to connect the dots and realise just how much Evelyn wanted this festival, and the business itself, to be a success. Aimee wanted her sister to do well. This shop was her dream and even Aimee understood that the drive behind the business is what gave Evelyn focus and hope. She'd noticed that during her work training the week before. Her sister's synergy and deep connection with the shop was obvious. Evelyn knew the place inside out.

Over cocoa the night before, Evelyn had opened up; a rare occasion in itself, claiming that Joe was a better, more natural, boss that she could ever be. It surprised Aimee, because that was not what she had witnessed. Evelyn lived and breathed the place and what's more, she was good at her job.

Feeling a spark of pride for her sister, Aimee took a sheet of paper from behind the till and jotted down the customer's compliments while she still remembered them. Placing the list next to the till she peered out across the shop to the colours, noise and festivities visible through the window.

It was then that she saw a familiar figure. And it was then that she gasped out loud.

*

'They're selling candy floss near the town hall,' a girl of about fourteen told Evelyn and Joe. Her mouth was full of the sugary mixture and she treated them to a bright pink, crystallising grin, transforming her back into the child-like persona she had only recently grown out of.

'Great. Do you want to buy a book?' Joe asked with enthusiasm, never one to miss a selling opportunity. 'We have some great teen fiction and Young Adult titles.'

Evelyn left him to it, shifting her attention to the full competition form. She replaced it with an empty sheet. The next author was due to start in an hour and she regretted not having the foresight to secure a third author to fill the gap. She hadn't wanted to overbook and risk being too busy to focus on sales, but now there was a lull with fewer people congregating around the table, and as a result fewer books heading off to new homes.

She considered visiting the shop and seeing how the others were getting on. The young girl didn't seem interested in parting with any more of her pocket money, and not even Joe's friendly demeanour and easy conversation would change that.

A shadow passed across the table, catching Evelyn's attention.

'Are the sales going well?'

With a visceral tugging of her heart she grabbed onto the table for support. That voice. That tone. For the briefest second, but one that felt like the longest of pauses, she couldn't bear to make eye contact. Her head seemed jammed at its angle, heavy as if sodden as a sponge, almost impossible to move. Time slowed. Memories rushed like a torrent. She sensed, if not saw, Joe's curiosity and the thought made her hysterical, bubbles of laughter threatening to burst forth if she failed to keep them under control.

With deliberate, measured movements she raised her eye line. Her gaze fell on the light brown skin, skin that had once anchored with hers. Skin that she had held and kissed and dreamt of in years past.

And here he was, in her tiny corner of the countryside, miles from the city where it had all fallen apart, where their relationship had gone to die. Here in her place of sanctuary stood the man, that even after a marital separation and the sale of their flat and the divisions of the profit, she now saw as clear as a tranquil stream that she wasn't over. It wasn't over.

All the hurt, all the fear, all the years of allowing themselves to fail and now she realised she didn't want to. She didn't want them to die.

His crooked smile was filled with uncertainty. The sun in her eyes made it hard to see more of his expression, but the shape of him was there in strong silhouette before her. A shape that was so familiar. Gulping down at the knot forming in her chest, Evelyn tried to focus.

'What are you doing here?' It hurt her throat to say the words, her voice choked and unrecognisable to her own ears.

Ishmael stepped to his right, the action casting light into the shadow that had prevented her seeing him clearly. Stubble decorated his chin, something in itself so rare for his character, and his eyes darted across the contents of the table, back to Evelyn, briefly at Joe, before locking in on her again.

'I know I should have called first, but I thought this would be better in person.'

'What would be better?' she asked, the nerves plummeting through her stomach. 'And yes, you should have called. As you can see we're in the middle of a festival.' A flash of anger punctuated her anxiety at having been taken unawares.

'I'm sorry, I thought being a Friday things would be quieter than the weekend and I had some leave to take. Can you spare an hour?'

'No, I cannot.'

Ishmael rubbed the stubble with his forefinger and gave a surreptitious squint towards Joe. 'Please Evelyn,' he pleaded. 'Couldn't your friend man the table for a while?'

'We have an author about to arrive,' she said, desperate to delay. 'They'll expect me to be here to greet them.'

'Then I'll wait.'

Ishmael stood back, planting his feet on the tarmac below, as if planning to stand in front of the table for as long as it took. His white checked shirt flapped in the breeze as he gazed around at the activity in the street. He put his hands in the pocket of his khaki trousers.

'I can manage, if you want to… you know,' Joe whispered. She appreciated his loyalty. He didn't want to speak louder in case she didn't want to go with the figure standing in front of them.

'I'm going to have to, aren't I? He's come all the way here after all.'

She was annoyed, irritated and shaken by Ishmael's presence. Anxiety trickled through her at the realisation of why he could be here.

'You can wait at the house,' she blurted. 'I'll be along when I can. The place is empty, except for Randall.'

'Are you sure?'

'Yes, it is fine,' she said, feeling that it was anything but. 'You remember how to get there?'

Ishmael nodded.

'Then I'll get you a key.'

Evelyn left her post, forcing herself to not glance over her shoulder at her estranged husband. She felt drunk, aware of every footstep, and had to concentrate on walking in a straight line. Raucous laughter rang out to her left, jarring with the turmoil of her emotions. A small child skipped by, holding on to his mother's hand, their chatter sounding blurred as if a long way away. The bunting flapped aggressively over her head as Evelyn reached the path and entered the open shop doorway, the instant quiet submerging her.

There were a few customers browsing inside and Evelyn passed them, catching Aimee's eye on the way. The shock on Aimee's face proved that Ishmael's sudden arrival hadn't gone unnoticed.

'Can I have your key for a bit?' Evelyn asked in hushed tones.

'Why?'

'He's going to wait for me at the house. Please don't ask me what he wants.'

'Right, I'll go get it then.'

Evelyn straightened the display books. It was therapeutic. The metallic ting of a key ring alerted her to Aimee's return. She took it, her fingers shaking slightly.

'I'm going to settle the next author, then Joe will bring him in for the signing afterwards, so Lucie can swap and man the outdoor table for a while. Depending on how busy it is, Joe will let you know where you need to be.'

'Evelyn,' Aimee said, placing a hand on Evelyn's retreating arm. 'I know we don't always get along, but we do have something in common. We both know men. And we both know how they can hurt us. If you want to crack open a bottle later either to commiserate or to celebrate, then let me know and I'll pick one up.'

'Thanks, but I don't want to jump ahead of myself just yet. I have a feeling this afternoon is going to be the longest of my life.'

Chapter Forty One

'You found everything okay?'

Ishmael held his mug up and nodded. 'I needed the caffeine boost. I set off early this morning to get here.'

She moved further into the kitchen, her fingers trembling as she clasped them in front of her, too anxious to make eye contact with the figure sitting at her kitchen table. He looked good. The stubble enhanced his dark features. She was unsettled enough, without the bolt of attraction on top.

'You sound like a man on a mission,' she laughed, nervous.

'The train took nearly two hours, without the commute either side. I had to get a taxi. You're not easy to get to.'

'That's what I like about the place,' she replied, putting the kettle back on to boil. 'Other than the fact I grew up here of course. It's like another world compared to London.'

'Was your life with me there so bad?'

Her eyes widened. 'Is that what you thought, that I hated being there with you?'

'No Evelyn, I'm not saying that. But we both know London was my plan.' He carried his empty mug to the sink and gave it a wash with the dishcloth. He placed it upside down on the drainer and stepped back, lengthening their distance. Every movement seemed slow and deliberate.

'I followed you willingly.'

'I'm grateful for that.'

'Did you…' Evelyn paused. She was uncertain she wanted to bring up the topic that had caused their last argument, the argument that led to their separation and the division of their life together. 'I have to know. Did you ever consider what I wanted? Did you ever consider my dreams?'

His eyes flashed and she knew he was remembering that last night. She'd said things she regretted. She'd hurt him. The fire in his eyes flickered out, as he hunched over and clasped the back of a kitchen chair with both hands. His closed fists paled with tension.

'We've had this conversation before. You felt disregarded and not listened to. My need to prove a point to my father blinded me to your unhappiness. Isn't that about right?'

'I did sometimes feel like that. I kept it in so long, that when it came out, it came out all wrong.'

'You shouldn't have brought my family into it.'

'And why not?' she said with a laugh of indignation. 'It drove you to excel at work, and it drove you to London to prove you could do it all by yourself. Those are facts Ishmael, you've said so yourself. I just didn't understand why you needed to bring me with you…'

'Because I loved you, Evelyn!' he exclaimed. 'Why else?'

'Perhaps I was only part of the point you were trying to make.'

It was the crux of all the self-doubt she'd accumulated over their relationship, and if she couldn't say it now, when could she?

He stared at her, stunned. 'Do you honestly believe I would have taken you to London and married you if it had just been some exercise to stick a finger up at my parents? I thought you knew me better than that.'

Her eyes swam with tears and tried to compose herself. During their last fight she'd failed to properly express her concerns, fleeing instead to Caren and Adrian's with a small overnight bag. Many weeks later, after the sale of their flat, she fled London for good. She'd messed it up back then, insulting Ishmael instead of explaining herself. She didn't know his reason for being here, whether he had divorce papers or whether he wanted to give their marriage another chance, but she knew her words might affect the outcome. She willed herself to speak carefully.

'Ishmael, I don't doubt you loved me. But our marriage became all about your work. It was all about succeeding. You resented the flat because of your father's contribution and it was obvious you hated living there. Towards the end we only ever communicated if we were entertaining friends. You remember how we would fall into silence as soon as they left? I never said anything and I should have done. But we both went silent on each other. We ignored the problems.'

'But that was in London,' Ishmael pointed out. 'What about before? You thought I invited you there on false pretences? If you thought that, then why didn't you just end it?'

'I didn't think you invited me there on false pretences! I told you I was willing. I loved you and I wanted to believe you loved me too.'

'But you had doubts, even back then?' he asked, his jaw tightening in anger. His shoulders hunched, his frame broken and defeated.

Evelyn emitted an abrupt sob. The kettle roared behind her, but not enough to muffle the sound of her sorrow.

'There were nights where you came to bed, after hours working at the kitchen table, and you wouldn't even make eye contact with me. I would sit in bed with a book and you'd just ignore me. Ishmael, I didn't stay up late to read, I stayed up to try and connect with you.'

He faced her, pain across his features. 'I never knew that. I didn't want to disturb your reading.' This was followed with a hollow, mirthless laugh. 'I worked hard so we could buy a bigger place, so we could have a family. And yes, Evelyn, I admit I wanted to prove myself worthy. I wanted to prove to my father that I could control my own life. But you were never a point. You were my first independent decision and I was proud of that. I was proud of us.'

Ignoring the kettle and the empty mug, Evelyn slumped onto a chair. How had it all got so tangled, so confused?

'I was hasty to suggest we move to London. I should have considered you more. I'm sorry you felt you had to run after me. I can't excuse it, other than I was twenty-two years old and thought I knew everything.'

'I'm sorry I ignored what was happening between us and didn't tell you how I was feeling,' she said, brokenly.

Having reached an impasse, Ishmael poured her drink, placing it in front of her and joining her at the table.

'I should have let you know I was coming.'

'It's not the first time is it?' She asked, taking a small sip from her mug. 'I saw you before, back in May.'

'Adrian told me you knew.'

'He didn't tell me why you were here though.'

Ishmael leaned forward, his hands clasped together across the table. She could see the tension in his forearms.

'I needed to know.' He peered around the kitchen, distracted. 'I remember this place well,' he added, with a wistful note.

'What did you need to know?' Evelyn drew a deep, steady breath. It was all she could do to keep her emotions in check.

He closed his eyes briefly. 'I needed to know that I was making the right decision. I needed to know whether there was still something there, something between us.'

'And, what is your conclusion?' Her voice came out as a wobble.

He touched her hand with his for the shortest moment, before the physical chasm returned between them. She waited.

'I want a divorce, Evelyn.'

Shock waves went through her entire body. The reaction was primitive, a combination of her thought process shutting down, her emotions twisted and frayed and raw. Her eyesight blurred with salty tears. She knew it was coming, she'd helped instigate it two years before, yet the hope, oh how the hope had kept her buoyant. Now she felt she was drowning.

'It's been almost two years.' He spoke fast. 'We've had a chance to build our own lives now. Seeing you here in your home town just confirmed it. You're happy here. Happier than you ever were with me.'

'That's not true,' she managed to choke. 'I loved you.'

'I loved you too, but in May when I saw you in the street, you were so relaxed and happy. You glowed. I hadn't seen you glow like that in years.'

'You make it sound like we were never happy. We were. We had lots of happy times.'

'Yes, but they didn't stay happy. And we never did enough to put it right.'

'I would have been willing to try again,' she said, her voice small.

He pulled back, surprised. He stared at her for a moment, deep longing flashing through his eyes for the briefest of seconds.

'I have a girlfriend,' he admitted gruffly, withdrawing his gaze. 'You and I need a clean break Evelyn. There's been enough time to talk this through, to work things out if we'd wanted. We've had two years. Neither of us made that step.'

The truth in his words hit her. They'd had their chance. What had she expected after all this time? Had running back to Suffolk cost her, or had it been the proof needed that the marriage was over? Was it only the distance, the memories of their years together that kept her believing they could overcome their issues, or had it all been a silly fantasy, spurred on in her quieter moments in the shop while daydreaming out of the window and watching life pass by?

Drained by the situation, she wanted to crawl under her bed covers and cry into the silence and darkness until sleep overtook her. But an entire conversation was stretched before them, the most important conversation of their lives, and she had no choice but to push through the swamp of her emotions and face up to the reality of the mess they'd both made.

Chapter Forty Two

'Evelyn? Are you awake?' Ethan's voice sounded muffled against the wooden door.

The hour was late, the house cast with twilight shadows, light from downstairs reaching the lower inches of the landing carpet. Evelyn's door had remained shut throughout the evening, despite the enticing scent of Aimee's famous Thai Green curry and the hushed voices discussing the events of the afternoon.

'Darling, I just want to make sure you are okay.'

He heard an indistinct noise from within the bedroom and knocked. 'Evelyn?'

Heavy footfalls padded across the carpet on the other side of the door. He stood back as it creaked open. Evelyn, wisps of tear-stained hair pasted to her face, her eyes tired and burdened, appeared before him. The cerulean-blue summer dress she wore was crumpled from lying down. Beyond her the room was dark, the curtain pulled across the window but not meeting in the middle.

'I've had a rough day.'

'So I heard. Aimee told me that Ishmael showed up. I can't imagine how hard today has been for you.'

'So you saw what was coming then? Have I been so blind?'

'I think you knew Evelyn. There's a difference between knowledge and acceptance. That's something I'm learning myself.'

He saw the pain stretched across her brow, the heaviness of the realisation that she could no longer hide from the truth.

'Aimee mentioned you didn't go back to the festival. Was Ishmael here for long?'

'No. He only stayed an hour. I couldn't face going back to the shop. What kind of boss does that make me?' She laughed, mirthless.

'Joe managed. They all said it went well.'

'Good. Daddy…' she began to speak then threw her hand over her mouth. Alarmed she pushed past him and ran for the bathroom.

He followed a few moments behind as soon as the retching ceased. She knelt on the lino, arm draped over the toilet seat. Tears streamed down her face.

'He doesn't want me anymore,' she said with a hiccup, her voice barely audible above the rim of the toilet bowl.

Ethan reached down and stroked her hair, a soothing technique he used to employ when she was a child. It was unlike Evelyn to display such vulnerability, to admit that despite her new found independence, she still hurt with the realisation that her husband no longer wanted her. It was a painful, crushing realisation and he knew few words would be sufficient to console her.

She wept, drawing back from the toilet, raising her knees toward her chest, leaning against the bath. Ethan sat down too and drew her closer. Kissing her forehead, he let her grieve.

Much later, with the sound of the television blaring from the living room below, the darkened sky reduced the lamplight downstairs to little more than pin pricks. The shadows in the bathroom were silent and brooding. Ethan eased himself to his feet, laying Evelyn to the side. She'd fallen asleep on his shoulder.

'Sweetheart,' he whispered. 'Let's get you to bed.'

She moaned, allowing him to lift her into a standing position. Leading her to the bedroom, he steadied her as they crossed the top of the stairs. The bed covers were still drawn back and she slid between them and the tear-stained sheet.

'Night, honey,' he said, drawing the door closed until he heard the minute click of the lock.

*

'We're going to have to manage without Evelyn today,' Joe said, as Lucie popped her head through the door.

'Can we?'

'If it's as busy as yesterday, then we should be fine.'

'But today is Saturday. It'll be the biggest day of the festival.'

Joe looked beleaguered for a second. 'We'll have to muddle along. Aimee will arrive in an hour.'

'So it's just us for a bit?' Lucie asked, feigning innocence.

Joe blushed. Their dinner out the previous week had gone well, but they'd decided to wait until after the festival to go out again. The memory of his chaste goodnight kiss on her cheek lingered, the memory of it as powerful as if they'd had a proper embrace.

'It'll be busy, I'm afraid. We have a lot to set up.'

'Oh,' Lucie replied, a little disappointed. 'Well is it okay if I…'

'If you what?'

'Just this,' she said, her smile growing closer in his vision, before she carefully planted her lips on his for the briefest of moments.

She pulled away. 'Sorry. I've just wanted to do that since our first date.'

'Don't apologise,' he said with a grateful laugh. They stood, a little uncertain, a little embarrassed, both thrilled.

'Shall I pop the kettle on?' He asked after a long pause.

She beamed.

*

'How's Evelyn?' Lucie asked.

Aimee shoved her bag into the office and shut the door. She shrugged. 'I haven't seen her. She didn't come down for tea or breakfast. Dad said he spoke to her last night. He didn't seem to get much out of her. Not anything he was willing to share at least.'

'I hope she's okay. I can't imagine what I'd feel if my ex just turned up in public with no warning.'

'Why? What did he do?'

'Nothing much,' Lucie said, in haste.

'It was that bad, was it?' Aimee asked, with a mischievous glint.

Joe entered the shop. The table outside was set up and waiting. A few curious members of the public already milled around and he didn't want to miss out on the chance of an early sale.

'I'll be out here for a while. We'll swap a bit later, once we know how busy it's going to get.'

'Dad said he can come and help if it's needed,' Aimee offered.

'Great. I think we're going to need all the extra hands we can get.' An expression of trepidation flickered across his brow and he retreated back to the stall.

'Ishmael's timing was utterly brilliant,' Aimee said, scoffing. 'Of all the days to pitch up, he chose the biggest local event of the year.'

Lucie nodded. 'We've got the creative writing workshop in here this morning. Annie, the author, should know what to do without too much handholding from us. Joe will be doing his storytelling session this afternoon. Your dad can slot in around all that. I might need to assist Joe. We don't know how many little ones to expect.'

'That sounds terrifying. Rather you than me. I'm sure Dad and I can manage outside for a bit. He used to do markets with Mum when she went through a ceramics phase. You and Joe seem quite close,' Aimee observed.

'Do we?' Lucie turned her face away to hide the blush to her cheeks.

Saved by the arrival of an elderly couple, Lucie grabbed their attention, grateful at the distraction. 'Yes, how can I help?'

*

'Just tell me where to stand and what to do,' Ethan said. His voice was almost inaudible above the chatter of the busy street. 'You'll remember that I did the odd shift to help Evelyn out in the beginning. I'm sure it'll come back to me quickly.'

'Well, let's keep you outside with me,' Joe answered. 'The workshop is about to start indoors, and to be honest, it is quite busy out here.'

'I can see. This is a great footfall. There have been some pretty dismal years in the past. Some years the festival's been rained out. I'm glad they extended it to the arts this year, it's made a massive difference.'

'It's impossible to tell for sure, not until we've sat down and worked it out, but I reckon we've sold three times as many books than a normal Saturday morning.'

'Evelyn will be thrilled to hear that.'

'How's she doing?'

Ethan exhaled and pushed his hands into his pockets. 'I saw her before I left. She doesn't appear to have slept much. She didn't say a lot either.'

'I don't want to pry.'

'It's Evelyn's story to tell. But you can probably gather that the man was Ishmael. Her husband,' he clarified.

'I guessed it was. Are they…?'

'They've been separated a long time, but as I said, it's Evelyn's story to explain, not mine. She considers you a friend Joe, not just a colleague,' he added, sizing up the younger man. 'Perhaps it would help to have someone in Taverton she can open up to.'

He left the hint hanging in the air, and dropped his gaze, sweeping the contents of the table. 'Right, fill me in on what I need to know.'

*

'How many of you here like rabbits?' Joe asked a chorus of noisy small people. Sifting through the cacophony of exclamations, he nodded. 'That's right! We all do. Now the story I am going to read is about a family of rabbits. Are you ready to hear it?'

Another loud burst of confirmation filled the air and Joe took his seat in front of the dozen or so children. They all stared up at him, wonder on their faces as he showed them the cover of the book.

'Come on!' one child called out, and they all laughed, including Joe.

'Thank you for that. And with no further ado, let's dive in.'

Lucie stood behind the till. She couldn't ignore the stirrings of hope as she watched him, someone she'd always assumed to be endearingly socially awkward, react with confidence towards his young audience. Would it be too much to imagine that he might respond well to her son? Was it too soon to even think like that?

A ripple of delighted laughter emanated from the packed carpet. Parents sat on or around the sofa, some with coffee cups in hand. No one had approached the till yet, that would come at the end of the story time, so Lucie relaxed a little. There hadn't been time to stop all day. She laughed along with the children as Joe adopted the gruff voice of the father rabbit. He was a natural storyteller.

'He's good isn't he?'

Lucie put her hand to her chest in fright. 'Evelyn!'

'You're all so engrossed you didn't even notice me come in.'

'But, why are you here? None of us expected you.'

The dark, swollen eyes of a tearful sleepless night were evident, despite the attempt to cover up with makeup. Evelyn's hair was held up in a simple, wavy, yet erratic ponytail. She wore a black t-shirt and matching trousers. She usually wore smarter clothing to work and favoured blue. It appeared to Lucie as if she'd thrown on the first thing she'd found. Either that or the effort to dress up had been too much.

'I need to be here. It's my business. Although today has shown me that this is a family effort. You've all been brilliant. But, I don't expect you all to cover for my personal problems. You've done enough of that lately. I should have dragged myself out earlier.'

'We understand.'

'Thanks,' Evelyn squeezed her arm in gratitude. 'But I still should have been here. This is my responsibility. You'd think someone had died, for crying out loud. Listen, I need to go and speak with my dad and Aimee. Can I have just five more minutes?'

Lucie nodded.

'You're a star. So is Joe. I'm sure you agree,' she added with the tiniest, painful, concession of their emerging relationship, leaving Lucie to blush for the second time that day.

*

'This may be too soon,' Ethan warned.

'My alternative is to sit at home with a cat who hates me.'

'Why don't you go to your office? Start tallying up the sales from yesterday. It'll give you a distraction and you won't have to deal with members of the public.'

'Stop trying to protect me. Besides the worst has already happened,' she reduced her voice to a whisper, as a customer stepped up to the stall. 'When the storytelling hour is finished, we won't need another pair of hands anyway. Joe can be back on the stall with me and you'll be free to go.'

'Not one of us minds if you take the day off, Evelyn.'

'That's not true. One of us minds very much.'

'I wasn't including you.'

'Well, I was.'

Ethan recognised the stubborn expression on his eldest daughter's face. 'You're only human, remember that.'

He took a proffered book from the customer and gave him his change. Evelyn turned to Aimee, who was being uncharacteristically quiet. 'You can join Lucie when Dad has gone. It's good for me to be here. At least, I'd rather be here than back home on my own.'

'Call me if you change your mind. I have no other plans this weekend. I can come back.'

'Thanks Dad, but I think that right here, right now, is exactly where I am meant to be. As much as that might hurt, I cannot shake off the feeling that with my business, I've got something very right for once.'

Chapter Forty Three

Ethan visits every day. I like his visits, but I am not stupid; the silk flowers, the gentle smiles, the way he kindly avoids the subject of Laurence as if knowing that the conversation might break me. I am convinced that he likes me.

I cannot imagine ever wanting to fall in love with anyone again. It is too painful. But Ethan's friendship is welcome. Caroline has gone away for work. Ethan is studying at university, but he comes home most weekends. And he always pops in to see me.

I am bored of being at home and I think he realises that. My other friends are busy with work, or with studying and don't visit often. I spend a lot of time thinking about how I almost threw my future away for Laurence, and almost had it taken again by the accident. In one foul swoop, it was almost lost to me twice.

It has been a huge relief to find out that I can go to college next year. Because of my injuries my place has been deferred until September. When the letter arrived with confirmation, I cried. In a strange, confusing way the car accident has been a blessing. Had Laurence and I gone away I would not be able to start my teaching degree. My time convalescing has reminded me how much I do wish to teach. I now cannot believe I would have been happy to leave my world and run away with Laurence. It aches to admit that. But the sheen of lust has peeled away. He has made no attempt to contact me. There has been no communication at all. Those niggling doubts that I liked him more than he liked me strengthen with each passing week. He would have been in contact if he loved me.

His family have put their house up for sale, and the rumours are that they don't even live there anymore. According to Ethan the place seems vacant.

I still love Laurence. I still miss him. But I was a summer romance. I know that now. Perhaps he wasn't aware of it himself – after all, we had planned to run

231

away together. But our romance is now consigned to the memories of hot sunny days, salty sea air and the strong arms which embraced me.

I guess some memories are best left in the past. Left behind where they belong, where they help mould my character and my understanding of the world. I am now planning ahead. I have a second chance and that won't go to waste. I won't let it.

Chapter Forty Four

'We should go away on holiday together,' Aimee said. She shovelled a generous spoonful of egg fried rice onto her plate from the takeaway container.

'But, of course. The solution to everything,' Evelyn replied, her tone sardonic. Her own plate was still empty and her stomach grumbled in agitation. She picked up a serving spoon, nudging Aimee over to reach the chicken noodles.

'I'm about to move to the other side of the world. This may be our last opportunity to get away and have some fun.'

'I thought you were saving all your money for New Zealand.'

'We could get a cheap last minute deal. We only need a place to crash at night. It doesn't have to be a fancy hotel. You have some leave coming up right? You need a holiday after the weekend you've just had.'

Evelyn finished dishing up and grabbed her glass of white wine off the counter.

'We don't get on most of the time. Why on earth would we go on holiday together?'

'We get on well enough when we want to,' Aimee replied sagely.

'Save some for Dad.' Evelyn nodded at the Chinese takeaway as Aimee dug in for another large scoop of sweet and sour pork. 'He said he'd be five minutes.'

Ethan had been waylaid by their neighbour Gordon, who was keen to set up a regular cards night. He'd remained on the driveway chatting, as Evelyn and Aimee transported the takeaway into the house. They'd all chipped in. None of them felt up to cooking. The festival was finished, Sunday proving even busier than Saturday. They were all worn out, including Ethan who'd helped pack away.

'Have a think about the holiday. But don't think for too long, I want to start searching.'

Aimee had an excitable glint in her eye and Evelyn laughed. Her sister, about to head out into the world and take responsibility, would never completely grow up. She realised that despite their differences she would miss her. Perhaps a holiday together wasn't a ridiculous suggestion after all.

They'd make new memories, try to forget old unfavourable ones, and drink to the future. With the divorce papers weeks from arriving and the painful void left by seeing Ishmael that last time, Evelyn needed a dose of fun. Aimee was the last person she'd imagine having a holiday with, but with a season of crossroads and changes, perhaps it was time to start carving out a new direction and a fresh way of doing things.

'I have to phone Caren tonight. She'll want to know what's going on with Ishmael. But we can start to plan tomorrow evening.'

'So, that's a yes then?'

'Yes, it's a yes,' Evelyn confirmed with an enormous gulp of wine.

*

The garden was cast in a golden hue as the sun lowered toward the horizon. Collared doves cooed in their roosting spots in the trees and the leaves rustled in harmony. Beyond the fence the harvested wheat fields smelled of scorched earth. A gentle breeze stirred the dust beneath where the crop had once grown. The meadow in the distance enticed with licks of yellow, amber and scarlet wild grasses, visible even from where Ethan and Evelyn were sitting. It was all Evelyn could do not to jump up and follow the trail, to where she knew peace, nature and beauty melded together in synergy. She remembered her walk there in June, where she'd felt crumpled, broken, and where she'd prayed.

She didn't feel dissimilar now, but after an hour on the phone to Caren, who'd cut short the call because her eldest started vomiting, she still had the urge for company and distraction.

'Do you think we'll see Aimee again this evening?' Ethan broke the silence with a joke. 'That was a rhetorical question, by the way.'

Aimee was on a video chat with Liam and had been since her last mouthful of takeaway food. Previous experience suggested that they wouldn't see her again until the next morning.

'Probably not,' Evelyn said, pulling her cardigan tighter around her and snuggling deeper into the deck chair.

'And Caren knows everything now? It must be reassuring to have her to chat to.'

'You make me sound like a loner.'

'We've both had our moments there,' he said. 'It's time we allowed life to continue, and not just for everyone else, but for ourselves too. We both need to get back out there.'

'I hope you're referring to seeing friends and not dating again,' she exclaimed, frowning as she watched the rabbits in the field chasing each other. 'I'm not ready for anything like that.'

'I did. I think you'd be more than entitled to wait for the ink to dry on your divorce papers before thinking about dating.'

'What about you? It's been over three years.'

'I fell in love with your mother when I was seventeen. I have only loved one woman my entire adult life. That's a hard act to follow.'

'Seventeen… I thought you got together in your early twenties?'

'We had a few obstacles to overcome first.'

'That sounds mysterious.'

'Not really.' He raised a half empty bottle of beer to his lips. 'She was in a serious relationship before me. In fact it wasn't even that serious… more all-consuming.'

'Isn't that one and same?'

'She was all-consumed by him. It turned out the feeling wasn't mutual.'

'Oh. Was she hurt?'

'Very. I had to be patient and wait. She needed to work her life out first. I…' he paused, glancing in Evelyn's direction. 'I found some pages of her journal when I started sorting through her belongings. There was always a small part of me that wondered…. I know she loved me, I never doubted that. But he was like a sports model, whereas I was always a safe and comfortable family car in comparison. Ironic considering….'

'Why is that ironic?' Evelyn leaned towards him, her face cast into shadow as twilight approached their peaceful spot.

'There's no reason you shouldn't know. Your mother had a car accident. The boyfriend was driving. He always drove like a demon through these streets. She…. Evelyn, I don't want you to see your mother in a bad light. She was eighteen then and well, if you ever wondered where Aimee got her liveliness from, be confused no more.

Helen was spontaneous and at times stubborn. The accident made her grow up and she changed a lot.'

'The truth was she was running away with him. She thought he was everything and she couldn't see sense. We all tried to talk her round. It took a near death experience to learn a painful lesson.'

Evelyn's eyes widened. 'It was that bad?'

'Yes, she spent ten weeks in hospital. She needed physiotherapy to help her walk again.'

'I never knew....'

'It wasn't a huge secret. It just wasn't part of her life anymore. Laurence Scott and his damn car and empty promises were in the past. She wanted them to stay there.'

'But doesn't that give you your answer? He wasn't as important as you became to her.'

'She stopped writing her journal before we got together. Or at least I can't find evidence of any other journals. Until I read them I never understood how deep her love was for him. It shocked me, in all honestly.'

'Dad,' Evelyn said in exasperation. 'Perhaps her journals were just an idealistic lie. Just fantasy and teenage hormones mixed together. The actual reality was you, and she lived it. She didn't need to write about it. She loved you, Daddy. I have no doubt of that. As a child, you two were my heroes. I couldn't wait to grow up and have a relationship like yours. There was nothing fake about it. It was genuine through and through.'

'Thank you.' Ethan's voice was hoarse. They sat in companionable silence for a while.

'Evelyn,' he said, reaching out to squeeze her hand. 'I am so very sorry about you and Ishmael. I liked him. So did Helen. We hoped very much you would be happy together.'

'But you knew we wouldn't?' she injected, voice cracking.

'No,' he paused, his brow crinkled in confusion. 'We didn't know anything of the sort. We knew that you loved each other. We saw the potential.'

'But....'

'Oh my darling,' he sighed. 'I think that maybe Ishmael was so busy trying to control his own life that he ended up controlling yours too. We hoped you'd both see the signs before it was too late and act upon them. I am very sorry that didn't happen.'

She sank back into the chair, diverting her attention to the gentle glow of dappled sunshine across the field. It was a good reminder that despite all the mistakes, all the issues that humans endeavoured to overcome, nature carried on regardless. There was peace on her very doorstep. And this was home, at least for now. No matter how well the bookshop had done at the festival, it would be a while before she could afford her own place. But she would get there, she reasoned.

Ethan was right. It was time. She could now plan ahead. And while the future would be different to what she'd imagined, at least now she knew. That would have to be enough.

Chapter Forty Five

Joe admired the way the light from the window highlighted Lucie's cheekbones and added golden sparkles to her blonde hair. She leant over the desk, tracing a finger along her scrawled notes as she typed her latest review into the computer browser with her other hand, oblivious to his examination.

The shop was empty after a late morning surge and Joe enjoyed these quieter moments. Even though they weren't talking and all Lucie's concentration was on her task, it was still time together, just the two of them.

Going out for dinner had progressed to walks in the evening and takeaway coffees. Despite the short commute home, they always managed to find a way to dawdle. And with Evelyn away on holiday Joe and Lucie had worked together every day for the entire week. It had bonded them.

She finished typing the last few letters and with a flourish pressed the enter key. 'There,' she said, satisfaction brightening her whole face.

I love this woman, he thought.

It was such a sudden and unexpected realisation that for a while he just grinned inanely as she regaled a summary of the review she'd just typed.

'Would you like a cup of tea?' she asked in conclusion, the question going unheard in between the muddle of Joe's thoughts.

'Would you like a cup of tea?' she repeated, louder this time.

He jumped. 'Yes. Yes, please.'

She laughed. 'What's on your mind?'

He reached a hand to the crown of his head and scratched self-consciously. How did he answer that one? Stepping up to the desk, Joe uploaded the finished copy while the question lay unanswered and heavy in the air. Lucie shrugged and filled the kettle in the kitchenette. She brought the steaming mugs back into the shop a few minutes later.

He took his drink and waved a polite goodbye to the solitary customer he had just served. They'd bought a large Encyclopaedia of the area after viewing Evelyn's display of local history and reference books. She was keen to make it a regular feature; yet another method to diversify and make the bookshop stand out from other competition.

'I was thinking the other day, after our walk through the fields, about how...' Lucie said, pausing.

'Yes?'

'Sam is a very important part of my life. And now you are also becoming an important part. And I am very aware that this is all very new and I would not want you to do anything you are not ready for yet.'

'Ready for what, exactly?'

Lucie seemed frightened and he wanted to reassure her. He just wasn't sure how.

'I come with responsibilities. Some might say I come with baggage. A lot of men wouldn't want to take that on... and I am not saying you have to,' she added with gusto, as if pre-empting any accusation of searching for an easy father figure. 'Sam is my responsibility, not yours. I just need to know, if and when, you might be ready to meet him.'

The bell above the door rang out before Joe could answer and Lucie grimaced at the interruption.

'We'll talk later,' he whispered. 'The bookshop isn't always the quietest place for a serious conversation.' He gave her arm a squeeze and she nodded in reply.

A flurry of customers prevented further discussion and only at closing time was Joe able to lock the door and proclaim; 'Right, let's chat.'

Hovering over by the till, Lucie's uncertainty became clear. He saw the fear behind her eyes and all he wanted to do was comfort and reassure her.

'Lucie, I like where we are...'

'But you don't want to spoil it.'

'Hang on! Don't answer for me. That's not at all what I was about to say. Lucie,' he started again. 'The last few weeks have been incredible. I love dating you. I think we get on brilliantly and if that sounds a bit too mild, well it's because I haven't wanted to frighten you off with how I truly feel.' He coughed to clear his throat. 'You're not the only one with difficult topics to discuss.'

'Like what?' she asked, her cheeks reddening.

'It's very early,' he warned.

'Go on. I want to hear it.'

'The truth is, I… well I have liked you for months and now that we're dating, I know that my feelings have deepened… and… I'm at risk of making a hash of this, but so be it… I am falling in love with you.'

The words hung between them like an echo in a cave. Lucie's expression was one of delight, mingled with fear and a dash of disbelief too.

'I know that isn't what you asked,' he continued, on a roll now and not wanting to pause in case he lost the nerve to carry on. 'But the point of saying all this, other than the fact that it needs to be said… well, it's also to demonstrate that I accept you as you are and all that goes with your life. Like Sam, if that wasn't clear enough.'

'Really?'

'Yes, really.'

'Joe?'

'Yes.'

'I am falling for you too,' she paused, as Joe's heart soared. 'And I am so relieved,' she added, 'to hear you say it, and to know that you have no problem with meeting Sam too.'

They grinned.

'You should kiss me now.'

'I was about to suggest the same thing,' he replied in jest, crossing the floor, pulling her into his arms and kissing her.

Neither noticed Betty Longhorn walking past, hunched over the walking aid the doctor now insisted she take everywhere. Tutting to herself, she whispered 'young people today,' before giving a whiskery smirk and shuffling on.

Chapter Forty Six

Summer is here. The air smells warm and full of promise and I am delighted. I have been home for months now, watching the seasons change out of the window, waiting to begin a new chapter. Now the summer has reached us. A whole year has passed since I first met Laurence and I can finally hope for a new start.

My body still bears the scars of the accident, but I am strong and the doctor says that youth is on my side and will help my healing. I have a future now. I can walk, I can breathe, I can dream.

In little over two months I will be heading to pastures new. I cannot wait to train to be a teacher. This last year has taught me so much and I believe that my experiences will help me be a better teacher than I'd have been otherwise.

Ethan continues to visit, although these days there is wariness there, as if he worries he has given away too much. I admit I know he likes me. That has been evident for a long time. Even before my accident I think in some small way I knew. He is a dear friend and I will miss him when I am away. I do not know that I can offer him more than friendship.

I have grown older than my years. My time with Laurence has left me cautious. I fear the depth of the feelings I had for him and I worry that I will never love another man the same way again, or that I wouldn't want to.

Caroline is home for the summer. Today we walked across the fields chatting of the years we grew up here. I will miss her for I suspect she will not return for a long time after this holiday. Our conversation was steeped in nostalgia, as if she has already confined Taverton to her memories and plans to stay in Cambridge forever.

The family she is a nanny for are good employers and she loves living with them. She is happy and I am thrilled for her.

I wonder what my own journey will be. Perhaps I will never return either. Yet that thought leaves a little niggle. I am not sure why. I was so keen to leave the place last year, but now I am not convinced that I would want that at all.

Today was a long day. It was always going to be. My father had hauled the last suitcase out of the attic and told me to give careful thought about what to pack. I also had my old school satchel. With both I had to stuff the most important of my worldly possessions. It was strange to decide which of my belongings were worthy to accompany me on a new life and how much will get left behind. What if I forgot something important?

But I digress. I spent the morning sorting and packing, the bubble of nerves and excitement building, knowing that in just a few days I would be leaving for teaching college. I found a book full of my poetry, another with dozens of sketches. They were the first items I packed.

A year is a long time to wait for something that you have learned is your dream. But this is all now thrown into a muddle, for Ethan arrived late morning and he was sent up to my bedroom with two cups of tea by my mother. He was nervous and I think I knew what was coming.

I cannot untangle it all. I am not sure of many things, other than I need to get my life back. I told him this and he said he understood. I know he did. He is a rare gem and a wonderful friend. He would never stop me pursing my dreams. In all the uncertainty I know that to be true.

I worry that I will never get to the point. My mind is racing with his words and my words and all the emotion that poured off us in between. But it is as he said; he will wait for me. He loves me and he will wait. He wants to marry me, if I want him and when I am ready.

I could not give him an answer. It is beyond me right now. I hope it will not remain that way. I hope I can give him an answer when it matters and that he will not be wasting his time and his life on an empty hope.

But right now I have to focus. I have to go away and start what should have been started a year ago. I have to replace what was stolen in that crazy haze of summer love, Laurence Scott and screeching car brakes.

I can only see what is in front of me, the next step I need to take, but it is this that'll lead to all the rest. And that is the true beauty of it.

Chapter Forty Seven

2019

September arrived with a roar of thunderstorms and pelting rain showers. The greedy scorched earth soaked up the deluge and a peaty smell permeated the fresh air, assaulting Evelyn's nostrils as she walked to work. Her umbrella kept the icy raindrops at bay and she skipped in between the gathering puddles.

It seemed odd to still sport a summer tan while avoiding the wet weather and the sudden arrival of autumn. It was even stranger to return home, from ten days spent on sun loungers, sipping cocktails and reading books, to the sodden English countryside. It had been fun to hang out with Aimee, to chat until the early hours, to eat out in the local markets and restaurants, to admire the architecture, to explore the town's history (Aimee did her own thing on those occasions), to just stop and relax around a sparkling hotel pool.

Thoughts of Ishmael, their marriage, the guilt over her part in its failure, were lessened by the eye-watering sunlight and endless blue skies overhead. Coming back to England wasn't a chore. She was ready to get stuck into the business and start initiating the changes she'd planned. But the holiday had come at a time when she needed to lick her wounds and regain her energy.

The vibrating phone in her pocket woke her from memories of the trip. She dug her hand into her waterproof jacket pocket, retrieving the phone within. Caren's name flashed across the screen.

'Hello.'

'You're back then?'

'We got back on Sunday.'

'That was three days ago! You should have called me.'

'Am I being a rubbish friend again?'

Caren snorted. 'I don't think I can complain. How many times have I cut short an important chat to deal with the little monsters that live under my roof?'

'Sorry, it's been nonstop since I got back. I had to do all the paperwork for the business, including the sales for the festival. And Aimee is already packing. I'm not sure my dad knows how to react to that. She came home from our trip with this scary determination. She wants to fly out to Liam as soon as possible.'

'I dread to think what you two spoke about on holiday.'

Evelyn laughed while dodging another puddle.

'We talked a lot about men. Specifically Ishmael and what went wrong and of course her perfect, flawless Liam. Let's give that a few years. She has the new love haze and nothing I say will dampen that. Not that I'd want to,' Evelyn said with conviction. 'I want her to be happy. And for what it's worth she didn't judge me on my relationship woes. She actually listened. My little sister is growing up.'

'Well, I am happy that the holiday wasn't a disaster. It was a bit of a risk going away with a sister you don't get on with.'

'I'm hoping we're past that now.'

Evelyn crossed the main street and stepped onto the pavement the other side. The bookshop façade was visible ahead through the dense sheet of rain.

'I'm almost at work. I can call again later?'

'Oh don't worry.' Caren's voice was muffled against the competing noise of the rain and traffic. 'I called to let you know that I'll be coming up on Saturday.'

'To Taverton, you mean?' Evelyn asked in excitement.

'No Scotland! Of course I mean Taverton. My train arrives about ten thirty. Would you mind picking me up from the station?'

'No, I don't mind picking you up! I can't believe you're actually visiting.'

'On my own too, without children. I can barely believe it myself.'

'How did you manage that?'

'I told you Adrian owed us after that nonsense with Ishmael. I told him he needed to deal with the kids for a weekend. Let's say, I just cashed my favour in!'

*

246

Ethan took down the shoe box for the last time, ran his hand along the lid, and placed it into a large cardboard box. He'd thought on Evelyn's words the last few weeks, deciding she was right. He'd never know for sure whether Helen had loved him in the same way she'd loved Laurence Scott. After college she never mentioned Laurence and Ethan had never asked.

But it now seemed silly to have allowed the curiosity of the shoe box to make him doubt the years they'd had together. Helen had been happy. Even if his offer before she went away to study hadn't been as exciting as Laurence's, as wild or heady or lustful, it was solid and came from the heart. And he had waited for her.

And ultimately Helen had chosen him. She'd left to train, their friendship carrying on during the long periods of absence through letters and phone calls. She'd never told him to move on or give up. Ethan knew she wouldn't have allowed their budding relationship to continue had there been no hope, or had there been any lack of sincerity to her feelings.

Evelyn had made a good point. Helen lived the reality of their relationship. She hadn't needed flowery poetic declarations as she had with Laurence. Perhaps the man had been her first love, but it hadn't been enough. Not by far.

It was time to let go, to put aside the little niggles of doubt which had hampered Ethan's progress of sorting her belongings. Perhaps that's all it had been, a distraction, a way for his brain to process his loss, amid clearing away the physical trace of her existence.

He closed the cardboard box. The contents would be going to the tip. He'd taken a long time to make the decision, wondering if it would be disrespectful to her memory to get rid of them. But he also knew as long as the shoe box remained in the house, he would be tempted to re-read, to keep analysing, hoping for hints of what just wasn't there and Helen would have hated that.

She was a doer. She always looked to the future. She'd learned not to stay stagnant, not to dwell on the past or even on the present. Perhaps her accident had taught her that, Ethan mused. He knew she wouldn't want him to dwell there either. And with that thought the decision was made. It was time to say a final goodbye. It was time to move on.

Ethan picked up the large box and carried it to the front door, where several others were already waiting. Lifting the car keys from the hook he took the smallest of the boxes in the crook of his arm, manoeuvring it into a secure position with the help of his knee and opened the door.

A weak burst of sunshine greeted him, the rain clouds puttering above and the floor still damp below his feet. Loading the car, Ethan heard the footfall behind him and knew instinctively who it was.

'Good afternoon Janice.'

She peered at the boxes in curiosity. 'Home again on a weekday?'

'Yes, I have taken a day off to finish what should have been finished weeks ago.'

'So that's Helen's stuff in there?' Janice's eyes hadn't strayed from the boxes, and Ethan wondered if she believed them to be a barrier between Ethan and herself. It was time for some honesty.

'She wouldn't have wanted them cluttering the place up. She was a remarkable woman and moving her things out won't change our memory of her.'

'No, of course not,' Janice said, her voice stiff. 'But it will allow you to move on.'

She made eye contact with him then and noticing the desperation behind her eyes he took pity.

'I won't be moving on in that sense,' He hoped his meaning was clear. 'I was with Helen a very long time. I am not searching for a replacement.'

'Oh, I see,' she said, dropping eye contact and nodding towards the boxes in the boot. 'Perhaps I ought to let you get on with it.'

'I appreciate your concern, and I need to thank you for being such an attentive neighbour,' Ethan added, trying to soften the blow. 'And your banana bread is out of this world! The girls and I have really enjoyed your baking. It's kind of you to think of us.'

'Yes, yes,' she interjected, backing away down the drive. 'It is a lovely thing to be neighbourly.'

'Indeed. So thanks again.' Ethan gave her a cheery wave as she disappeared around the hedgerow. He felt bad, but honesty was needed.

In that instant he imagined Helen smiling at his concern. His every action, thought and word was still measured by how he thought she would have responded. She'd always be with him. He finished packing the boxes and shut the car boot, a smile on his face.

*

248

'Wow, there's no denying you live in the countryside.'

They drove past open arable land, a lone green tractor far off to the right. The car windows down, Caren surveyed the landscape, distracted by a flock of seagulls lifting in unison from a ploughed field.

'Now I can understand why London was such a shock to your system.'

'You make me sound like a true country bumpkin,' Evelyn remarked.

'I think perhaps it's inbuilt. After all you lived in the city for a long time, yet...' Caren paused, observing her friend. 'I may have just arrived, but I can see you are settled here. It's in your entire,' she flapped her hands trying to think of the right word. 'Being... it's in your entire being.'

'But that doesn't mean I hated my life in London.'

'You loved Ishmael. I believe you would have followed him anywhere.'

'Does that make me a doormat?' Evelyn asked, slowing the car down as she reached a crossroad.

'No, I don't think so. I think it's just part of who you are. You saw the promise and potential. No doubt you saw the same for your business.'

'I think you might be right,' Evelyn mused, never having had her personality summed up before. She turned the steering wheel to the right, her gaze flicking over the sign for Taverton. 'We're nearly there. Then the weekend can get started.'

'Don't you have to get back to the bookshop?'

'Yes, but you are coming with me. You want to see what my life is like now? Then Taverton Tales is where we shall start.'

'Sounds like a hell-raising weekend ahead.'

'Indeed,' Evelyn joked.

*

'You know that Adrian and I won't take sides. Both you and Ishmael will remain our friends. Although between you and me,' Caren added, leaning in. 'I know who I prefer.'

Evelyn grinned. 'I wouldn't expect you to take sides. Besides living in Suffolk, I realise that you'll see more of him than you will of me. I can get upset about that, or I can just accept that it is what it is.'

They lay on a picnic blanket watching a herd of geese fly over the mirror-like lake. A reprieve in the early autumnal weather lent the day a final hit of summer sun. Determined to enjoy it while it lasted, she'd bought some picnic food and drove Caren out to a local beauty spot.

They'd spent most of the previous day at the bookshop, Caren noting the pride in Evelyn's voice as she showed her around, before Caren slipped off to explore and shop while she completed her shift. After work they dined together at the pub. Caren admitted the food was on par with any bistro kitchen she'd eaten in in London and marvelled how affordable it was in comparison.

She'd be heading home on the late afternoon train, and Evelyn felt a pang realising how much she missed their friendship. With the long hours of running a business she'd yet to make new friends back in Taverton, with the exception of Lucie and Joe. Now that she knew her future was here perhaps that would change in time.

'For what it's worth, I don't think the new girlfriend will make him happy.'

Caren's comment lay charged between them.

'Don't.' Evelyn said. 'There's no point going there. What he does now is his business. We're not in each other's lives any more. I can't go there, I just can't.'

'Okay,' Caren nodded. 'I mean it, but I'll drop it. For you,' she added, unapologetic; which was exactly why Evelyn couldn't resist loving her friend. 'It'll come right. It might seem like the end, but this is just the beginning for you. I'm not a sentimental type, but I truly believe that.'

'Thank you.'

Evelyn watched a circle of ripples burst forth from the pond. A fish broke the surface, but she was too far away to make out its features. A few seconds later the surface resumed its glass like state, reflecting the pale blue sky above. She sat, pulling her legs towards her, and resting her chin on her knees.

'I'm going to be fine,' she admitted, feeling for the first time that that was true. 'I'll be absolutely fine.'

Chapter Forty Eight

'I'm meeting Sam later,' Joe whispered, as Evelyn reached for her handbag. The morning was drawing to an end and she was leaving early to get to the airport.

'Wow, that's big. Things must be going well.' She had been surprised to hear about Lucie's young son, but the revelation made a lot of sense. It was as if a puzzle piece had been missing and found down the back of the sofa.

'It is going well.' Joe blushed. 'I hope he likes me,' he confessed.

'I have not met a child yet who doesn't like you. The storytelling hours are proof enough. You're a hit!'

'This is more important though.'

'I know.' She gave him a reassuring pat on the arm. 'Just be yourself and take Lucie's lead. She knows her child. Listen I need to run. Dad is driving us to the airport and he said it'll take hours to get there this time of day. If there are any problems I have my phone with me.'

'We'll be fine,' Joe said, a grin playing the corners of his mouth. She knew Lucie joining him for the afternoon was behind it.

Oh, young love, she thought. She remembered it well. 'I'll be back in the morning. Thanks Joe.'

'Send Aimee my regards,' he called, as she exited the shop. She waved back to show she'd heard.

*

Ethan and Aimee waited on the driveway, accompanied by Gordon who was regaling a bored Aimee with tales about an old work colleague who just happened to be from New Zealand, didn't she know? Evelyn ran the last few steps, the relief erupting across Aimee's face making her burst into laughter.

'I thought you'd never make it,' Aimee berated.

'Sorry, Joe needed a pep talk. Are you all ready?'

Aimee's gaze fell onto the now packed boot, a flicker of anxiety passing her features. 'I think so.'

'Liam has Dad's tick of approval and for what it's worth mine too. If this is what you want, then go for it. These things are always terrifying at first.'

Aimee stepped forward and gave her a tight hug. 'I'll miss you, you know.'

Stunned, Evelyn returned the embrace. 'You know what? I'm going to miss you too.'

'All right girls, we need to head off,' Ethan interrupted. 'If you don't mind I'll save my hugs and tears for the airport, otherwise I'm not sure I'll be letting you leave at all.'

'Have a safe trip then Aimee,' Gordon called, as Evelyn waved her sister into the front seat, taking her place in the back.

Securing his seatbelt Ethan addressed his youngest daughter. 'Right, let's go, before any of us have a chance to change our mind.'

*

The airport buzzed with a combination of excitement, the dread of long haul journeys, and the stoicism of business travel. After checking in, the trio found the nearest restaurant, placed an order, and tried to relax. But the nervous energy affected them all amid the stirring of pre-flight jitters and tearful goodbyes.

'It won't be long now,' Ethan said. He squinted at his watch for the seventh time since their arrival.

Aimee pushed her burger around the plate, only taking the occasional nibble. She took a long draw of her orange juice, her body giving a little shiver.

'It's okay to be nervous,' Evelyn said, remembering how she'd felt moving to London. Moving to a new country, even with Aimee's prior experience, was far bigger.

'I know.' It came out as a squeak.

'We'll video call as soon as we know you've arrived,' Ethan reassured.

She nodded with a weak smile on her face. 'I can't wait to see him again. It's been so long. I know once I'm in his arms all the nerves will disappear.'

'I'm sure they will.'

Ethan placed his hand over hers. 'It is time for you to find your path Aimee. When you and Liam come back in the spring, you'll have a plan to work to. I am proud of you. I admit there have been times when I have worried that you were destined to wander through life, but you have shown a determination I never gave you credit for. You have established a career, without us even knowing, and now you have chosen someone you want to build a future with. We'll miss you greatly, but I think we all know deep down that you belong there with him, not here with us.'

Evelyn nodded in agreement as Aimee sniffed.

'It's funny to think that we have all been waiting for something. And now, we're all moving forward at the same time. Well maybe not forward, perhaps we're all moving in different directions now, but that's how it should be. We each have our own path to walk.'

'Thanks, Dad,' Aimee responded, the crack in her voice giving her away.

Evelyn discreetly wiped away the tear that rolled down her cheek.

*

Joe opened up the shop as a brand new morning ushered in. He often set up these days. Evelyn trusted him enough to get the shop ready for the shift ahead. She'd be in soon, having started her working day ploughing through paperwork at home.

He sat on the chair behind the desk and awaited the first customer. His mind wandered to the other evening when he'd met Sam for the first time. The little boy was shy. But soon enough, with Lucie's prompting Joe managed to engage the toddler into a game of peekaboo. Using Sam's favourite teddy to hide behind, it wasn't long before the tiny child, with his tight bronze curls and cute button nose, erupted into uncontrollable giggles. Joe had laughed too. It was impossible not to. There was something about a child's laughter that was infectious.

Lucie was a good mum, he saw that. Patient, but firm when she needed to be, he'd watched her with a growing sense of awe. This was the woman for him, he just knew.

The tinkling of the shop bell announced a customer's arrival and Joe felt the fuzzy feeling abandon his stomach as Betty Longhorn shuffled across the shop floor.

'What can I do for you, Mrs Longhorn?' he asked, trying to ignore his trepidation.

'Are you and that girl here courting?' she asked, a frown deepening across her forehead, sterner than he'd ever seen her.

Alarmed, he almost made an excuse. But remembering Lucie's bravery, how she'd trusted him with the truth about her little boy, stopped him in his tracks. Now wasn't the time for covering up. Not anymore.

'Yes, Mrs Longhorn. Lucie and I are together.'

She studied him for a moment, making a subtle but still noticeable clucking noise in her throat, before diverting her attention to the bookshelf on her left.

'I want to purchase another one of those Austen books. I might as well read them all before I die, and I'd like the full collection to leave to my granddaughter. She's an author herself you know. About to have her first book published this winter.'

Joe grinned behind her back, his relief sharp and instant. He'd expected her to complain or make a fuss about inappropriate work place relationships.

'Is that so Mrs Longhorn? You must tell me more. And let's see what we can do for you. If you follow me, I'll show you what we have in stock.'

Acknowledgements

Thank you to all the readers who pick up this book and give it a chance. I hope you enjoy reading it!

A massive thank you goes out to the writing community who have shown me support this last year. Particular mention to Lizzie Chantree, Fiona Jenkins and Sue Baker, who all work tirelessly to support and encourage readers, writers and bloggers. An extra thanks to Fiona Jenkins for her advice regarding the book cover.

Thank you to my editor/proof reader Sophie Wallace and to my beta readers. Your feedback is always so spot on. As this book is about an independent bookshop – an additional thanks to those who prop up the industry. It is a challenging profession, especially in an era of online retailers. I wish you all success.

Lastly, thank you to my husband and children. Writing full time as an indie author can be stressful. Knowing you have my back makes it all worthwhile.

Other Titles

The Things We Regret

After suppressing childhood memories of her grandmother Edie, Jules prides herself on her resolve and independence. But when her personal life turns sour she is left with unanswered questions, a broken family unit, and a vacant house in a small seaside community in Cornwall.

In post-war Britain, a young Edie must learn to adapt to the changes of a desolate country. Stepping up to the responsibilities of the family business, amid a blossoming courtship with local fisherman Henry, she soon discovers that life can still be harsh and struggles to cope with the tragedy that befalls them.

.

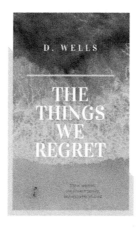

6 Caledon Street

In an attempt to escape her painful past Sarah Miller moves into a beautifully restored Edwardian property in Caledon Street. Soon her life intermingles with not only her concert pianist neighbour, and her landlord, but also upon the discovery of some dusty journals written by an original occupant of the house.

Recognising parallels in her life and the young teenage girl's among the crisp pages of the journal, Sarah is faced with the choice to overcome her past, or allow it to hinder her future.

Thank you for reading Where Our Paths Meet. Please feel free to leave a review on Amazon or Goodreads. Don't underestimate the power of the review. It really does make a difference. It needn't be long – sometimes the best reviews are one-liners!

You can find D. Wells on Facebook at
www.facebook.com/authorD.Wells/
On Instagram at www.instagram.com/d.wellsauthor and
On Twitter at @dwellsauthor

Or at https://dwellsauthor.weebly.com

Other titles by the author

6 Caledon Street
The Things We Regret

Short stories, written under the pen name D. van de Merwe

Red; a collection of short stories about relationships
12 Days of Christmas
The Heart of Christmas

Printed in Great Britain
by Amazon